CARNOSAUR

I0633107

HARRY ADAM KNIGHT was the pseudonym of JOHN BROSNAN (1947-2005). Brosnan was born in Australia but lived most of his life in Britain. He published many books about films and filmmaking (including the particularly well-regarded *Movie Magic*, *Future Tense*, and *James Bond in the Cinema*). Three of his horror books (*Carnosaur*, *Slimer*, and *Bedlam*, the last two written with Leroy Kettle, all under the pseudonym Harry Adam Knight) were made into movies. Their most successful book was *The Fungus*. Two other horror books were published as by Simon Ian Childer, *Tendrils* (with Kettle) and *Worm*.

Brosnan also wrote several science fiction novels – the *Skylords* trilogy, *The Opoponax Invasion*, and *Mothership*, as well as a range of SF thrillers such as *Torched* (with John Baxter) and *Skyship*, and comic fantasy novels *Damned and Fancy* and *Have Demon, Will Travel*.

He wrote a much-liked column for the U.K. magazine *Starburst* and scripts for the comic 2000 *AD*, as well as a range of TV novelizations.

WILL ERRICKSON is a lifelong horror enthusiast and author of the *Too Much Horror Fiction* blog, where he rediscovers forgotten titles and writers and celebrates the genre's resplendent cover art. With Grady Hendrix in 2017, he co-wrote the Bram Stoker Award-winning *Paperbacks from Hell*, which featured many books from his personal collection. Today Will resides in Portland, Oregon, with his wife Ashley and his ever-growing library of vintage horror paperbacks.

HARRY ADAM KNIGHT

CARNOSAUR

INTRODUCTION BY WILL ERRICKSON

VALANCOURT BOOKS

Carnosaur by Harry Adam Knight
Originally published in Great Britain by W. H. Allen in 1984
First published in the United States by Bart Books in 1989
First Valancourt Books edition 2022
Published by arrangement with Tor Books/Macmillan Publishing Group

Published by Valancourt Books, Richmond, Virginia
http://www.valancourtbooks.com

ISBN 978-1-954321-72-4 (*trade paperback*)
Also available as an electronic book.

Cover art copyright © 2022 by Lynne Hansen

Set in Dante MT

INTRODUCTION

'Young boys tend to be dinosaur mad. I know I was at his age. I had a big collection of plastic ones and could give the correct name for each one.'

I was a mean dinosaur fanatic when I was growing up in the Seventies. Family trips to science museums in Philadelphia and New York allowed me to see the immense fossils in person; relatives would ask me the names of the various prehistoric animals, which I could rattle off (and spell!) with the unselfconsciousness of a precocious child. Visits to the local library were never complete without a stack of books on these fantastic, near-mythic creatures. Most of these titles were from the Fifties and Sixties and out of date by the time I was reading them, illustrated with timid little black-and-white pencil sketches of what were in essence giant tail-dragging lizards. Tom McGowan and Rod Ruth's *Album of Dinosaurs*, published by Rand McNally in 1972, boasted in full color the leaping, devouring, attacking creatures, pure catnip for kids like me.

More kid-friendly dinosaur ephemera: there were model kits from Revell in a line called 'Prehistoric Scenes'. Lots of tiny multi-colored plastic toys that your little cousins visiting from the country could easily swallow and choke on. I was obsessed with the original *King Kong*, Saturday mornings and *Land of the Lost*, Doug McClure stranded in *The Land that Time Forgot*, and especially a bottom-of-the-barrel TV movie called *The Last Dinosaur*, with a drunk Richard Boone battling a Tyrannosaurus (that is, a dude in a suit, Godzilla-style) and other archosaur baddies in a land deep inside the earth's core. Jules Verne's *Journey to the Center of the Earth*? Sir Arthur Conan Doyle's *The Lost World*? You bet. I know I attempted my own version of all these stories. And who can forget good old Ray Bradbury's masterful time-travel tale 'A Sound of Thunder' and its chilling climax? Not I, friends, not I.

But it wouldn't be until the Nineties before real dino-mania took over the popular culture, and while you're certainly right about what caused it, there was another bit of forgotten prehistoric lore that deserved excavation, this lovely preserved fossil you now hold in your hands: a book originally published in 1984, entitled *Carnosaur*, by one Harry Adam Knight.

*

'Harry Adam Knight' was a pseudonym used for a handful of pulp throwback novels by a writer named John Brosnan. Born in Perth, the capital of Western Australia, in 1947, Brosnan got his start in the fertile grounds of science fiction fandom, eventually moving to London to follow this passion. Making his name with books about genre movies – *James Bond in Cinema* (1972), *Movie Magic* (1974), *The Horror People* (1976), *Future Tense* (1978) – as well as popular movie review columns in science fiction magazines, Brosnan moved on to writing pulp fiction.

His first horror novel was 1983's *Slimer*, written with fellow fandom scribe Leroy Kettle. Together they wrote four novels, including 1985's *The Fungus* (aka *Death Spore*), sometimes using the name Simon Ian Childer as well. But *Carnosaur*, however, was Brosnan's baby alone. In the e-book *You Only Live Once*, a collection of his nonfiction, Brosnan talked about the genesis of his primeval horror thriller:

> In 1983 a film journalist colleague of mine, Alan Jones, returned from a visit to Hollywood with the news that the next big Hollywood trend would be dinosaur movies. A whole, big line-up of dino pics were on the drawing boards, he told me. So I immediately came up with a clever and cunning plan. I quickly whipped up an outline about genetically engineered dinosaurs being created in a private zoo owned by a deranged aristocrat . . . as hack novels go I thought, and still do, that *Carnosaur* was pretty good and I also thought, at the time, that it might do well. It didn't . . . it sank without a trace.

Such is the life of a pulp writer. Fortunately, Brosnan was sanguine about his career prospects and wasn't too perturbed by his lack of bestsellerdom. He remained in London and kept writing, under his own name and even more pseudonyms: pulps with Kettle, science fiction, TV novelizations, humor, guides to the *Scream* and Hannibal Lecter movies. Afflicted by depression and alcoholism, Brosnan died of complications from pancreatitis in 2005, aged only 57.

*

A fleet-footed, old-fashioned, no-frills, Fifties monster movie-inspired tale with plenty of gore and action, *Carnosaur* is as solid a vintage paperback science-gone-mad novel as one could want. James Herbert vibes abound as Brosnan ticks all the boxes and doesn't muck about with the unnecessaries; the ride you're in for is mean, nasty, brutish, and short. Even the characters moan and groan, so glumly rude you think, Jeez, doesn't anyone have a nice polite word to say? Everyone's all Johnny Rotten all the time.

Our tale begins at 2:17 a.m. sharp when a poultry farmer is woken by his wife because their chickens are squawking up a ruckus. *'Fat lazy cow,'* he thinks first off. (See what I mean? So rude.) Of course, you're reading a book called *Carnosaur*, so you know what's about to happen when our farmer goes out to investigate. And it does. A great beastie, *'the colour of dried blood,'* lurches out of the darkness amidst the unholy screech of upset fowl and makes short work of old Rudie McRuderson. The locale of this attack will prove to be apropos later.

Then the action switches to two teens getting it on in the back seat of a car, straight out of a Fifties monster movie, and it's more of the same, with some class-consciousness woven in as British pulp always seems to do: *'She'd been flattered to have been picked up by someone who was so upper class. Well, sort of upper class.'* Dino arrives, makes short work of teenage boy, girl drives off in terror and crashes into a tree: a tale as old as time.

Daytime: David Pascal is a twenty-something bloke working as a 'journalist' at a newspaper that's barely a newspaper in the small English town of Warchester, *'where nothing exciting ever happened.'* He's just dumped his wonderful girlfriend, a colleague named Jenny, because of his dreams of leaving for a job on a Fleet Street scandal rag. Who knows when that'll happen, since those folks keep ignoring his desperate applications. So here Pascal is, still working on a paper that's practically a free local business flyer and having awkward moments with Jenny in the office. But you're reading a book called *Carnosaur*, so you know that Warchester will offer up something soon that Fleet Street dared never dream.

Warchester's wealthy eccentric, the big-game hunter Sir Darren Penward (erroneously referred to as 'Sir Penward' throughout the novel; 'Sir Darren' is the correct nomenclature), has his own personal zoo on his vast estate, filled with exotic and dangerous animals. This includes his ravenous 'nympho' wife, Lady Jane. Jane is referred to by locals as Lady Fang, and Brosnan notes that she looks *'like something out of* The Story of O *'*, well known for her penchant for seducing younger men while her husband tends to his menagerie.

The bodies of the chicken farmer and the teens are found; the 'upper-class' boy is the son of a respected MP. Suspecting one of Penward's large felines, police begin their investigation, and 'Sir Penward' blames the attacks on an escaped Siberian tiger. Pascal suspects a cover-up when he and one of the police officers notice blood has been cleaned up around one of the bodies at the chicken farm. Later Pascal questions a little boy who says his family was killed by a dinosaur: *'Simon watched his mother die without comprehending what he was seeing . . . it was as if he was watching something on television.'*

Penward's men capture and kill the escaped tiger, but Pascal is skeptical. Along with a reluctant Jenny, Pascal begins an investigation of his own. He tries to learn more about Penward and his zoo, finding the men who worked for him drinking in a locals-only pub. *'They seemed almost to worship [Penward] . . . Like that of a High Priest and his disciples. Pascal suspected they were all crypto-fascists who were attracted both by Penward's autocratic style and his well-publicized Darwinian social theories that were so reactionary they made Nietzsche seem a wet liberal by comparison.'*

Of course, these aren't the type of blokes who talk to nosy reporters, and they hand Pascal his ass for his trouble. Nursing his wounds, Pascal drives back to the newspaper offices only to find, alas, his ex Jenny in a tryst with another coworker. *'The ultimate wimp,'* Pascal is thinking of himself, feeling Penward is responsible for this sudden downward trajectory in his life, both personal and professional. *'One way or the other, he was going to bring Sir Penward and his little empire tumbling down no matter what the personal cost. He would do it even if it killed him.'*

Pascal has a confrontation with Penward in which all is revealed about how these extinct monsters are suddenly alive again: the painstaking genetic process that the obsessed Penward explains like a Bond villain (recall Brosnan literally wrote a book on James Bond) which leaves Pascal muttering, *'Incredible. Chickens into dinosaurs.'* Penward got the idea of loosing dinosaurs upon the world from a chance comment made to him by a biologist at a science convention – 'genetic engineering' and all that. Outside, Penward might be a man of power and authority but inside he's a kid playing with dinosaur toys. And of course in keeping with Bond villain energy, Penward reveals to Pascal that Pascal must die for his trespasses at the zoo. Fortunately for the reporter, the dinosaurs escape – or are they released? – before that can happen . . .

'The residents of Warchester – the ones still alive – woke up to a world that was vastly different to the one they'd gone to sleep in.' Brosnan intermixes scenes of Pascal and Jenny rushing around Warchester, trying to alert authorities to the dangers, with scenes of dinosaurs appearing incongruously in everyday life. Behold: Tarbosaurus, a Tyrannosaurus Rex in everything but name, traipses through backyard gardens; Deinonychus, with its scythe-clawed foot that it uses like a prehistoric exponent of kung fu, to unzip hapless folks' guts from neck to groin; an ankylosaur faces off with a military tank; a baby brachiosaur is befriended by a boy; and a plesiosaur joins a boating party that none of the invitees will soon forget: *'After a long, stunned silence a man's voice said, with an edge of hysteria to it, "Well, you've got to say one thing for good old Dickie; he sure throws a hell of a party . . ."'*

*

I'd be remiss if I didn't mention the original Eighties editions of *Carnosaur*. Not a single paperback of it had a cover that could be called 'interesting' or 'eye-catching' or 'good'; personally, I think they are some of the poorest of the era, considering the dreadful dino damage within that could have inspired an exciting illustration right out of that *Album of Dinosaurs*. Its initial publication was in 1984 by Star Books, a paperback division of W. H. Allen, based in London. To me, it looks like a giant bloody bird claw busting through a door; maybe it's an ostrich, an eagle, an egret, I don't know, but it implies none of the specifically saurian menace within. In 1989, the obscure, primed-for-liquidation Bart Books released it in the United States, featuring an even less impressive cover: I think it's a big bird opening a window shade from the outside? And a desert sunset? At least both use the word 'prehistoric' front and center. Then there are two movie tie-in editions for the woebegone 1993 Roger Corman movie adaptation, for which Brosnan wrote a screenplay that was all but ignored.

*

Before I sign off, I have to address the thirty-ton brontosaurus in the room: one cannot talk about *Carnosaur* without mentioning that other cultural behemoth, the book and movie *Jurassic Park*. The ground zero of dino-mania, the aftershocks still strong three decades later (the trailer for the latest installment arrived as this piece was being written). Brosnan's unassuming little paperback preceded Michael Crichton's bestselling hardcover novel by five or six years and is also filled with many facets that would become famous, indeed iconic, when Steven Spielberg's adaptation was released in 1993. Chase scenes, close calls, and especially the agile killer Deinonychus – literally akin to the velociraptor – are all first seen in Brosnan's work. The scientific basis of resurrecting prehistoric creatures is also nearly identical in both titles. After reading *Carnosaur* you may wonder if Crichton first read Brosnan's book . . . or if it's simply a case of a great idea whose time had, like the mighty dinosaurs you're about to encounter, come round again.

WILL ERRICKSON
February 2022

I

'Des, wake up!'

Des Cartwright tried to ignore his wife's hand tugging on his shoulder. He wanted desperately to sink back down into his sleep. He'd been having a wonderful dream and being wrenched out of it was almost too much to bear. 'Leave me alone,' he growled, still half asleep.

'Des!' she cried again, shaking him harder. 'The chickens! Something's upsetting them!'

'Something's *always* upsetting them,' he muttered. But he was fully awake now and the dream was fading from his mind like the tantalizing after-taste of some beautiful flavour. He couldn't remember what the dream had been about but he felt a sharp sense of loss.

Feeling strangely sad he turned over on his back and listened. Julie was right. The chickens were in a hell of a state. What was scaring them, he wondered. A fox? Or one of the local dogs? But how could any animal have got in? He'd checked the fences only a couple of days ago.

He sighed, sat up and switched on the bedside lamp. The alarm clock said it was only 2.17 a.m. '*Shit.*' He got up and put on his dressing-gown. Julie was sliding back under the covers, eyes screwed shut against the light. He felt a momentary wave of revulsion wash through him. *Fat lazy cow,* he said to himself as he looked at her and then immediately felt guilty. It wasn't her fault she'd been sick the last couple of years and put on so much weight. *I still love her,* he told himself definitely, but he knew it wasn't true. He hadn't felt anything like love for her in years. Even before she got sick.

He tried to shut out these unwanted thoughts as he walked through to the kitchen. The chickens were continuing their frantic squawking. If anything they were making more noise than before. Then he heard a crash as a heavy object hit the floor in one of the sheds. A cage had been overturned. He stopped thinking of foxes. It had to be one of the local dogs. A big one. Or perhaps more than one.

He went to the cupboard by the back door and took out a 12 bore shotgun. He loaded it with cartridges kept in a kitchen drawer, then went outside. It was a warm August night and the air smelled of summer. It brought back memories of summer nights long ago as he walked across the yard towards the three large buildings that housed the chickens. Unexpectedly a frag-ment of the dream flashed through his mind. He had a mental image of a girl's face. She seemed very familiar but he couldn't remember who she was. Was she someone from his school days, he wondered. A girl he'd had a crush on? Or was she merely a figment of his imagination? The feeling of familiarity could be a trick of the mind. Dreams were funny things . . .

The noise was coming from the middle shed. He opened the door and went inside. The long, narrow building contained over a thousand birds and every one of them seemed to be squawk-ing. Cartwright paused at the doorway and stared down the central aisle. The lights were on – as they always were – and he could see all the way to the end of the building, but there was no sign of any animal. Holding the shotgun ready he walked to the top of the next aisle. In the distance he could see that a whole section of cages had been knocked over. They had been ripped open and there were feathers all around. He began to walk towards the wreckage, curious to see what had caused all this damage. He didn't feel afraid. He was confident that the shotgun was adequate protection against any dog, no matter how large. And by the look of the cages it *was* large. He tried to think of anyone nearby who owned a large Alsatian or Dobermann, but couldn't.

Then he became aware of the smell. He stopped walking. Suddenly he was very frightened but he had no idea why. The smell was unlike anything he had ever experienced before but it produced an atavistic terror within him. He started to shake. He knew he had to get out of there . . .

He turned and began to walk quickly back up the aisle towards the doorway. The skin on his back tingled unpleasantly and he could feel his scrotum tightening but he fought the urge to break into a panic-stricken run. *Keep calm,* he told himself, *once you get outside you'll be safe . . .*

It stepped out between a gap in the row of cages, blocking the aisle ahead of him.

Cartwright froze. He couldn't believe what he was seeing.

It stood about six feet tall and was the colour of dried blood. Cartwright was absurdly reminded of some kind of giant plucked bird, like an ostrich, but this was definitely no ostrich. It had the head of a reptile. The partly open mouth revealed rows of curved, pointed teeth and the eyes that coolly regarded him from beneath two bony protective ridges were also reptilian. They were cunning eyes too, almost intelligent, and this scared Cartwright more than anything. Even more than its claws . . .

He'd noticed the claws right away. The claws on its forelimbs were bad enough. There were three on each 'hand' and they were huge but it was the claws on the creature's feet that made it seem that the thing had been specifically designed by some sick mind: the middle toe on each three-toed foot pointed upwards to form a seven-inch long natural blade, like a scythe.

Man and creature stood about ten feet apart staring at each other. The man was aware of several things simultaneously: his pounding heart, the slippery feel of the shotgun within his sweaty hands, the curious, bellows-like motion of the creature's chest as it breathed rapidly in and out, the fetid stink of its body, and above all the awful surety that he was going to die.

They stared at each other for a full thirty seconds, though it seemed much longer to Cartwright. Then the creature's tail, which had been sweeping back and forth restlessly over the floor, suddenly stiffened and rose into the air behind it. This had the effect of pulling the upper body back until the creature was standing almost as straight as a man.

Even as part of Cartwright's mind began to register this new development, the creature charged him. Emitting an ear-splitting screech it covered the ten feet with just two strides of its powerful hind legs. The claws on its forelegs grasped Cartwright by the shoulders and lifted him into the air. At the same time one of the hind feet rose up and slashed him down the length of his body.

The scythe-like middle claw opened up Cartwright from neck to groin before he even realized what was happening.

Then he was lying on his back on the floor and staring up at the lights on the ceiling. He felt terribly cold. He was dimly aware that the shotgun had gone off but he had no idea if he'd hit the creature. Perhaps the noise had scared it away. He wondered how badly he was hurt. He didn't want to look and see . . .

The creature's head suddenly moved into his field of vision. It was bending over him. As the head came closer he felt its hot breath on his face. The stink was awful. The teeth closed on his neck and Cartwright knew nothing more.

First the weird animal cry and then the boom of the shotgun. Julie sat up in bed, convinced that something was very wrong. What kind of animal made a sound like that? She suddenly felt very worried for her husband.

She got out of bed and hurried through the house. By the time she reached the back door she was already panting badly – since she'd put on so much weight the slightest exertion made her short of breath.

She ran across the yard towards the middle shed. 'Des!' she cried, 'What is it? Are you all right?'

Gasping, she staggered in through the doorway, and immediately froze. Her mind refused to accept the sight that met her eyes.

Some yards away down the central aisle lay the body of her husband. He looked like some farm animal in the process of being cleaned and gutted. A hideous wound ran down the entire length of his torso, exposing his internal organs . . .

And standing over him, straddling his body on two manlike legs, was something out of a nightmare. It was all teeth and claws and it was *eating* him. Even as she stood there looking, the monster pushed its snout into her husband's open stomach and tore out a length of intestine.

She shut her eyes, threw her head back and screamed.

Startled, the creature looked up, saw her blocking the doorway and, feeling trapped, sprang at her . . .

Julie Cartwright felt something heavy slam into her. She was sent sprawling backwards and landed heavily. She opened her eyes to see one of the creature's large hind feet narrowly miss her head as it stepped over her. She heard its terrible screech again – it was like the squawk of a parrot magnified a million times – and then the thud of its footsteps were fading across the yard.

She tried to rise but couldn't. There was a crushing pain in her chest. A steel hand was gripping her heart, harder and harder. . .

Pat Housemann was rapidly coming to the conclusion that sex wasn't all it was cracked up to be. True, this was only her second experience of *real* sex, as opposed to just playing around, but it was just as unsatisfactory as the first one and she couldn't really see how things would improve with practice. For one thing it was damned uncomfortable, especially on this occasion. They were doing it in the back of Jeremy's father's car and even though it was a Bentley there didn't seem to be enough space for this sort of thing. Her left foot was resting on the back of the driver's seat and her right one was protruding out through the open rear window. She already had a cramp in her right leg and felt suffocatingly hot under Jeremy's sweaty bulk.

Isn't he ever going to finish? she wondered impatiently. It seemed she had been watching his enormous bare bottom go up and down for hours. This was very unlike the previous time with the boy from next door, Roy. He had been so fast it was all over before they'd really got started. 'Is that it?' she'd asked him and he'd got very angry. Not that she was enjoying Jeremy's approach any better. On the contrary it was beginning to get rather painful . . .

She wished Jeremy had agreed to make love outside on the grass as she'd wanted. It was a warm night, it would have been more comfortable – and at least they could have taken off all their clothes. As it was her dress was bunched up under her chin and he still had his shirt and jacket on. She guessed his reason for doing it in the car was that he was frightened of someone seeing them. That was silly, of course, because the car was parked in the woods a long way from the road. She supposed it was the fact that she was so young that made him nervous. He had almost driven off the road when she'd told him she was only fifteen. She knew she looked much older.

Well, at least she'd have something to tell Josie and Sarah in the chemist shop, where they all worked, tomorrow. They'd have been home for hours now. They left the dance at 12.30 to catch the last bus back to the village. She'd told them to go on without her because Jeremy had already promised her a lift home in his car. Or rather his *father's* car. She knew what he had in mind though – it was obvious – and she had been happy to comply. Not that she found him all that attractive. He had a round, red face that always seemed to be shiny with sweat. He had pimples too. And he also had the beefy, chunky type of body she didn't particularly like. She preferred boys who were slim. And dark. Jeremy had blond, wispy hair which he was already beginning to lose even though he was just twenty-one.

If she was really honest with herself she had to admit the only reason she was letting him make love to her was the Bentley. She had never been in such a luxurious car before. And there was also the fact that his father was a Member of Parliament, and rich. She'd been flattered to be picked up by someone who was so upper class. Well, sort of upper class.

But the novelty was rapidly wearing off. And as she watched his bottom bob up and down for what seemed the millionth time, and noticed that he had just as many pimples there as on his face, she wondered how she could bring matters to a speedier end. Perhaps she could moan a little faster . . .

It was then that she saw something move past the open window. She only saw it briefly – it was just a shadow – and she thought she might be imagining things. Perhaps it was a branch being moved by a breeze, she told herself as she craned her neck above Jeremy's wide expanse of back to see. He, meanwhile, kept his face buried in her collarbone and continued his rhythmic thrustings.

Something touched her bare foot. The one protruding through the window. Something warm and dry. Something alive.

She screamed and struggled to pull her foot inside the car.

'Wha – ? What's the matter? What did I do?' asked Jeremy, startled.

'There's someone out there!' she screamed. 'They touched my foot!' By now she had managed to get her foot inside.

'Yeah? Are you sure?' He pulled out of her and began to squirm round on the seat. 'If there *is* anyone out there I'll break their necks...'

Trying to pull up his pants with one hand he leaned towards the window, one of his knees digging painfully into her stomach as he did so.

She heard him gasp, 'Jesus H. Christ!' and then saw, to her amazement, a large arm with three long claws on the end of it snake in swiftly through the open window. The claws hooked into Jeremy's throat under his chin and then the arm slowly withdrew, taking him with it. Jeremy struggled wildly but seemed power-less to prevent himself from being dragged out of the window like a hooked fish.

Pat, screaming, tried to sit up but one of Jeremy's flailing feet caught her a hard blow on the chin and her head fell back onto the upholstery.

'*Oh Jesus help me!*' she heard him gasp as his kicking legs disap-peared through the window.

She tried to sit up again and this time succeeded. Fearfully she looked out of the window. Jeremy, still struggling frantically, was being dragged along the ground by something that looked like a large lizard that walked on its hind legs like a man. Its jaws were clamped around Jeremy's head and as it pulled him over the ground it shook him back and forth violently. Suddenly there was a distinct crunch of bone and Jeremy stopped kicking his legs...

She watched the thing drag Jeremy into the bushes and then sprang into life. Muttering half-forgotten prayers in a childlike voice she wound up all the windows and then scrambled into the driver's seat. She had never driven a car before but vaguely knew the basics.

Even so it seemed like an eternity before she finally got the car to start. Looking anxiously over her shoulder at where the creature had vanished with Jeremy among the shrubs she pushed her foot down hard on what she hoped was the accelerator. It was. The car lurched forward and was soon travelling at an unex-pectedly high speed. Already in a state of panic Pat's mind went blank. She had no idea what to do next.

She was still sitting there frozen behind the wheel when the powerful Bentley crashed head-on into an oak tree. Her body was catapulted out through the windshield and she ended up lying across the crumpled bonnet, her neck broken.

2

David Pascal drove into the small Cambridgeshire town of Warchester and parked his car in front of the office of the local newspaper. He went inside and looked around the open-plan office. No one else had arrived yet apart from Mrs Fleming, the editor's secretary. He called good morning to her as he went to the coffee machine, the first step in his ritual.

The next step was to take his coffee over to the telex machine and skim all the items that had come through over the wire services during the night. The more interesting ones he took to his desk to read more closely while he finished his coffee. By the time he'd read them it was almost 8 a.m. The third step in the ritual was to go and collect all the London papers from Mrs Fleming and start reading them as well.

The high point of my day, Pascal told himself wearily. He felt bored and depressed. That morning he'd woken up experiencing an anticipatory tingle, as if he knew something exciting was due to happen that day but had forgotten what. The feeling had lasted until his car had entered the outskirts of Warchester and then faded away as the overwhelming familiarity of the scene etched itself into his mind yet again. Nothing exciting ever happened in Warchester. *Nothing* ever happened in Warchester.

Well, that wasn't quite true. Newsworthy stories were happening all the time – sex scandals and small-town corruption affairs, for example – but they weren't the sort of things that Pascal would be permitted to write about in the *Warchester Times*. Its editor, and Pascal's boss, the ultra-conservative Digby Brown-lowe, ran the paper as a bland appendage to the business community. It was more like the house journal of the local Chamber of Commerce than a newspaper. Nothing was allowed to ruffle the image the paper presented of the town as a prosperous utopia populated by law-abiding asexuals.

Pascal desperately wanted to get away from Warchester. His ambition was to get a job with one of the Fleet Street newspapers but so far all his applications had been unsuccessful. Now, at 26, he felt life was passing him by and he would be stuck in Warchester, and on the *Warchester Times* for good.

His fear was that he would finish up like Johnny MacGibbon who handled the sports section of the paper. Pascal liked MacGibbon – he had a sharp sense of humour and was, for the most part, an enjoyable working and drinking companion – but he knew the fifty-three-year-old journalist considered himself to be a failure. MacGibbon's hale and hearty façade concealed a deeply depressed man who was close to becoming an alcoholic. The idea that MacGibbon was him in twenty-seven years' time terrified Pascal, but he knew that would be his fate for sure unless he got out of Warchester.

He was halfway through the papers when Jenny Stamper came in. She was twenty-three years old, tall, slim and possessed of a unique kind of beauty. She wasn't pretty in the conventional sense; her nose was a little too broad and one of her front teeth was slightly crooked but the combination of large green eyes, wide, sensuous mouth, flawless skin and shoulder-length tumble of curly black hair was irresistible.

Pascal's attitude to her was ambiguous: half the time he admitted to himself he was in love with her, the rest of the time he strongly resented her. She had joined the *Times* less than a year ago, ostensibly as his assistant on the local news section even though there was hardly enough work to keep him busy. But everyone knew the reason she got the job was because her father was an old friend of Brownlowe's. When she'd left Cambridge with a First Class Honours degree in Politics and Economics, but had been unable to get into television journalism as she'd planned, Brownlowe had offered her the job as a favour to her father.

It was originally intended to be a temporary arrangement but eleven months later she was still with the *Times*. Also she'd given up the idea of television; working on the *Times* had given her a taste for newspapers and now her ambition was the same as Pascal's – to get a job with one of the Fleet Street quality papers.

To Pascal's annoyance he knew her chances of realizing this ambition were far better than his. Apart from the advantage of her university education she was also a very good writer. A better writer than him, he realized, though it pained him to admit it. And she was probably even a better journalist than him too – she certainly had a knack for getting people to open their hearts to her – but on a paper like the *Times* which didn't require real journalism it was hard to say.

Nonetheless he was confident that she would soon make the breakthrough into Fleet Street and be off and he would be left behind to fester indefinitely on the *Times*. It was partly because of his envy of her that he brought their love affair to a premature end, but it was also because he knew that losing her was going to be all that much harder to bear if they remained lovers. And he was certain he *would* lose her. When that acceptance from Fleet Street finally arrived he was sure she wouldn't hesitate to go, no matter how deeply involved they were. He knew that because he would do the same if the positions were reversed.

So six weeks ago he had calmly told her that he thought their relationship was a mistake. She'd been terribly upset and demanded an explanation but he'd refused to elaborate and from that moment on had treated her with a studied coolness. For the first week she made several attempts to breach the invisible barrier he'd erected between them but then gave in and treated him with equal coolness. Since then their relationship had been one of strained politeness that sometimes slipped into childish hostility.

He had very quickly regretted the ending of their affair. The two months of intimacy had been very sweet indeed, he had to admit, and he missed it badly. He particularly missed it on mornings like this one when Jenny looked so beautiful. She was wearing brushed denim trousers and jacket and a man's blue-and-white striped shirt, and positively glowed with good health and desirability. Just looking at her made his blood sing and he wondered again if rejecting her had been such a wise manoeuvre. In retrospect it often seemed the action of a madman . . .

Unwanted, the memory of the last time they'd made love together surfaced in his mind. They'd done it on the floor of

Brownlowe's office, as they had many times before. It was about the only place in town where they could have any privacy – Jenny lived with her parents and he still lived at his mother's house – yet another disadvantage of being young in Warchester.

'Hello David,' she said brightly as she sat down opposite him at her desk. 'How are you?'

'Fine,' he answered, his mouth suddenly dry. He was remembering her writhing naked on Brownlowe's carpet, her back arched, her skin shining with sweat ... She had a splendid body, the best he'd ever seen in the flesh, so to speak, and seemed designed to fit all his personal erotic requirements. Each time he undressed her he experienced a sexual jolt that remained constant in its impact. Jenny Stamper, he now realized with a sick feeling, was about as close to his sexual ideal as he would probably ever get.

'You don't look fine,' she told him as she took off her jacket and hung it on the back of her chair. 'You look grumpy and miserable as usual. What's the matter?'

He tried not to watch the play of her muscles beneath the fabric of her shirt as she moved, nor look at those high, perfect breasts. 'I'm fine!' he snapped.

'You sound it. You should change your brand of muesli. There's definitely something wrong with your blood sugar level in the morning.'

He rose to his feet and said stiffly, 'If Brownlowe wants me I'll be in the station.'

'As usual. You spend more time in that place than you do here. You should have joined the police force instead of becoming a journalist.'

'I may join it yet,' he told her as he walked out of the office.

The police station was only three buildings away along the high street and it was Pascal's custom – part of his morning ritual – to drop in and see what was happening in the district. Usually nothing was.

There were three young officers in the duty room when Pascal entered and he knew them all well. One of them, Constable Keith Driscoll, he'd been to school with and was probably his oldest friend. The other two he drank with regularly on most weekends.

'Hello, look out,' said Driscoll as Pascal came in the door. 'Hide all the secret papers, here comes that investigative reporter again.'

Pascal forced himself to join in the laughter. More old jokes. Everything we do and say around here has become so damn predictable, he thought wearily. Like wind-up robots following a preordained script. And his next question, he knew, was part of that same script . . .

'What's new?'

Driscoll leaned back in his chair and gave him a sly look. 'New? You know nothing ever happens around here.'

Pascal felt a small jab of excitement. Driscoll was playing games. Something was up.

'Okay, what's going on?' he demanded. 'What's happened? I'm not leaving here until you tell me.'

Driscoll glanced at his two colleagues. They all grinned at each other. Driscoll turned back to Pascal and said, 'Sorry, Dave, it's all a bit too sensitive and juicy for the ears of a reporter.'

'Don't piss around,' said Pascal impatiently. 'If it really is juicy you know old man Brownlowe wouldn't print it anyway. So give. Tell me what's up.'

Driscoll pretended to think it over. Pascal knew he was going to be told what was going on; he just had to endure this silly game first.

Finally Driscoll said, 'We got a call from Stanley Pitt this morning. Said his son hadn't come home last night.'

'Jeremy?' Pascal vaguely knew the MP's son. He didn't think much of him. Jeremy Pitt was an arrogant, thick-headed snob with too much money. The only thing he was good at was rugby.

'Yeah. Pitt was worried he might have had an accident but if you ask me Pitt's more worried about his car than his son. Young Jeremy had borrowed his Dad's Bentley for the night. He's already wrecked two cars of his own during the past year – '

'*Has* he had an accident?'

'Not that we know of. No reports of any accident and we checked the hospital. But get this: we also got a call from the Constable at Tricklewood saying that a woman by the name of Mrs Housemann reported her daughter, Pat, was missing. She'd come into town with a couple of friends to attend the charity dance at the social club and never came home.'

Pascal frowned. 'What's the connection with Pitt?'

'You'll love it. The Constable questioned the missing girl's two friends and they told him she was going to get a lift home with none other than our young Pitt.'

'I'm beginning to get the picture,' said Pascal.

'No, that's not all,' said Driscoll and smirked. 'The girl is only fifteen years old.'

'Oho!' Pascal smiled. 'I *like* it. Does Pitt the Elder know about this yet?'

Driscoll shook his head. 'Nope. When he does he'll probably break poor old Jeremy's neck.'

'Yeah,' agreed Pascal, still smiling. Pitt was highly sensitive about his image as a stalwart guardian of public morals and a campaigner against the 'permissive society'. 'Hey, you don't think Jeremy's gone off somewhere with the girl, do you?' he asked hopefully.

'You mean run off with her? Nah,' said Driscoll. 'Nothing like that. Most likely they parked somewhere off the road, went at it hammer and tongs and then passed out from a mixture of exhaustion and booze. Right now they're probably just waking up and wondering where the hell they are.'

'Is anyone out looking for them?'

'Yeah. The Sarge and young Hazelmere. They're driving along the route Pitt would have taken from the social club checking the woods. I expect we'll hear they've been found any moment now.'

Pascal went and helped himself to a mug of coffee from the pot that was kept topped up and hot all the time. He couldn't stop smiling. So Jeremy Pitt was in the shit! What a great headline that would make. And it couldn't have happened to a more deserving person.

He felt considerably more cheerful than he had a few minutes before. Perhaps his anticipatory tingle hadn't been a psychic false alarm. Perhaps this *was* going to be a good day.

The phone on Driscoll's desk suddenly rang, making Pascal jump. Driscoll answered it and seconds later sat up straight in his chair, his expression becoming grave. Pascal heard him mutter

'Jesus Christ . . .' Then, 'We'll be right there. Stay where you are . . . oh, and don't touch anything.'

The other three looked at him expectantly as he put the phone down. Pascal noticed that he looked a little dazed. 'That was Tom Gooch who works out at the poultry farm. He just arrived for work and found the manager, Des Cartwright, and his wife dead. He thinks they might have been murdered.'

There was a momentary silence in the duty room, then one of the other officers gave a low whistle of surprise.

Murdered. Pascal couldn't remember the last time anyone had been murdered in Warchester. Certainly not since he'd been working on the newspaper.

Driscoll was putting on his jacket and cap hurriedly. 'Nigel, you come with me. Terry, you stay here and hold the fort. Oh, and raise the Sarge if he's in his car and tell him what's happening. Keep trying until you get him.'

As Driscoll headed out towards the car park at the rear of the station Pascal followed him. 'Okay if I tag along?' he asked.

Driscoll gave him a distracted glance and, after a pause, said, 'Sure. Why not.'

The Cavendish Eggs Poultry Farm was just over four miles out of town. It was a fairly isolated establishment: its nearest neighbour was a farm house about a half a mile away. On three sides the poultry farm was bounded by open pasture land but at the rear lay thick woods.

As the police car pulled in through the front gate a man came running over. He'd obviously been standing in the yard waiting for them. He was in his late twenties with longish hair and was wearing a pair of grey, dirty overalls. His thin face was very pale and his eyes were dull with shock.

'They're dead!' he cried through the open window of the car. 'Both of them! There's blood everywhere . . . !'

'Okay, take it easy,' said Driscoll as he got out. 'Show us where they are.'

Driscoll, Constable McCaffrey and Pascal followed the agitated man round the side of the house. Pascal felt a mixture of dread and excitement. His main fear was that he might embarrass himself by reacting badly to the sight of the corpses. Driscoll would never let him live it down if he fainted, God forbid. He had seen dead bodies before, such as the old tramp who'd been found frozen to death in a field last winter, but he suspected that these were going to be particularly gruesome.

They saw the woman first. She was lying on her back in the doorway of one of the poultry sheds. She was a big woman aged about fifty. She was dressed in a pink nightgown, the hem of which was caught up around her upper thighs, exposing most of her legs. They were very fat and very white. On her left foot was a pink slipper with a faded pom-pom. The other slipper lay inside the shed. Her eyes were wide open and her face was frozen in a grimace of pain and surprise.

This isn't too bad, thought Pascal as he stared down at her. Thankfully there were no gaping wounds and no sign of any blood. Then he looked into the shed and saw the man . . .

Driscoll had already stepped round the woman's body and was walking down the aisle towards the other corpse. McCaffrey followed him and, after a long pause, so did Pascal. He didn't want to – he'd already seen enough from the doorway – but he had no choice. It was a matter of pride.

The noise from the chickens was deafening as Pascal moved between the two rows of cages. He was beginning to feel lightheaded and sick. And the feeling of nausea increased as he neared the body.

It was dressed in pyjamas and dressing gown and lay on its back in an enormous pool of dried blood. A swarm of flies rose into the air as Driscoll and McCaffrey approached the corpse but Pascal could still see other flies crawling on the dried blood and over the coils of intestines that lay spilled out across the dead man's groin.

Pascal came to a halt at least ten feet from the body. Even there the smell was overpowering. He shut his eyes briefly as a wave of dizziness swept through him. Then he forced himself to look again at the ghastly sight on the floor.

The hideous wound extended all the way up to his neck. And the neck itself had almost been severed from the body. It looked as if something had tried to chew through it. Pascal could actually see teeth marks in the flesh. It reminded him of photographs he'd seen of shark bite victims.

'An animal!' he cried over the noise of the chickens. 'An animal did this!'

Driscoll and McCaffrey turned and looked at him. Both their faces were completely white. Driscoll nodded.

Pascal returned his gaze to the body. But what animal in the world, he wondered with a growing sense of fear, could do *that?*

3

Police Sergeant Harry Monroe was feeling uneasy. The day had begun like any other normal day but now it seemed to be going completely mad. The call from Blake at the station about the Cartwrights had unnerved him. *Murdered?* It couldn't be so! Why on earth would anyone want to murder a poultry farm manager and his wife? More likely it was the tragic result of some domestic trouble. Maybe Cartwright had murdered his wife then committed suicide. Terrible, yes, but easier to take than the idea that there was a killer on the loose in Warchester.

Monroe was impatient to get more details on what had happened. He knew he should have abandoned the search for young Pitt and headed off to the Cartwright place himself as soon as he received the call, but he'd assured Jeremy's father he'd find the boy personally, and one thing he'd learnt in recent years was that you had to keep Stanley Pitt happy if you wanted a quiet life. He could only hope they found the young idiot soon.

'Hey, Sarge, I think I saw a glint of something through the trees over there,' said Hazelmere, pointing to the right. Monroe slowed the car and stared but couldn't see anything. He sighed. 'Probably just a broken bottle but we'd better go look . . .'

He pulled off the road onto the grass and stopped. They both got out. It was going to be another hot day. It was only 9.15 a.m. yet the temperature was in the low seventies already by the feel of it.

'Beautiful day, isn't it Sarge?' said Hazelmere as they walked into the woods. Monroe grunted.

A few minutes later they found the Bentley. And Pat House-mann. Monroe didn't need to touch her to know she was dead. His feeling of uneasiness became more acute. He could see the headline: 'MP's Son and 15-year-old Girl Killed in Drunk Driving Accident.'

He looked into the car, expecting to see Pitt's body, but it was empty. Then he noticed that the position of the girl's body on the bonnet indicated that *she* had been driving when the car hit the tree. Monroe frowned. More complications. As if it wasn't messy enough already.

'What do you think happened?' asked Hazelmere in a strained voice. He was staring at the dead girl as if hypnotised. Monroe remembered he hadn't been in the force for very long.

'Beats me,' he said, but he already had a growing suspicion about what had happened and sincerely hoped he wasn't right. He opened one of the rear doors and checked the back seat and floor. He saw the girl's shoes, tights and panties. They made him even more depressed. It looked as if young Pitt had tried to get the girl to go further than she wanted to; perhaps he'd actually tried to rape her. Perhaps he *did* rape her. Anyway, there was a struggle, somehow she pushed him out of the car and drove off. Straight into a tree.

He shut the door and stared thoughtfully into the woods behind the car.

'Where do you think the lad is?' asked Hazelmere as he joined him.

'Good question,' Monroe grunted. He began to follow the car's tracks along the ground. Another possibility had occurred to him. Perhaps the girl had hit him with something – a rock, a spanner – and they would find him lying in the woods either unconscious or dead. Then again he might have panicked when he saw the girl drive off and had gone into hiding. But whatever the answer, mused Monroe, it spelt a lot of trouble.

The two police officers walked in silence through the woods until they came to the place where the Bentley had obviously been parked. From there the tracks led towards the road, only a short distance away. There was no sign of Pitt.

'Hey Sarge,' said Hazelmere, 'Why do you think she was driving the car deeper into the woods instead of heading back to the road?'

Monroe wasn't paying any attention. He'd noticed flies buzzing round something on the ground. He went over to it. He saw it was a patch of dried blood. A big one. Then he saw another, smaller, one. It looked as though someone, bleeding badly, had dragged himself through the grass.

He followed the trail of blood into a clump of bushes, his face grim. Judging by the amount of blood his theory was right: young Pitt *had* been injured by the girl. And badly.

As he walked through the bushes, searching for more blood, Hazelmere came running after him. 'What's up, Sarge? What have you found?'

'Nothing . . . yet,' Monroe muttered darkly.

Hazelmere fell into step beside him. A short time later Monroe came to a frustrated halt. They were standing in a carpet of bluebells and the trail seemed to have gone cold. He had no idea which direction to go in next. Then suddenly Hazelmere bent down and picked up a man's shoe.

'Look, Sarge . . .'

Monroe took it from him. It was almost new and well-polished. It was also unusually heavy. Monroe peered into it and saw the reason why. Part of the foot was still in it.

'Jesus . . .' gasped Hazelmere.

Monroe heard a sound behind them. Someone was coming towards them through the woods.

Pascal wanted to get out of there. The incessant screeching from the chickens, the heat, the flies and the smell were combining to make him feel increasingly ill. But he continued to stand there, trying to look nonchalant. He wondered if Driscoll and McCaffrey felt as bad as he did.

Driscoll repeated the question they'd all been asking since seeing the body. 'What sort of animal can tear a man up like this?'

'A big cat, maybe. A lion or a tiger,' suggested Pascal, trying to avoid looking directly at the corpse.

'There haven't been any reports of an animal escaping from a zoo or circus,' said Driscoll.

'Doesn't need to be from a zoo or circus. Might be an escaped pet. It's happened before. Someone raises a lion cub secretly until eventually the thing escapes and the owner is too frightened to tell anyone.'

'Yeah, perhaps,' said Driscoll doubtfully.

McCaffrey pointed at the shotgun lying near Cartwright's remains. 'You think he wounded it?'

Driscoll shook his head. 'The chickens are probably all he hit by the look of it.' There were a number of dead chickens in the cages on the right side of the aisle. They had apparently caught the full force of the shotgun blast. Pascal guessed that the gun had gone off when the animal had sprung on Cartwright. Too late . . .

Then he became aware of something puzzling. There was a large pool of dried blood around the body and yet there were no animal prints leading away from it. How could that be? he wondered. There was no way the animal could have avoided the blood. He pointed this out to Driscoll. Driscoll frowned. 'Yeah, you're right,' he said. 'There are no prints at all.'

Driscoll headed back outside. Pascal followed him with relief. The fresh air smelt marvellous. Driscoll went over to Gooch who was hovering nervously in the yard, keeping as far away from Mrs Cartwright as he could.

'Gooch, you haven't done any cleaning up in there, have you?' Driscoll asked him.

Gooch looked at him in surprise. 'Cleaning up? What do you mean?'

'Like cleaning blood up off the floor.'

'Hell, no. I took one look at Des and I haven't been in there since.'

'There's been no one else around here?'

Gooch shook his head. 'Nope. Not that I've seen.'

Driscoll took off his cap and rubbed the back of his head. 'Very strange,' he said worriedly.

'You think someone murdered Cartwright and then tried to make it look like the work of an animal?' Pascal asked him.

'It's possible, I suppose.' He glanced back towards Mrs Cartwright's body. 'She certainly wasn't killed by any wild animal. Not a mark on her.'

'Then how do you think she died?'

'No idea.'

'She had a bad heart,' Gooch volunteered. 'If you ask me she dropped dead of a heart attack.'

Driscoll considered this and nodded. 'It's possible. She comes out here, sees her husband being attacked and the shock kills her. But if it was a wild animal why didn't it eat her too? It was obviously hungry.'

'Perhaps her arrival scared it off,' said Pascal. '*If* it was an animal.'

Driscoll sighed. 'To be on the safe side I have to assume it was, for the time being. That means issuing a major alert and sealing off the whole area. We're going to have to warn the public and organise a big-scale operation to hunt it down. Means bringing in reinforcements from all over the county, police marksmen, helicopters . . .' He shook his head wearily. Pascal guessed he wasn't overly happy about being responsible for starting up such a large police operation.

McCaffrey came out of the shed and joined them. 'I had a look at those wrecked cages. The metal's in shreds. Whatever did it is fucking strong.'

'That settles it,' said Driscoll. 'We raise the alarm that a suspected wild animal is on the loose, possibly an escaped lion or tiger. Nigel, you go see if you can spot where it got into the premises. Take Mr Gooch here with you. I'm going to call in.'

Pascal accompanied Driscoll back to the patrol car parked in the front yard. He leaned against the side of the Austin Allegro while Driscoll climbed into the hot interior and contacted the station on the car radio.

As Driscoll talked Pascal heard the familiar sound of Jenny's MG approaching the front gate. He watched expressionlessly as she drove into the yard and pulled up alongside the police car.

'That was quick work,' he said after she had switched the motor off. 'How did you find out about this?'

'Brownlowe wanted to talk to you,' she said with a smile, 'I called the station and Terry told me you were here. What's going on? Terry said something about a murder.'

'We don't know that yet but there are two dead bodies out the back. It's possible they were killed by some sort of wild animal.' Then he added maliciously, 'Why don't you go take a look? They're in the middle shed.'

She hesitated for a moment then said, 'All right, I will.' She got out of the red sports car and, after giving him a suspicious look, walked off towards the rear of the house with a determined stride. He immediately felt guilty. He debated whether to call her back or at least warn her what to expect but did neither.

He forgot about Jenny when Driscoll slammed the car door so hard the vehicle shuddered violently. He came round the side of the car swearing under his breath. Pascal looked at him questioningly. 'What's wrong now?'

'It's a wild animal all right,' said Driscoll grimly, 'the alarm has already been raised. By the Sarge himself. He radioed in a few minutes ago. He said he just ran into some of Sir Penward's men. They told him they're hunting an escaped animal. It got out of Sir Penward's zoo last night. And guess what it is – a bloody great Siberian tiger!'

'Shit,' said Pascal. Sir Darren Penward's private zoo was Warchester's one and only claim to fame. The eccentric, and egocentric, Sir Penward had accumulated the world's most unique collection of dangerous animals in the large zoo that had slowly grown around his stately home, Penward Hall. Occasionally, over the years, people had voiced their disquiet at the presence of so many wild animals on Sir Penward's estate, but the zoo had a perfect safety record – until now.

'And it looks like the Cartwrights weren't the only ones to have been attacked last night,' continued Driscoll. 'The Sarge and Hazelmere found the remains of young Pitt in Ashton Woods. The girl is dead too.'

Pascal felt shocked. Just over an hour ago Pitt and the girl's disappearance had been a cause for jokes and now it had suddenly become a tragedy. Yet while he felt sorry for them Pascal couldn't help being excited by the news. Nor could he help realizing he was in at the start of a story that was going to be of national interest . . .

'Keith, do me a favour and let me use the Cartwrights' phone,' he said urgently.

Driscoll frowned. 'I don't know if I . . .'

'Look, if I can be the first to break this story it will be a big boost for my career. Every second counts. I've *got* to use that phone!'

'Well, okay, go ahead,' said Driscoll doubtfully.

'Thanks! I'll return the favour sometime, I promise!' cried Pascal as he ran across the yard towards the house.

He found the phone in the living room. First he rang the office to get the Associated Press number in London. He spoke to Mrs Fleming who, while she looked up the AP number for him, informed him that Mr Brownlowe wanted to see him as soon as possible. 'It's about the church fête on Saturday . . .'

'Fuck the church fête,' muttered Pascal after he'd hung up. He quickly got through to the AP office, identified himself and began to recount the morning's events. He hadn't got very far when the woman on the other end of the line broke in. 'Hold on, we've already got this story.'

'What? But how? The local police only found out about it a few minutes ago.'

'A spokesman for Sir Penward issued a press statement half an hour ago. All the wire services have it. A three-year-old female Siberian tiger called "Pokey" escaped from Sir Penward's private zoo in the early hours of this morning by climbing two fences that were previously thought to be unclimbable. The animal's escape wasn't discovered until 7 a.m. Sir Penward and his staff immediately set off in pursuit. The animal has been tracked to a wooded area near the town of Warchester and Sir Penward is confident it will soon be recaptured without further loss of life.'

'Further loss of life,' repeated Pascal, dazed. 'You mean you know about the victims already?'

'Yes,' said the woman crisply, 'their names were included in the press statement. Mr and Mrs Des Cartwright, Jeremy Pitt and Patricia Housemann. Sir Penward is accepting full responsibility for all four fatalities and has promised full recompense to the families concerned.'

Pascal put the phone down feeling totally confused. How had Sir Penward found out about the deaths so quickly? The AP woman had said the statement was issued 30 minutes ago. That meant Penward had known about the Cartwrights *before* the police. How?

Then Pascal remembered the missing animal prints in the shed. Someone *had* been here. Penward and his men. They had cleaned up the prints and left without reporting the Cartwrights' deaths to the police. But why?

What had they been trying to cover up?

4

Jenny was waiting by her car when Pascal came out of the house. She looked annoyed, and as he neared her he saw that there was a distinct greenish tinge to her complexion.

'You bastard,' she told him, 'You could at least have warned me what to expect.'

'I'm sorry,' he said distantly, his mind on other things.

'You look it. Well, just for that I'm not going to give you a lift to Ashton Woods.' She turned and swung her long legs over the side of the MG and settled herself in the driver's seat.

'You know about Ashton Wood?' he asked, surprised.

'Keith just told me.' She started the engine. 'See you later. I'll tell you what happens.'

'Hey, wait!' he cried anxiously. 'Take me with you, please Jenny. I *have* to see this thing through.'

She regarded him coolly, a hint of mischief in her green eyes. 'Give me one good reason why I should help you after what you just did to me?'

He thought quickly. 'I've got some information that will fascinate you. Really.'

After a long pause she nodded. 'All right. I'm making a mistake but hop in. And it had better be good.'

'It is,' he said as he quickly jumped into the car beside her.

When the MG was speeding down the country lane away from the poultry farm Jenny said, 'Well, what is this fascinating information?'

Pascal hesitated before replying. He didn't want to share it with her and regretted his moment of rashness. But now he had no choice, so he told her of what he'd learned from the Associated Press. Her first reaction was to call him a bastard again.

'You were going to take all the credit without even telling me,' she accused him.

'I didn't know we'd agreed to work as a team on this thing. Besides I was first on the story. You would have done the same thing in my position.'

She gave him a quick, cold glance. 'No, I wouldn't have. That's the difference between us. Or *one* of them at least.'

'Look, forget all that,' he said impatiently. 'The important thing is to try and figure out what Penward and his lot are playing at. I'm sure they were at the Cartwright place first. They found the bodies but didn't report it to the police. Yet for some reason they cleaned up the tiger's footprints. Why?'

'They were trying to hide the fact that the tiger had escaped?' she suggested.

Pascal frowned. 'But why? The news was going to come out sooner or later. You couldn't keep it a secret after it had actually killed people. Besides, Penward announced it to the press himself . . . but before he told the police. I don't get it. I think he's covering something up.'

'Oh David, you're probably just suffering from your Bernstein and Woodward syndrome again. You tend to see conspiracies everywhere, even in Warchester. There's most likely a simple explanation for it all. You know how arrogant Sir Penward is; he still thinks he's the feudal lord of the manor around here and regards the police as his private property.'

Pascal considered this. 'Well, it's true Penward still thinks he owns Warchester and everyone in it, including the police force, but even he must have realized there would be serious repercussions in not telling the police the moment it was discovered the tiger had escaped. It's as if there's something else he doesn't want them to know.'

'What do you mean?'

'I'm not sure yet. But we could be onto something big. This tiger-on-the-loose is going to attract a lot of interest – in a couple of hours Warchester is going to be crawling with journalists and TV cameramen. Now it's too late for either of us to exploit *that* story but if we can find another angle on it, or uncover whatever it is that Penward's trying to hide, then we've got ourselves an exclusive. We can then take it to one of the nationals and make a name for ourselves.'

'Oho, *now* you're suggesting we team up,' she said, laughing.

'I don't have much choice, do I? Besides, I'm going to need your help on it.'

'So big of you to admit it.'

'So what do you say?'

'I'll think it over. I'm not even convinced yet that Penward *is* hiding something.'

They didn't have any difficulty in locating the search party. Half-way along the road that cut through Ashton Woods they came across a number of vehicles parked beside the road. Two of them were police cars, the rest were Land Rovers and trucks with the Penward coat of arms, a rampant dragon facing a gryphon, on their sides.

As they got out of the MG they were startled by the sound of a helicopter flying low overhead. Pascal thought at first it was a police helicopter but then he recognised it as one of Sir Penward's. It was a big Sikorsky S-76 that Pascal had seen flying about Warchester several times before.

At first sight it certainly seemed as if this was a Penward operation rather than a police one. His men, all wearing the same white overalls and white caps, far outnumbered the few police officers who were present. Pascal had always been intrigued by the men who worked at Penward's zoo – none of them were locals, all were in their mid to late twenties, heavily built and with the same short-back-and-sides haircuts. They gave Pascal the impression they had come out of the same mould, as if perhaps they were all ex-soldiers. They kept very much to themselves and never mixed socially with the residents of Warchester. Some were in the habit of using a pub called The Phoenix Arms, which was right near Penward's estate, but even there they only talked amongst themselves. A few of them were married, but what the others did for female company Pascal had no idea. Went elsewhere, presumably.

Another thing they had in common was an obvious admiration for Sir Penward. They seemed almost to worship him. It wasn't the normal relationship between employer and employees, but more like that of a High Priest and his disciples. Pascal suspected they were all crypto-fascists who were attracted both by Penward's autocratic style and his well-publicised Darwinian social theories that were so reactionary they made Nietzsche seem a wet liberal by comparison.

Pascal soon spotted Sir Penward. It was hard to miss him. He was undoubtedly a striking figure. Over six feet tall, he was broad-shouldered and powerfully built. His long patrician face was olive-skinned and his hair jet black apart from some touches of white at the temples. He looked hard and ruthless. Put him in a suit of chain-mail and you would have a Norman conqueror just up from the Battle of Hastings.

The man he was talking to was the exact opposite. He was short, round, fair-headed and red-faced. At the moment he was very red-faced and very angry. His name was Inspector Bodycombe and he was Warchester's senior police officer. Pascal, followed by Jenny, walked closer to the two men to hear what was going on.

'But dammit, Sir Penward, your actions have been inexcusable!' Bodycombe was spluttering. 'This is a police matter! You must wait until the units from Cambridge arrive!'

'We can't wait, Inspector. My men are specialists. They can work better on their own than with your hordes of clumsy policemen,' said Penward calmly.

'Clumsy . . . *clumsy?*' Bodycombe's face went even redder. Penward's expression remained one of supreme indifference.

Pascal took the opportunity to step forward and say loudly, 'Sir Penward, is it true that you and your men were the first to discover that Mr and Mrs Cartwright had been killed by your escaped tiger but that you failed to notify the police of this fact?'

Penward turned and looked at him. Pascal saw a glimmer of anger in the grey eyes and felt his courage rapidly deserting him. It was as if he was a schoolboy again standing before his headmaster.

'Who are *you?*' asked Penward coldly.

'Oh, that's just young Pascal,' said Bodycombe irritably. 'Works on the paper. One of Brownlowe's people.'

The grey eyes stayed fixed on him. It was like being scanned by a pair of security cameras. Then Penward turned back to Bodycombe. 'Tell the idiot to go away,' he told the Inspector.

To Pascal's dismay Bodycombe made a dismissive gesture towards him and said, 'Yes, go away, Pascal.'

Pascal took a deep breath and said, 'Not until Sir Penward answers my question.'

Bodycombe's look of irritation increased. 'Pascal, I won't tell you again – *piss off!* This is police business. Go away or I'll have you arrested for obstruction.'

His face burning with embarrassment, Pascal pointed a finger at Penward and said, '*He's* the one you should arrest for obstruction.' Then he turned and strode away before either of them could say anything.

Jenny came after him. 'Well handled, Mr Woodward. All the subtlety of a sledgehammer. Now you've put both their backs up. You should have let me have a go at them.'

He ignored her words. 'God, I wish I worked for a *real* newspaper,' he said angrily. 'I'd crucify the pair of them.'

Fiona Smythe-Graves, aged nine, was riding her small pony Robbie through the woods near her home. They were following their usual route but on this particular morning the pony had been acting strangely. Several times it had come to an abrupt halt and only after much urging from its young mistress on each occasion had it continued along the bridle path.

'Robbie, what is the *matter* with you today?' cried Fiona in an exasperated voice when the pony came to a stop yet again. 'Come on, *giddap!*' She dug her knees into his well-covered ribs and gave him a slap on the rump, but he just whinnied nervously and refused to move.

She was about to give him another slap when, about ten yards ahead of them along the path, something stepped out of the bushes. Fiona only caught a glimpse of it before her pony reared up with a high-pitched cry of terror. Taken by surprise, she found herself falling backwards . . .

She hit the ground hard and lay there winded as the pony wheeled round and galloped off back down the path the way it had come. Then she saw something run past her very fast on two legs. It seemed to be some kind of enormous lizard, taller than a man.

As she struggled to draw breath into her lungs she heard Robbie give a heart-rending shriek of pain. She sat up and looked round. The creature had caught up with Robbie; it had pulled him down onto his forelegs in a kneeling position and was in the process of biting a large chunk of flesh out of the pony's shoulder.

Fiona Smythe-Graves didn't hesitate. She got to her feet, picked up a large branch lying beside the path and ran to help her beloved horse.

'Leave Robbie alone, you horrible thing!' she cried as she hit the creature on its back with the branch.

The creature gave a startled snarl and spun round, letting go of the pony. As she looked into the eyes of the thing and saw its rows of fearsome teeth the girl's courage began to fade away. She took a step backwards, holding the branch up defensively. The creature, making an ominous sound deep in its throat, continued to size her up.

Meanwhile, behind it, the badly mutilated pony seized its chance. It struggled to its feet and ran off. This spurred the creature into action; having decided that Fiona presented no threat it suddenly lashed out with one of its fore-claws. The girl died instantly, her skull completely crushed. Then the creature turned and set off in pursuit of the pony again . . .

Teresa Smythe-Graves, Fiona's mother, was just finishing the morning's muck-out of the pony's stable when she heard the animal's frightened whinnying in the distance. Puzzled, she went to the stable doorway and looked out. There was no sign of either the pony or its rider. She called to her eight-year-old son, Simon, who was playing with his toy trucks in the garden: 'Simon, did you just hear Robbie then or am I imagining things?'

Without looking up from his toys Simon said, 'I heard him too Mummy.'

Frowning, Teresa scanned the row of trees along the edge of the paddock that lay sloped beyond the big back garden. Then she saw the pony suddenly emerge from the woods at a gallop. Her heart gave a painful kick when she saw that Fiona was missing. *The damn animal must have thrown her!* she thought as visions of Fiona lying hurt beside the bridle path seared her mind.

Then, behind the pony, she saw something else emerge from the woods. At first she thought it was a man dressed in some kind of ridiculous costume but then she noticed the long tail that extended rigidly from its rear. Simultaneously she heard its shrill, terrifying cry and knew that she was seeing something totally beyond her experience. The creature *shouldn't* exist.

But yet there it was, running after the pony, its clawed forearms extended in front of it. And the pony, blood streaming from an unbelievably large hole in its shoulder, was heading straight towards its stable – its sanctuary. It had almost reached the end of the paddock . . .

'Simon!' she screamed. 'Come here! Run!'

He didn't seem to hear her. He stayed crouching among his toy trucks, apparently mesmerised by the approaching pony and the apparition pursuing it. The pony was now running over the rows of lettuces at the edge of the garden.

'Simon!' she screamed again, running towards him. She knew she'd never have sufficient time to get to him and carry him back with her. But then, with agonising slowness, he stood up, turned and began to run to her.

Robbie was only five yards away – the thing behind it a further ten yards – when Teresa scooped up her son in her arms and headed towards the open stable. It was their only chance. The house was too far away.

The pony hurtled past her, almost knocking her down. Now there was nothing between them and the pursuing creature. A quick glance over her shoulder revealed that it was closing fast. She saw its head clearly for the first time and realized it was some kind of extraordinary reptile. Its lips were pulled back from its rows of long, curving teeth. It appeared to be *grinning* at her . . .

The pony ran into the stable ahead of them. When Teresa got there mere seconds later Robbie was cowering against the far wall, his flanks heaving painfully. There was already a lot of blood on the floor from his ghastly wound.

Teresa dropped Simon onto the hay and slammed both top and bottom stable door shut. She was just in time. The whole building shook from the impact as the creature collided with the heavy wooden doors. Robbie made a sound like a bleating sheep. Simon began to cry.

For a short time nothing else happened and Teresa was daring to hope that the thing had gone away. But then the doors shuddered again and a long claw suddenly came through the wood. Teresa screamed.

After that it became a total nightmare within the stable. The dying pony was driven into a frenzy of panic by the repeated blows on the door and began to buck and rear, kicking out with its hooves. Blood spraying from its wound covered both Teresa and her son as she tried to shield him from the crazed horse. And all the time the curving, scythe-like claw was making an ever larger hole in the door . . .

As the wood splintered inwards Teresa's only thought was for her son. She shoved him behind her into a corner and turned to face the thing that was thrusting its blood-red body through the remains of the door. She screamed at it in a mixture of terror and sheer rage.

The thing screamed back at her. The three-toed hind leg made a lightning kick outwards. The cruel, razor-sharp middle claw slashed through Teresa's neck and deep into her chest. She was already dead by the time her body fell backwards onto the blood-soaked hay.

Simon watched his mother die but without comprehending what he was seeing. The ripped bundle of flesh and clothing at his feet had nothing to do with his mother. It was as if he was watching something on television. It was interesting, but it didn't really concern him.

With the same detachment he watched the creature seize Robbie and sink its teeth into the back of the pony's neck. Robbie squealed and struggled then blood began to pour from his mouth. Slowly, he fell over and lay on his side kicking feebly. The creature was already tearing off long strips of his flesh.

Simon's blank expression didn't change even when the two men wearing some kind of armour appeared in the stable doorway. They carried rifles with unusually thick barrels. They aimed these at the creature but the bangs Simon was expecting didn't come. Instead there was a muffled *phhhfftt* sound and two bright yellow feathery tufts suddenly sprouted from the creature's back.

It straightened with an angry screech so loud that it made Simon's ears hurt. It turned towards the two men but before it could take even one step its legs began to buckle and it collapsed onto the floor with a deep sigh. It wasn't dead – Simon could see its chest moving as it breathed – but it didn't get up again.

One of the men stepped round the creature and came over to where Simon sat in the corner. He bent down and picked him up. 'Don't worry son,' said the man, his voice muffled behind a mask made of wire and thick plastic. 'This isn't really happening. It's all a dream.'

'I know,' said Simon.

The man carried him out of the stable, away from the dead thing that looked like his mother; away from the dead thing that looked like his sister's pony. Away from the sleeping monster . . .

He wasn't even surprised to see the big red and yellow helicopter sitting in the middle of the back garden, its rotor blades still slowly turning. There were other men in the garden, some dressed in armour, others in white overalls. Four of the latter ran past carrying a big net. They went into the stable with it.

The man set Simon down. Another man came over. 'What shall we do with him?'

'We can leave him be,' said the man who carried him out of the stable.

The other man frowned. 'Is that wise? He's the only witness.'

'He's only a child. Who will believe him? I say let him be.'

'I don't know,' said the other man doubtfully. 'I think I'd better ask the chief.' He turned and ran back towards the helicopter. Simon yawned. The film, or dream or whatever, was getting boring. He wondered where his mother was.

5

'Something's happening,' said Pascal.

He and Jenny were leaning against the side of her MG and trying to look inconspicuous. After the altercation with Bodycombe and Penward he'd expected to be ordered out of the area but no one had paid them any further attention. Now, some fifteen minutes later, it seemed that the tiger had been sighted. One of Penward's men had summoned him urgently to a Land Rover equipped with a powerful-looking two-way radio. Penward's expression gave nothing away during his brief conversation but then he had hurriedly waved Bodycombe over and pointed out something on a map. The already flustered police inspector became even more agitated and ran off towards his car, yelling orders.

'What now?' asked Jenny. 'Shall we follow them?'

'Yeah, but let's give them a bit of a head start.'

Penward's men were jumping into their own vehicles as the police cars moved off at speed, their sirens sounding. Pascal watched as Penward's Land Rover rushed past them and turned onto the road after the police cars. Penward's face was as stony and unreadable as ever. 'Okay, let's go,' Pascal told Jenny.

They followed the convoy along the winding road through the woods, maintaining a discreet gap of about one hundred yards between them and the final vehicle. As the woods began to thin out the convoy turned right into a side road. There were houses around now – expensive ones with large gardens. Known as Flagonglen, this was one of Warchester's more up-market residential areas.

There was a familiar clattering noise overhead. Pascal looked up and saw the Sikorsky S-76 again. It was low and flying in the direction of the Penward estate. Slung beneath its red and yellow fuselage was a tarpaulin-covered object in a net.

'Looks like they got the tiger already,' said Pascal, disappointed. 'We've missed all the excitement.'

About three quarters of a mile down the road the convoy pulled into a lane leading to a large house on the edge of the woods. 'Oh God,' cried Jenny, 'that's the Smythe-Graves' house!'

'You know them?'

'Friends of my parents. I hope nothing's happened to them.'

There was hardly any room in the driveway when they arrived. Jenny parked the MG behind one of the Penward Land Rovers and they got out. There was no sign of anyone, but they could hear voices coming from the rear of the building. Pascal followed Jenny through a rose garden along the side of the old, comfortable-looking house which he guessed had once been a farmhouse. The setting was so English it was hard to believe that so alien a creature as a tiger could have been in the vicinity only minutes before. But then the whole day was beginning to seem unreal and dreamlike to Pascal.

The large rear garden was swarming with men. The centre of all the activity seemed to be a small building half-way down the garden. 'The stable,' said Jenny. 'They keep Fiona's pony there.'

Pascal guessed what had happened. The horse must have attracted the tiger . . .

'Let's see if we can get closer for a look,' he said. They began to walk towards the stable. They were only a short distance from the rear of it when one of Bodycombe's constables noticed them and hurried over. 'Sorry. You can't go in there.'

'Hey, come on Ian,' pleaded Pascal. 'Just one quick look.'

Constable Ian Nolan shook his head. He was younger than Pascal and had a round, earnest face and very blue eyes. Pascal noted that he looked paler than usual. 'No, Dave, can't do,' he said, 'Bodycombe would have my guts for garters. Besides, I'm doing you two a favour. It's like a slaughterhouse in there.'

'What happened?' asked Jenny anxiously.

'The bloody tiger killed a woman. Tore a horse apart, as well . . .'

'Oh no!' Jenny put her hand up to her mouth. Pascal gave her shoulder a squeeze. 'She knows the family,' he explained to Nolan.

'What about the children?' asked Jenny.

'They found a boy in the stable. Unharmed – physically, at least, but he must have seen his Mum get killed right in front of him. What other kids are there?'

'A girl. Fiona. About nine years old, I think,' said Jenny.

Nolan looked grim. 'Apparently there's a trail of blood leading up from the woods. Theory is that the tiger attacked the pony in the woods then chased it up here. Penward's mob are down in the woods now, searching for the rider.'

Jenny gave Pascal an anguished look. 'David, this is *awful*. Not Fiona too.'

'Look Jenny,' said Nolan quickly, 'how about helping us out by sitting with the boy for a while until someone comes for him? Probably help him to see a familiar face, and a woman's at that. Pete's got him up at the house, in the kitchen.'

Jenny nodded. 'Of course I will.'

As she hurried back up the garden towards the rear of the house Pascal asked Nolan how the tiger had been captured. Nolan took off his cap and ran his fingers through his sweaty blond hair. 'We don't know yet. The Inspector is still trying to get the full story out of Sir Penward. I've never seen the old man so hopping mad.' He pointed to the end of the garden where Body-combe could be seen talking angrily to Penward who appeared as unruffled as ever. 'All we know is that Penward's boys managed to shoot the thing with anaesthetic darts. They arrived in time to save the boy but not his mother.' He shook his head with distaste. 'Awful sight she is too. Terrible . . .'

'They certainly didn't waste any time in carting the tiger away,' said Pascal. 'I saw it being flown out as we were driving here.'

'Yeah. That's another reason the old man's so mad. He wanted to examine the animal.'

'So what was the almighty rush?'

'Beats me,' said Nolan. 'Maybe the anaesthetic wears off quickly or something. But I don't understand why they just didn't shoot the damn thing dead on the spot. It's going to have to be destroyed anyway.'

'Yes,' said Pascal, nodding. 'That *is* a good question.' Once again he had the strong feeling that Penward was covering something up. But what?

'Uh oh.'

Pascal followed Nolan's gaze and saw the reason for his utterance. Two of Penward's white-suited employees were coming out of the woods. They were carrying a small bundle. Pascal realized it was a child's body. Even from that distance he could tell it was lifeless.

'Victim Number Six,' he muttered. 'Sir Penward's liking for exotic animals is sure costing the community a lot today.'

'They'll close his zoo down after this,' said Nolan gloomily.

'Not that it will do these poor bastards any good.'

'I'd better go break the news to Jenny that they've found the girl,' said Pascal, not looking forward to the task.

As he walked up to the house he heard the sound of approaching sirens. Either more police cars or ambulances, he wasn't sure which. He wondered what it was that Penward was concealing. He couldn't imagine what it might be. Whatever it was it had to be more important, or more potentially embarrassing, than a tiger that escapes and kills six people . . .

The boy looked remarkably composed. Pascal had expected to find him in tears, but he was seated at the kitchen table calmly drinking a glass of milk. Jenny was sitting beside him; Constable Pete Davenport, an overweight young man with the battered face of an ex-boxer, was standing nearby and staring awkwardly at his shoes.

'How is he?' asked Pascal.

'He's fine,' said Jenny quickly, giving Pascal a warning glance. 'Aren't you Simon?'

The boy nodded sombrely. He looked at Pascal without any curiosity. Pascal felt unnerved by the blankness in the boy's wide eyes. 'When's Mummy coming back?' he asked in a clear, calm voice. Pascal realized then that the boy hadn't taken in what he'd seen in the stable. His mind had refused to accept his mother's death.

'Soon,' answered Jenny, 'but your father will be here even sooner.'

Simon gave a childish shrug. Evidently his father's presence was a matter of indifference. 'Where's Fiona?' he then asked.

Jenny looked questioningly at Pascal. He shook his head. Jenny winced but said brightly, 'Fiona is with your Mummy, Simon. You'll see them both soon . . .'

Someone was ringing the front door bell. Constable Davenport shambled off to let them in. 'Ambulance probably,' he muttered as he went.

On the spur of the moment Pascal decided to do something that he knew would upset Jenny. 'Simon,' he said quietly, 'did you see the tiger?'

'David!' cried Jenny before the boy could answer. 'Don't be horrible! Leave him alone!'

'It's all right, Jenny,' he said placatingly, 'I'm not upsetting him. Am I Simon?'

The boy shook his head disinterestedly.

'You don't mind talking about the tiger, do you?' persisted Pascal. 'You know it was only make-believe anyway . . .'

'David!' Jenny's voice rose almost to a shout. 'Not another word! Get out of here right now or I'll never speak to you again.' Her face had gone bright red with anger. Pascal had never seen her so furious about anything before. Nonetheless he went on. 'Did you see the tiger, Simon?'

Jenny got up and rushed towards him. She gave him a hard push in the chest with both hands. *'Shut up, David!'*

Pascal stumbled backwards, surprised. There were voices and the sound of approaching footsteps coming through the house. There was little time left. 'Simon, the tiger . . .' he called as he tried to prevent Jenny pushing him out the back door.

Very clearly, and in the same unconcerned tone of voice, the boy said, 'It wasn't a tiger. It was a dinosaur.'

'You're a bastard,' said Jenny. 'And to think I once thought I might be falling in love with you.' It was an hour later and they were heading back towards town in her MG.

'Look, Jenny,' he said, 'be reasonable. I didn't upset him. I could tell he'd detached himself from the whole experience. It was all unreal to him. Like talking about something he'd seen on television.'

'Yes, but by making him talk about it you could have forced

him to face the reality before he was ready to. You might have done him terrible emotional damage.'

'But I didn't, did I? It didn't bother him in the least.'

'You had no right to take the risk. And it was all for nothing anyway.'

Pascal said slowly, 'I'm not so sure about that.'

She gave him a look of exasperation. 'David, he told you he saw a *dinosaur.*'

'I know.'

'He was obviously imagining things. It was part of his shield of make-believe. He turned the tiger into a fantasy creature to make it seem less real.'

'Possibly,' admitted Pascal, 'but surely a big tiger turning up in your back garden would seem fantastic enough to a little boy. Why would he have to change it into a dinosaur? And he sounded so matter-of-fact about it . . .'

'He probably doesn't even know what a dinosaur is. It's just a word he's heard on TV or the radio.'

'I don't think so. Young boys tend to be dinosaur-mad. I know I was at his age. I had a big collection of plastic ones and could give the correct name for each one. I wouldn't mind betting that young Simon knows more about dinosaurs than you do.'

'Are you saying you believe he saw a dinosaur?'

'No. I'm saying I believe *he* believes he saw a dinosaur. And whatever it was it definitely wasn't a Siberian tiger. Sir Penward is lying.'

'Why?' she asked.

'That's what *I* want to know.'

She sighed. 'Poor little Simon isn't the only one who's retreated into a fantasy world. You're so anxious to get your hands on a big, exclusive story you're making one up.'

'It's not my imagination that someone cleaned up the animal's prints in the poultry shed. And look at the way Penward's men were trampling all over the ground behind the Smythe-Graves' house. I bet by now not one clear print exists. And what about the way the "tiger" was whisked away by helicopter before the police arrived? All bloody suspicious if you ask me.'

Jenny frowned. 'Well, yes, it is a *bit,*' she admitted reluctantly.

'But the idea that Sir Penward is hiding a living dinosaur in his zoo is just absurd.'

'Penward is always financing expeditions to hunt for rare wild animals. Perhaps one of them came back with something *very* rare.'

'David, dinosaurs are extinct,' she said, her tone patronising, 'they became extinct millions and millions of years ago. It's impossible that a species of dinosaur somehow managed to survive until the present day. The idea is pure sci-fi . . .'

'Look,' he persisted, 'I'm not saying that whatever Penward has in his zoo is a bona-fide dinosaur, I'm just putting the theory forward that it's some kind of rare animal that *resembles* a dinosaur. Maybe it's a big lizard or perhaps even some previously unknown species of mammal.'

'Then why is he keeping it a secret?' she asked.

'Who knows? He might have smuggled it out of its home country illegally, or maybe it's because he's a typical collector. Collectors are obsessive types: when they get something really rare they like to keep it all to themselves, especially if their right to ownership is in doubt. If Penward has really got himself some animal unknown to science then every zoologist in the world is going to demand access to it.'

Jenny was quiet for a while, then she said, 'Okay, I admit you make it all *sound* kind of logical, but it seems so far-fetched. You've got no real proof at all, just some wild theories and the word of a poor child who's just undergone the most terrible experience.'

'Oh, I'll get the proof all right,' he said confidently, 'even if I have to break into Penward's damn zoo to find it.'

6

'I just can't believe he's going to get away with it,' muttered Pascal.

'You're learning an important lesson, David my lad,' said Johnny MacGibbon as he poured a small amount of water into his double scotch. 'There are some people in this world who can get away with anything. Sir Penward is one of them.'

They were in the Green Man, their local pub, having what was misleadingly termed a 'quick after work drink'. Pascal would be there for at least another hour while MacGibbon wouldn't be leaving the bar until closing time, as usual.

It was two weeks to the day that the 'tiger' had escaped from Penward's zoo and gone on its fatal rampage. The small army of journalists and TV crews that had invaded Warchester afterwards had since departed, but the story was still very much alive in the nation's news media. The latest development was that Stanley Pitt had agreed to drop the charges of negligence against Sir Penward even though a few days ago he'd made a press statement to the effect that he wouldn't rest until Penward had been brought to justice and his zoo shut down.

'Obviously someone has been putting pressure on him to back down,' said MacGibbon.

'On Pitt?' asked Pascal, surprised. 'But he's an MP. A *Conservative* MP for God's sake. If anyone has influence to burn it's him.'

MacGibbon chuckled gently and downed his scotch with one swallow. As he beckoned to Jaz, the barmaid, he said, 'Accept this in the best possible spirit, lad, but you're still somewhat naive when it comes to the realities of life.'

'For example?' asked Pascal, slightly annoyed.

'For example you're naive if you believe that politicians hold all the power in this country. We may be living in the 1980s but Britain hasn't really changed all that much. Most of the wealth, and a lot of the real power, is still in the hands of a small number of families. The British aristocracy is just as powerful as it ever was, it's just not as obvious about it as it used to be.'

'Oh, come on . . .' smiled Pascal.

'I'm not exaggerating, believe me. And Sir Penward is one of the richest men in England. His family owns chunks of Canada, Australia, South Africa and God knows what else.'

'Just because someone is very rich doesn't mean they can buy their way around the law. Not in Britain, anyway.'

MacGibbon regarded him sorrowfully. 'My, you *have* got a lot to learn, lad. But it's not just the money in Penward's case, it's his connections too. He has powerful friends. They stick together, the aristocrats. When one of their number gets into trouble, no matter how serious, they close ranks around him. Look at Lord Lucan. To disappear *that* completely he had to have help of a very special kind.'

Pascal nodded but didn't look entirely convinced. 'I don't see how these so-called powerful friends could have influenced the Health and Safety Executive.' The Executive, which is responsible for safety in private zoos in England, had taken out a summons against Penward but dropped it after their officials had inspected the tiger compound and declared it met their standards of construction. The fact that the tiger had somehow managed to scale the fence was no fault of Sir Penward's as far as they were concerned.

MacGibbon shrugged. 'Maybe they did, maybe they didn't. But I have heard whispers that the Director of Public Prosecutions took a personal interest in the case. And he's an old school friend of Penward's . . .'

'Are you suggesting . . . ?'

MacGibbon said slyly, 'I'm not suggesting anything. I'm just trying to make you see that Penward's influence extends a long way.'

'And you think he somehow put pressure on Pitt to drop the charges against him? How?'

'Who knows? But I'll tell you one interesting thing. You know that Penward has promised to increase the security around the estate even though he's under no legal obligation to do so?'

'Yes. We mentioned it in the paper. He said he's going to build a double row of fences round the entire estate. And the inner one is going to be electrified. It's to make sure that if any other animal escapes from the zoo it won't get off the estate. Costing him a fortune, so he keeps saying.'

'Right. And guess whose security company has got the contract to do the job?' asked MacGibbon.

'Not *Pitt's*?' said Pascal with surprise.

'None other.'

'God, you mean Pitt has let himself be bought off by Penward? But his *son* got killed by that animal.'

'Pitt's a business man first and foremost. Someone probably whispered in his ear it would be a choice between the carrot and the big stick. He chose the carrot. He's well aware that Penward could wipe him out financially with just a blow of his nose.'

Pascal shook his head disgustedly. 'And Penward's come to terms with the families of all the other victims too. He offered them huge cash settlements which they've all accepted, even Mr Smythe-Graves . . .'

'*And* he succeeded in smoothing Inspector Bodycombe's ruffled plumage,' said MacGibbon with reluctant admiration, 'which can't have been easy. The Inspector and his men were made to look like fools that day.'

'I know,' said Pascal. 'I can't understand why Bodycombe is letting the matter rest. He *knows* Penward delayed telling the police about the animal's escape, and that he tampered with the evidence at the poultry farm.'

MacGibbon put a forefinger to the side of his red nose and said quietly, 'Well, I have heard rumours that Bodycombe got the carrot and stick treatment too.'

'You mean Penward *bribed* the Inspector?' asked Pascal, somewhat shocked.

'No. Not exactly. Let's just say it was pointed out to him that his promotion prospects would be just that much better if he forgot the whole thing. On the other hand his career might come to a sudden halt if he didn't. Apparently there are a few skeletons in the Inspector's closet from his younger days as a policeman. I am told he made a few foolish decisions once upon a time.'

Pascal looked at MacGibbon with new respect. 'Where do you hear these things?'

'Oh, around,' said MacGibbon nonchalantly, 'people tell me things. Mainly because they don't take me very seriously. Certainly not as a journalist anyway.'

'Look,' said Pascal eagerly, 'why don't we write a story that will expose this wide open? With what you know and what I know we could really stir things up. At the very least we could force Penward to close down his zoo. He may have bought off the idiots who run this town, but a lot of people are frightened that another animal might escape one of these days, no matter how many new fences he builds.'

MacGibbon shook his head. 'Count me out. I don't have much

but I don't intend throwing it away on a hopeless cause, and I advise you to follow my example. I don't know why you're so obsessed with the matter – you seem to have a personal vendetta against Penward – but you're wasting your time. You can't win against someone like him, believe me.'

'We'll see,' said Pascal, disappointed that he couldn't rely on MacGibbon for support. He finished his drink, ordered another round, then stared moodily into his glass feeling depressed.

Pascal hadn't given up on his belief that the animal that had escaped and killed six people wasn't a tiger, even though Penward had displayed the dead carcass of a female Siberian tiger to the press the following day. It had been shot through the head with a single .303 bullet. Penward had apparently carried out the execution himself, even though he'd raised the tiger, called Pocahontas, from a cub himself. The members of the press were also, subtly, made aware of the animal's high value, which made Sir Penward's act of contrition even more impressive.

None of this convinced Pascal for a moment. It would have taken an examination of the contents of the tiger's stomach to persuade him it was the same creature that had partially eaten two people and a pony, but no one in authority had demanded such a post-mortem. And why should they? The only person who suspected Penward of substituting another animal was Pascal, and until he could get the evidence to uphold his suspicions he knew it would be useless telling anyone else about them.

And so far his efforts to obtain that evidence had been met with frustration. He had had no luck at all in gaining access to Penward's zoo since the incident. He hadn't even been allowed to join the other reporters who'd been invited to Penward Hall to see the tiger's corpse. He'd tried to get in, of course, but had been stopped at the gate by two of Penward's employees who'd told him, to his annoyance, that the *Warchester Times* wasn't on the list they'd been given, therefore they couldn't admit him. He'd tried to argue that surely a reporter from the town's own newspaper had more of a right to be there than all the other journalists, but in vain . . .

So the next day he'd called up Penward's private secretary, a man by the name of Charles Pearson, and asked for a personal interview with Sir Penward. Pearson said he would call him back.

What happened was that twenty minutes later Brownlowe summoned him into his office and demanded to know what 'all this foolishness with Sir Penward' was about. As calmly as possible Pascal had explained that the readers of the *Times* might be interested in hearing Sir Penward's version of the tragedy in his own words – he owed them that much at the very least – but it was like trying to talk to the coffee machine. Brownlowe had reacted with uncomprehending astonishment. 'What is the *matter* with you, Pascal? How can you think of pestering Sir Penward at a time like this?'

Pascal had opened his mouth to say that it was a reporter's job to pester people like Sir Penward at times like these but knew it would be a waste of breath. Instead he'd simply muttered, 'It's probably the hot weather, sir. Sorry . . .' And walked out of the office.

He couldn't see any other way of looking over the zoo. It had been closed to the public for an indefinite period which meant he had no legitimate means of access for the time being. And as for his rash boast to Jenny that he would break into the zoo, that was out of the question too, what with the new security fences already under construction.

Pascal had racked his brains for alternative avenues of investigation. The most obvious one would be to question the Smythe-Graves boy more closely, but his grieving father had taken him to stay with relatives somewhere in Devon. And anyway he doubted if he would be allowed to speak to him.

Finally he had come up with one possibility, and he intended following it through this very night . . .

'Look, there's Jenny.'

MacGibbon's words brought him out of his reverie. He looked round to see Jenny entering the bar. She was accompanied by Tony Chilton, the young manager of one of the local banks. They'd been seen together with increasing frequency of late, much to Pascal's irritation. Jenny had known him for about six months – she'd met him at her tennis club – but had always described him as 'just a friend'. Now it looked as if the friendship was developing into something else. Pascal knew he had no right to feel proprietorial about her, having ended their own affair himself, but that didn't lessen the sharp, jealous pangs he experienced whenever he saw her with him.

'Forgive my asking,' said MacGibbon, 'but what's up with you two? For a while there I thought you and Jenny were getting pretty close, then suddenly it all seemed to be over.'

'Oh, it was never more than a casual thing between us,' said Pascal offhandedly, not really wanting to talk about it. 'Never anything serious.'

MacGibbon tut-tutted. 'If you want my opinion, Davey lad, you're making a serious error if you let her slip through your fingers. Girls like Jenny only come along once in your life, and that's if you're lucky . . .'

'Once is enough,' muttered Pascal. He was watching her out of the corner of his eye. She was standing at the far end of the bar and laughing at something Chilton had just said. It was bad enough that Chilton was a tanned, athletic-looking hulk, but that he could make her laugh was even worse.

Their relationship had been even cooler than usual since the day of the 'tiger'. It was partly because, he knew, she hadn't forgiven him for the incident with the Smythe-Graves boy, but also because he'd deliberately avoided the subject of his theories about Penward's escaped animal. In fact he now regretted ever mentioning it to her. If his suspicions proved right he was onto one of the biggest stories of the decade, and the idea of having to share it with Jenny didn't appeal.

She was laughing again. Apparently Chilton was the banking world's equivalent of the Monty Python team all rolled into one. The sight helped to make up Pascal's mind. He finished his drink quickly and said, 'Must run, Johnny. I've got a small errand to take care of before I go home.'

MacGibbon raised his eyebrows in surprise. 'Not for the paper, I trust? I thought I'd trained you out of those kind of bad habits.'

'No, this is purely personal. I'll see you tomorrow.'

Pascal made a point of ignoring Jenny as he walked out of the bar. He half hoped that she would call out to him, but she didn't. She probably hadn't even noticed him go by, he decided sourly as he climbed into his battered Ford Cortina.

A few minutes later he was driving through the outskirts of

Warchester. His destination was the Phoenix Arms, the pub used by Penward's men.

7

Pascal rarely used the Phoenix Arms. He didn't like the pub much. It was usually full of 'Hooray Henrys' and the huntin' and fishin' brigade, rich farmers and the like. Also the staff were well known for their rudeness to anyone who wasn't part of the regular set of customers. They made sure you were aware that you didn't belong there.

He was pleased to spot four of Penward's employees as soon as he entered the main bar. They were instantly recognisable even though they were in 'civilian' clothes. As usual they were standing apart from the other people in the bar and talking only among themselves.

Pascal eyed them with interest as he ordered a pint of Guinness from a surly young barman. Once again he was struck by the way they all resembled each other with their short hair, muscular builds and complexions glowing with good health.

They're like clones thought Pascal as he approached them with his drink. 'Excuse me,' he said brightly, 'sorry for butting in but you're from the zoo, aren't you?'

Their conversation stopped and they turned as one towards him, their resentment at the intrusion obvious. Under the cold stare of those four pairs of arrogant eyes Pascal felt his resolve falter slightly.

Finally one of them said, 'That's right, we are.' His tone contained the unspoken: 'So what's it to you?'

Pascal pressed on. 'Awful about that tiger, wasn't it? Jolly good thing you people captured it so quickly – otherwise it might have chalked up a lot more victims . . .'

'Yes.' The four pairs of eyes continued to stare coldly at him.

'I understand Sir Penward shot the animal himself,' continued Pascal.

'That's right,' said the one who had done all the talking so far, such as it was. The temperature dropped even further.

'Must have been difficult for him. I've read how much he loves those big cats of his. Was it a very valuable tiger?'

'Very.'

Again the cold, questioning silence. Pascal gave them what he hoped was his most ingratiating smile. 'Isn't it odd that a tiger born and raised in captivity should become a man-eater?'

This time they all exchanged a brief glance before the unofficial spokesman replied. 'No,' he said, 'tigers are very unpredictable. They are the most dangerous of all the big cats.'

Pascal was impressed. It was almost a speech. He decided to try a different tack. 'Sir Penward must pay well for you to work in such a risky place.'

'It's a *privilege* to work for Sir Penward,' said the spokesman coldly.

Pascal was finding it hard to keep the smile on his face. This wasn't going at all well.

And at that precise moment, as if by telepathy, one of the four narrowed his eyes and said accusingly, 'I recognise you. You work for the newspaper.'

'You're right,' said one of the others quickly. 'He was at Ashton Woods on the day of the hunt. And at the Smythe-Graves' house later. With a girl . . .'

'What's your game then?' the spokesman demanded harshly.

'Game? I'm not up to any game,' said Pascal through his aching smile. 'I just want to ask you a few questions. I'm thinking of writing a piece about your zoo . . .'

'You'd better speak to Sir Penward about that. Not us.' They exchanged glances again and then all quickly finished their drinks. Pascal realized they were about to leave.

'Hey, wait, don't go yet,' he pleaded, 'let me buy you all a drink . . .'

They deposited their glasses on the bar and moved off without another word, leaving Pascal standing there by himself. The other customers watched Penward's men leave, then stared curiously at Pascal. Feeling foolish, he cursed silently to himself. It had been a total waste of time, coming to the Phoenix Arms. All he'd achieved was to arouse their antagonism towards him. *And* their suspicions . . .

There was the sound of a powerful motor starting up in the car park beside the pub. Pascal guessed it was their Land Rover. Then he saw the lights of a vehicle go past the front windows and head off down the road in the direction of Penward Manor.

'You make a habit of this, do you?'

Pascal turned and found himself looking into the round, flushed face of the publican, a big fat man with a handlebar moustache and an abrasive manner that was famous locally.

'Pardon?' said Pascal.

'You make a habit of scaring off customers? Because if you do I don't want to see you around here again.' He spoke loudly enough for his voice to be heard throughout the bar.

Pascal felt himself flushing with embarrassment. 'Don't worry,' he said with as much sarcasm as he could muster, 'I'm just going. And I won't be back.' He drank the remains of his Guinness and banged the glass down.

'You can bet on it!' called the publican to his departing back, provoking titters of amusement from the other customers.

Pascal was still seething with anger and embarrassment as he opened his car door. As a result he didn't notice that he wasn't alone in the car park – until it was too late.

The first blow caught him totally by surprise. For a few moments he had no idea what was happening: all he was aware of was a sudden impact in the side of his head behind his right ear. Then he was on his hands and knees beside his car watching a spectacular display of exploding lights. As he tried to get up a boot thudded into his left side and he went sprawling onto the gravel.

By then his dazed mind had grasped what was happening. He twisted round to get a look at his attacker, but this action coincided with another kick. The toe of the heavy work boot connected with the ridge of bone above his right eye. His head snapped back and he knew immediately he'd been hurt badly, even though there was no pain as yet.

He lay on his back staring up at the night sky. The firework display had grown even more spectacular. All his strength had left him. He was completely helpless. There was nothing he could do to defend himself. He waited passively for the next kick.

But it didn't come. Instead he heard two pairs of footsteps

moving away across the gravel car park. He lay there listening to them recede into the distance and then move onto the bitumen surface of the road. A short time later he heard a car door open and shut and an engine start up. It was a familiar sound.

He realized that Penward's men had stopped the Land Rover a short distance away from the pub and two of them had come back to lie in wait for him in the car park.

Slowly he sat up and began to assess the damage tentatively. He still didn't feel any pain but his head felt so strange he knew it was going to take more than a couple of aspirins and a cold compress to take care of it. He touched his face and discovered it was covered in blood. Already there was a massive lump under his right eyebrow and his eye was beginning to close up. More disturbing was a pulsating orange blob of light *within* his eye. Had the retina been injured, he wondered with sick anxiety. Detached even? He tried to remember if a detached retina meant automatic blindness.

He stood up and leaned against the side of the car. He debated with himself whether to go back into the pub and ask for help, but finally decided not to. For all he knew the publican himself had been in on the set-up. He had certainly made sure that Pascal's departure was a quick one.

Pascal climbed into the car and wondered if he was capable of driving back into town. He wasn't dizzy and could see all right out of his left eye. He decided to risk it.

He felt strangely calm as he drove along the deserted country road back towards Warchester, even though blood was continuing to trickle down his face from the gash in his eyebrow and the right side of his head was beginning to throb. The only thing that really concerned him was the inconvenience his injuries would cause him and not the possible extent of their seriousness. He guessed he was suffering from mild shock.

As he entered the town it occurred to him it might be wise not to go straight home. He didn't want to risk upsetting his mother until he had checked out how badly he looked. So he decided to go to the office and clean himself up in the bathroom first. If it was obvious he needed hospital treatment he would drive himself there and call his mother later.

By the time he'd parked outside the paper his right eye had closed up completely, but the pulsating red blob remained as strong as before. *That settles it,* he told himself, *I'll have to go to the hospital . . .*

He let himself into the darkened office, after switching off the burglar alarm, and made his way warily towards the rear of the building. He didn't want to turn on the lights for fear of attracting the attention of his friends in the nearby police station. The last thing he needed was to have to answer awkward questions.

As he was passing Brownlowe's office he thought his left eye had begun to act up as well because he thought he saw a glow coming from under the door, then he realized he wasn't seeing things – the light *was* on in the office. Surprised that his employer was working so late, particularly as Brownlowe hardly ever stayed back if he could help it, Pascal opened the door – and received his second major shock of that night.

Jenny was on her hands and knees beside Brownlowe's desk. She was naked. Behind her, also naked, was Tony Chilton. He was gripping her by her waist and thrusting violently into her offered rear – so hard that with each thrust of his pelvis Jenny would jerk forward and almost lose her balance. And each time she did that she would utter a low, animal-like moan. Pascal had never heard her make that sound before.

He stood frozen, not wanting to believe what he was seeing. The image, however, was burning its way through the layers of his consciousness like acid. Time seemed to become horribly elastic, the moment stretching on and on. And then finally Chilton opened his eyes and saw him. Chilton's mouth, already hanging slackly open, opened wider. He stopped moving and stared at Pascal silently.

Realizing something was wrong Jenny lifted her head. She peered out through the tangle of damp hair across her face with pleasure-dulled eyes. Then she screamed.

Pascal had been so surprised by the sight of Jenny and Chilton together that he'd completely forgotten about his injuries. When she started screaming he remembered he probably looked extremely alarming. Blood was still trickling down his face from the gash above his eye.

Weakly he raised a hand and said, 'It's okay . . . it's not as bad as it looks.' But as he spoke his knees buckled and he pitched forward on his face. *I'm getting blood on Brownlowe's carpet* was his last thought as he passed out.

When Pascal came to he was lying on the couch in Brownlowe's office. Jenny was bending over him with a wet, blood-stained cloth in her hand. Chilton was hovering in the background looking uncomfortable. Pascal saw that they were both dressed now.

He sat up and groaned. He felt awful. The throbbing in his head had become much worse and he also had a sharp pain in his left side.

'David, what happened to you?' cried Jenny, 'Did you have an accident in your car?'

'No,' he muttered, 'It was a fight. Sort of. You should see the other guys. Not a scratch on them.' He tried to focus on his watch but couldn't. 'What time is it?'

'Quarter past eleven. You were in a *fight*? Who with?'

'That's what I'd like to know.'

'We should get him to hospital. That cut above his eye needs stitches in my opinion,' said Chilton, trying to sound authoritative.

Pascal glared at him. 'Why don't you piss off home? You must be very tired after all the exertion.'

Chilton's tan went a shade darker but he didn't say anything else.

'He's right, David,' said Jenny, 'we've got to get you to hospital. You look terrible.'

'I'll drive there myself,' he said, getting off the couch and standing up. The room spun.

'You're in no condition to drive. Tell him, Tony . . .'

'*Tony* can keep his advice to himself. I'm going to the bathroom.' Swaying slightly, he pushed past Jenny and walked out of the office.

He almost fainted again when he saw his face in the bathroom mirror. He was unrecognisable. He looked like he'd gone through a car windshield. Possibly two of them. Both his eyes were black, his nose was swollen and bleeding, and the entire right side of his face was puffed out like an inflatable toy. Most alarming of all was the deep gash over his right eye which continued to ooze blood.

He opened his shirt and examined his side. A giant bruise extended across his ribs. He sighed. So much for investigative journalism.

When he returned to the office Jenny and Chilton were having an intense, whispered conversation. It ended abruptly as he came in and they turned towards him. Pascal noted that Jenny at least had the grace to look a little shame-faced. Chilton, on the other hand, had recovered some of his bank-manager's poise.

'I'm taking you to the hospital,' Jenny told him.

'No need. I said I can drive myself. You two stay and finish what you were doing.'

Jenny flinched. Chilton said quickly to her, 'You sure you don't want me to hang around?'

'No, I'll be fine. You go.'

'Okay. Take care.' He gave her a kiss on the cheek. 'I'll call you in the morning.'

'Yeah, you do that,' said Pascal bitterly.

Chilton gave him a look of open dislike and opened his mouth to say something but then thought better of it. With a farewell nod to Jenny he hurried out of the office.

When he had gone Pascal said, 'I guess I was lucky he didn't hit me. He's a big man. In good shape too. Must be all that tennis.'

Jenny sighed. 'You don't understand.'

He tried to laugh and failed. 'I don't *understand* ... My God! I may be blind in one eye, but I could still see well enough to understand what you two were up to in here ... and it wasn't practising your backhand!'

'Come on,' she said curtly, 'Let's get going before *I* hit you.'

At the hospital they put three stitches into his eyebrow, taped up his ribs and X-rayed his head. To his relief there was no sign of any fracture. And to his greater relief an examination of his right eye revealed his retina was undamaged. 'That glowing after-image you can see is probably caused by bruising on the optic nerve,' the doctor in Casualty told him. 'It's just a temporary effect. May last a few days at most.'

Afterwards Jenny insisted on driving him home to his mother's house.

'Are you going to tell me what really happened?' she asked on the way.

'I told you. I got in a fight.'

'But who with?'

'Two people who are better at that sort of thing than me.'

'You're not going to tell me.'

'No.'

They drove on in silence for a while. Then Jenny said, 'Look, about Tony and me...'

'I know. Don't bother telling me. You're just good friends. *Very* good friends. I mean I'd hate to think you were going through all that just to get an extension on your overdraft.'

'If you're going to take that attitude it's a waste of time continuing the conversation.'

'You bet it is.'

He stared out of the window, his thoughts in a turmoil. Now that his anxiety about his eye had been alleviated he was beginning to fill up with a dull rage. Events had conspired tonight to turn him into a helpless, foolish-looking victim. The ultimate wimp. He had been pulped into the ground with ridiculous ease by two neanderthal hulks and then, as the *pièce de résistance,* he'd been obliged to witness the spectacular servicing of his girlfriend by God's gift to the banking industry. True, Jenny was technically his *ex* girlfriend, but that didn't ease the pain, or the humiliation.

Pascal wanted to hit back, badly. He wanted to break Tony Chilton's neck, but most of all he wanted to get his hands on Sir Darren Penward. He had become the symbol for all that was going wrong in Pascal's life. One way or the other, he decided, he was going to bring Sir Penward and his little empire tumbling down, no matter what the personal cost. He would do it even if it killed him.

8

Dinosaurs were definitely extinct.

Pascal had to face that fact, after spending his week of convalescence reading every book on the subject that his mother could find in the local library where she worked part-time. All the books said the same thing – dinosaurs became extinct approximately sixty-five million years ago. The fossil record since then showed no further trace of their existence. The likelihood of a species of dinosaur somehow surviving to the present day was, according to all the evidence, out of the question.

'Why this sudden interest in palaeontology?' asked his mother one afternoon when they were sitting together in the back garden. He glanced at her warily before replying. A tall, thin woman in her early fifties, she had been a school teacher before ill health forced her into premature retirement. She had the uncanny knack of always knowing when he was trying to hide something.

'I'm thinking of doing an article on dinosaurs for the paper,' he said carefully. 'You know, one of those typical 'Silly Season'' things.'

She nodded approvingly. 'Good idea. Warchester has quite an historical association with dinosaurs.'

'It has?' he asked, surprised.

'I thought you knew. The area was rich in dinosaur fossils. In fact some of the first dinosaur bones ever found in this country were discovered in Warchester way back in the 17th century. They were dug up in a quarry. Of course no one at the time knew what they were. One theory was that they were the remains of giant *men . . .*' She laughed. 'Actually the bones belonged to a dinosaur known as *Megalosaurus,* one of the first of the giant *carnosaurs.*'

'You know a lot about the subject,' said Pascal curiously.

'I should do. I used to take my classes regularly to the quarry. Lots more fossils were found there in the 19th century and it was famous for a time. There was a big public interest in dinosaurs in the 1850s and Warchester became a magnet for amateur fossil hunters.'

'That's interesting,' he said slowly, wondering if this had any significance or was just a bizarre coincidence. 'Where else were they found, apart from the quarry?'

'A lot turned up in the clay pits that supplied the old Penward brickworks. The clay of Cambridgeshire and Bedfordshire was seabed sediment in the Late Jurassic era and contains a lot of fossils. Most of those found were of sea reptiles like plesiosaurs, which aren't technically dinosaurs, but a great many dinosaur fossils were also dug up in the pits. Obviously these came from the corpses of dinosaurs that had floated down river and been washed out to sea . . .'

He flipped through the pages of the book on his lap until he came across a colour plate of a plesiosaur. It was a long-necked creature with four large flippers. It was similar to the popular conception of the Loch Ness Monster. He showed it to his mother. 'I always thought these things *were* dinosaurs.'

She shook her head. 'No doubt they had a common ancestor but they were a different group entirely. Dinosaurs are a specific class of land reptiles and are distinguished by skull and limb structure. They were the most efficiently built, let's say, of the land reptiles, which was why they were so successful. And for so long.'

'One hundred and forty million years, it says here,' said Pascal, tapping the book. 'A hell of a long time. Yet now not a trace of them remains except for some old bones.'

'That may not be completely so,' said his mother.

'What do you mean?' he asked, raising his eyebrows.

'Well, some scientists believe that birds evolved from one of the dinosaur species. If that's true, then the dinosaurs are still with us.'

'Oh,' he said, disappointed. He looked at a sparrow that was hopping along the top of the garden wall. It seemed absurd that this harmless little creature was a direct descendant of the dinosaurs. But then it seemed absurd that this prosaic back garden with its rose bushes and deck chairs had once been at the bottom of a primeval sea. He was suddenly struck by the realization of how transitory everything really was: this permanent-looking setting had existed, and would exist, for only a fraction of a second in terms of geological time. The thought sent a slight chill through him.

'How long has it been since anyone found some fossils round here?' he asked.

'Oh, not for years. Nothing big at any rate, but people still occasionally come across small fossil fragments in the quarry. Bits of teeth and so on. I don't know about the clay pits. They've been closed to the public for 15 years at least. But I think the last major finds there were made in the 1920s by Sir Penward's grandfather – Oswald. Sir Oswald was a keen amateur palaeontologist and built up quite a large collection of dinosaur skeletons. He used to have them on display in the manor house – I remember seeing them when I was a girl. Heaven knows what ever happened to them. I imagine they were sent to museums after Sir Oswald died. Or perhaps they're still on the estate somewhere.'

'Curiouser and curiouser,' muttered Pascal, wondering again if this strange coincidence meant anything or whether he was just creating patterns where none really existed.

'By the way dear, you're not the only one in town to have developed a sudden interest in dinosaurs,' said his mother.

He straightened in his deck chair. 'I'm not?'

'No. Your friend Jenny came into the library this morning asking for dinosaur books. I said they were all with you. She didn't seem surprised . . .'

I bet she didn't, he thought angrily. 'She's helping me with the dinosaur article,' he said quickly. 'I'd better call her and tell her I've got enough material now and she needn't bother . . .'

'She's such a lovely girl.'

'Who?' he asked distractedly.

'Jenny, of course.'

'Oh . . . yes.' He frowned. So she hadn't forgotten about his dinosaur-like animal theory even though she hadn't mentioned it again since the day of the killings. Instead she was following up the story on her own, the bitch . . .

'You haven't brought her back here for ages. Nor do you talk about her much any more. I gather from that that you two are no longer such good friends?'

He smiled inwardly at his mother's prim choice of words. 'No,' he said, 'We're not.'

'What happened? An argument?'

He sighed. 'Yes.' He didn't want to discuss it with her.

'And that's it? You're not going to tell me any more?'

'I'd rather not, if you don't mind.'

She shook her head sadly. 'I *do* wish you'd confide in me, David. We never seem to *talk* together any more.'

He looked at his mother's gaunt face. You could still see that she had once been an attractive woman but now the skin was stretched unhealthily tight over her skull and she wore the habitual expression of nervous anxiety she'd had ever since his father had died twelve years ago. It was then that her migraines had begun too. Guiltily he said, 'There's nothing *to* confide, believe me. I'm living a very dull life at the moment.'

'Dull? I wouldn't call being dreadfully beaten up dull. And you still haven't told me who did that to you.'

'I told you I don't *know.* I didn't see their faces. It all happened so quickly.'

'And you have no idea why they did it?'

'Not a clue,' he said uneasily.

'You worry me, David. I don't want anything to happen to you. You know you're all I have left now.'

He winced. He knew the conversation would end up taking this embarrassing route. Stiffly he said, 'Nothing is going to happen to me.' He looked away from her and pretended to become interested in the sparrow. It was now upside-down on the wall and pecking at something in the gap between two bricks. Then suddenly there was a struggling spider in its beak. The bird flew triumphantly back to the top of the wall and swallowed its victim.

Pascal's first assignment on returning to the paper was to cover the church fête being held that Saturday. It was supposed to have been held weeks ago but had been postponed because of the tragedy.

Pascal arrived feeling frustrated and in a bad mood. He had run completely out of ideas for determining the truth about

Penward's escaped animal. The only way he was going to achieve that goal was by getting into the zoo and seeing what was in there for himself . . . but how?

The day before he had driven out to the Penward estate and spent a wasted couple of hours walking beside the high perimeter fences. The security, he quickly saw, had been greatly improved. Television cameras were mounted on top of the fence at regular intervals, along with other devices he didn't recognize, and now there was also an inner fence displaying signs that read: DANGER: ELECTRIFIED. Obviously Stanley Pitt's security company had been doing well here.

But as Pascal studied the fences he became convinced that the new safeguards seemed to be aimed more at keeping people *out* of the estate rather than keeping the animals in . . .

Later, while driving past one of the farms that lay adjacent to the Penward estate he had, on impulse, stopped and walked over to a farm worker repairing a water pump in one of the fields. The worker, a big man with the face of someone who didn't do much thinking, was not pleased at the interruption and answered Pascal's questions with increasing annoyance. No, he hadn't seen anything strange in the Penward grounds recently; yes, you could hear the cries of the zoo animals a lot of the time, depending on which way the wind was blowing and yes, it did upset the farm animals but that had been happening for years now. The smells from the zoo always upset them too . . .

When Pascal had asked him if he'd heard any *new* animal cries, or cries he couldn't recognize, the worker had looked at him as if he was crazy. 'What do you mean?' he asked.

'Well, an animal that doesn't sound like a lion or a tiger,' said Pascal helplessly, 'or anything else you normally hear there.' He could hardly say: *A cry that something like a dinosaur might make.* What on earth did a dinosaur sound like? No one knew. It was possible they weren't capable of making sounds at all. The fossil records, according to the books Pascal had read, gave no clue in this area.

He had quickly ended his futile quizzing of the farm worker and walked back to his car feeling foolish. It was times like that when he had serious doubts about the whole matter . . .

It was a hot day with the temperature in the low 80s, so he made his way towards the drinks tent as soon as he entered the churchyard. He was bored already, and resentful. Penward's zoo concealed what might be the biggest story of the decade and here he was having to write about a church fête. It was pathetic.

The tent was crowded. Pascal recognised the majority of the people there, including the paper's photographer, Henry Wates. Pascal didn't like Wates very much; he was a small, wiry man in his early thirties whose range of conversation covered only two subjects, sex and cars. Pascal found the latter subject boring and Wates' almost pathological obsession with the former somewhat distasteful. Anyone who talked so much about sex – his own experiences as well as other people's – and in such clinical detail, obviously had a problem.

Wates came over to him immediately. The inevitable Canon was hanging round his neck, as was the inevitable cigarette hanging out of the corner of his mouth. He was clutching a pint of lager too. 'Hello, Davey lad,' he cried, giving him his usual leer, 'You *do* look a treat. What happened? Her husband come home too early?'

Pascal gave him a pained smile. Wates hadn't seen him since the attack. 'You should have seen me a week ago. I look almost human now.' This was true. The swellings had practically gone and all that was left was some bruising around and above his right eye.

'So what's the true story?' asked Wates, lowering his voice to a conspiratorial whisper. 'You can trust old Henry . . .'

Patiently, Pascal repeated the same thing he'd told everyone else. He'd been jumped by two men in the car park of the Phoenix Arms. He didn't know who they were or the reason for the attack. Perhaps they mistook him for someone else; perhaps they were just drunk and in the mood for some aggro.

Wates looked disappointed. 'Is that all?'

'I'm afraid so,' said Pascal. He glanced around the tent and to change the subject said, 'So what's been happening here? Anything exciting?'

'Are you kidding? The most exciting thing to have happened so far is the bobbing for apples competition. You should have been here. The tension was unbearable.'

Pascal forced a laugh and went off to buy a pint of lager. When he returned Wates was busy scanning the female half of the tent's population, his leer even more pronounced than usual. He looked like a small, balding shark. Pascal had never known anyone before who was so blatantly lustful, but Wates seemed to get away with it.

As Pascal expected he then had to endure a sexual litany as Wates described the physical plus and minuses of most of the women present, adding intimate details in many cases which he claimed came from first-hand experience. Pascal had given up trying to work out how much of his sexual boasting was based on fact and how much was fantasy. He had to admit that despite Wates' unprepossessing appearance women did seem to find him attractive.

While Wates talked on Pascal's mind drifted back to the subject that had been plaguing him for the last few weeks – Penward's mystery animal. He was abruptly brought back to reality when Wates poked him in the arm and said, 'Aren't you listening to me, mate? I said, don't look now but Lady Fang herself has got her eye on you . . .'

'Pardon?' said Pascal, wondering what the hell Wates was talking about. 'Lady Fang . . . ?'

'Her worshipfulness,' he whispered impatiently, 'The Grand Dame. Lady Penward herself. Over there . . .'

Pascal followed the direction of Wates' furtive thumb and saw Lady Jane Penward standing some five yards away drinking champagne with the Mayor's wife. And she *was* staring straight at him. But as their eyes met she looked away.

'She fancies you, mate,' said Wates out of the corner of his mouth.

'Don't be ridiculous,' laughed Pascal. 'She's probably wondering where I got the black eye.'

'Listen mate, there was no mistaking the look she gave you. Believe me, you could be in there.'

'With *Lady Penward?*' Pascal laughed again at the absurdity of the idea.

'Davey, don't tell me you don't know about her. She's a bloody nympho. Goes through blokes like a threshing machine. Leaves nothing but the bones and a smile . . .'

Pascal grinned down into Wates' flushed, earnest face. 'You've got to stop believing everything you read on the back of toilet doors.'

'It's *true,*' protested Wates. 'She doesn't mess around here in her own patch, she does her trolling outside of Warchester as a rule – Cambridge is her main hunting ground. She even has a flat there. Ask anyone if you don't believe me . . .'

Pascal looked curiously back at Lady Penward and again their eyes met. Was it his imagination, fanned by Wates' words, or did her gaze linger on him this time? He *had* heard that her marriage with Sir Penward was a far from happy one and that she took lovers, but he'd always presumed that was just local gossip. Not that he would have been surprised to learn that her marriage really was an unhappy one – being married to Sir Penward couldn't be a lot of fun.

He had seen Lady Jane on numerous occasions before – usually at functions like this one – but had never spoken to her. Now, perhaps for the first time, he found himself studying her carefully. She was a striking woman. Handsome rather than attractive. She was tall – nearly five foot ten inches – slim and held herself very straight. She had coal black hair that hung down past her wide shoulders and an angular face with very prominent cheek-bones. Her eyes, her best feature, were large and expressive. It was a severe face in repose, but when she smiled it softened into something approaching true beauty.

As he continued his study of her she again looked directly at him. This time it was he who looked away. But there had been no mistaking the cool challenge in her stare . . .

'See, I told you,' whispered Wates hoarsely. 'You're in there, mate.'

Feeling both flattered and childishly excited, Pascal said, without much conviction, 'Oh, come on, it's your imagination. Why on earth would she be interested in me?'

'. . . because you're good-looking, and you're young. She likes 'em young, I hear. That's why she spends so much time in Cambridge. It's the students she goes after . . .'

'I'm not young. I'm twenty-six . . .'

'When you're knocking forty like she is, then twenty-six is

young. Besides, with your blond curls and blue eyes you look even younger. I sometimes fancy you myself.'

'Thanks. You've made my day,' said Pascal sourly.

'So what are you going to do about her?'

'Do? Are you crazy? I'm not going to do *anything* about her . . .' Then Pascal paused. The idea that had formed in his subconscious a couple of minutes ago had just broken through to the surface. It came almost as a blinding flash, shocking him with its audacity.

He looked at Lady Jane again, his heart beating fast. He saw her differently now; he saw her as the potential solution to his problem.

She was going to be his way into Penward's zoo.

9

The dinosaur slammed its two ton bulk against the titanium bars of the cage and let out an angry cry that was a cross between an ambulance siren and a giant fingernail being scraped down glass. The whole building vibrated from the impact, but the thick bars, set firmly in several feet of concrete, didn't budge.

The animal was a *Megalosaurus,* a successful breed of carnosaur that had flourished across England and France throughout the Jurassic period and part of the Cretaceous. Its skin was scaly and coloured a bright green. It stood upright on its hind legs and the top of its large head was some ten feet above the floor of the cage.

It was a young male, two years old and not fully grown. The reason for its belligerence was sexual frustration, which made it bad tempered and even more dangerous than when it was hungry. Unfortunately it would never have the opportunity of satisfying its desire, as no female member of its breed existed.

The dinosaur paced to the rear of its cage and swung its huge tail against the wall. Again the building vibrated. It repeated its air-splitting shriek of rage and frustration, forcing the two keepers beyond the bars to cover their ears with their hands.

'Jesus, what's *wrong* with it?' asked one of them when the noise had died down. 'It was only fed an hour ago.'

'Maybe it's sick,' said the other man. 'It's left a lot of its meal untouched.' He pointed at the three bloody sheep carcasses. The sheep, which had been fed live to the creature, had been killed but only partly eaten.

'It doesn't *act* sick,' said the first man, moving closer to the bars. 'Perhaps it's got a toothache.'

'Look out!'

He ducked back just in time as the dinosaur, moving with a terrible speed, turned and lashed out between the bars with one of its powerful forearms. The 'hand', with its three long claws, cut through the air with a swishing sound, narrowly missing the keeper.

'Jesus, that thing is *fast!*' he cried, obviously shaken.

'We'd better go and get Sir Penward,' said the other keeper. 'We're going to have to quieten this thing down somehow. He's beginning to excite the others.'

At this moment Pascal was driving out of Warchester. It was 7 p.m. He was heading towards the small town of Thrapham some eighteen miles from Warchester. He was wearing his best suit and was in a state of high excitement. He was also experiencing a strong feeling of trepidation. He wasn't sure how he was going to cope with what lay ahead that night.

And what lay ahead was Lady Jane Penward.

He still hadn't recovered from the surprise at how rapidly events had moved that afternoon. After fortifying himself with a quick beer he had gathered up his courage and approached Lady Jane, although she was still talking to the Mayor's wife. It was one of the hardest things he'd ever done in his life, and wasn't made any easier with the knowledge that Henry Wates was observing his progress with fascinated interest.

With a dry mouth he had introduced himself to Lady Jane and asked if she minded being subjected to a short interview. The Mayor's wife, a thin, haughty woman with delusions of grandeur, made it clear she resented the interruption, but Lady Jane had smiled warmly at him and said she'd be happy to talk to the *Warchester Times*.

Pascal had then asked her some mindless questions about the

fête and the subsequent benefits for the local charities and she had responded with some equally vacuous comments, though delivered with such practised skill and charm they had the illusion of substance.

After a few minutes of this the Mayor's wife was beginning to give him increasingly angry looks, even though Lady Jane seemed quite happy to continue the discussion. Pascal, however, felt himself starting to dry up. His supply of meaningless questions was rapidly running out and he knew he wouldn't be able to prolong the 'interview' for much longer. All of a sudden the whole idea seemed ridiculous – how in the world had he, even for a moment, believed *he* could proposition the wife of Sir Penward? And, even more incredibly, expected her to accept?

As his questioning began to falter he was gripped by panic. Now what? It was all hopeless. He'd end up standing there stupidly in front of the two women while they stared at him blankly, wondering what was wrong with him.

Then, unexpectedly, Lady Jane turned to the mayor's wife and asked if she'd mind fetching her another glass of champagne. The woman was only too happy to oblige. As she hurried away Jane then turned back to Pascal and said, 'Do you like trout?'

'Trout?' he repeated weakly. The conversation appeared to have veered off into totally bizarre areas. 'Uh, yes, I quite like trout,' he finally replied, hoping that was the right answer.

'There's a small country inn called The Three Suns just outside of Thrapham that serves the finest cooked trout in all of England. Would you care to be my guest there for dinner tonight? Say 8pm?'

Pascal thought he was hearing things. He stared into her eyes and saw immediately that they held a plain and unmistakable invitation that had nothing to do with trout, well cooked or otherwise.

He swallowed noisily and said, 'Yes, I'd love to.'

'Fine,' she said. 'That's settled then.' And at that point the Mayor's wife returned with the champagne. As Lady Jane took the glass she thanked her and then said to Pascal, 'Is that sufficient for your needs, Mr Pascal?'

'Pardon?' he asked, at a loss. Then he realized she was talking about the interview. He nodded violently. 'Oh yes, fine. Marvellous . . .'

'I must admit I'm impressed by your professionalism, Mr Pascal,' she added.

'Really? How do you mean?' he asked, frowning.

'You conducted the whole interview without once having to write anything down in your notebook. You must have a great memory.' Then, after giving him another smile, she resumed her conversation with the Mayor's wife.

Pascal walked back over to Wates in a daze.

'Well?' demanded Wates. 'What happened?'

'Nothing,' lied Pascal. 'We just made small-talk. About the fête. And trout.'

Wates looked at him suspiciously. 'Trout?'

Pascal gave a long sigh. 'I need another drink. Badly.'

He was late. He had got lost and been obliged to stop and ask for directions three times. By the time he reached the inn it was twenty past eight. He parked in the small yard beside the picturesque old building, which stood next to a stream, and hurried inside. He feared that Lady Jane had got tired of waiting and had gone already, but was relieved to see her sitting in the inn's tiny bar just off the main entrance. She was alone and dressed very differently from that afternoon. At the fête she'd been wearing a simple blue dress and a wide brimmed white hat; now she was wearing tight jeans, boots and an old blazer that could have come from the fête's jumble sale. The effect of this ensemble was to make her look years younger . . .

She smiled as he came into the bar and cut short his apologies and explanations as to why he was late. 'No matter,' she said, 'the important thing is you made it.' She finished her drink in one swallow and got off the bar stool. 'Let's go upstairs.'

He realized she was talking about the bedroom. The nervous flutter in his stomach grew more pronounced. 'Now?' he said, with surprise. 'Aren't we going to eat first?'

She paused and looked at him with one eyebrow raised, as if she suspected him of making a joke she didn't understand. Then she said crisply, 'You can eat later if you want,' and led the way swiftly out of the bar. Pascal followed reluctantly, wishing he could have at least had a drink. A double, preferably.

Lady Jane nodded to the cheerful-looking old lady seated behind the front desk as she went by. The old lady smiled and said, 'Good night Miss Bailey, good night sir . . .' He gave her a weak smile back, feeling unpleasantly exposed. It was obvious that Lady Jane was well known here – or rather Miss Bailey was. Presumably she brought a lot of her pick-ups to the inn. He wondered, with a prickle of embarrassment, what the staff thought of the endless parade of young men. And by now he was certain there *was* an endless parade of young men. In this case, at least, Henry Wates had been telling the truth.

She strode up the narrow, winding staircase. Pascal, hurrying to keep up, hoped he wasn't going to disappoint her. He felt like an actor on his way to a tough audition; if he failed to satisfy her he knew the relationship would be over before it had really started and with it would go his hopes of using her to discover her husband's secrets.

The palms of his hands had become sweaty by the time she ushered him into a small, low-ceilinged room. Most of the space was taken up by a double bed. As he looked at it he couldn't help wondering how they had managed to get such a huge bed into the place. He turned to make what he hoped was going to be an amusing remark to Lady Jane, but was surprised to see that she was already undressed apart from her bra, which she unhooked and removed as he watched.

Her body, though slim and muscular – the body of someone who took regular exercise – was showing signs of age. There were networks of stretch marks on her upper thighs and hips, her legs were further marred by varicose veins and her breasts, free of the bra, hung too low. Pascal felt his sexual desire, which had been mounting, begin to fade. He knew there was a strong element of fastidiousness in his make-up which manifested itself in his attitude towards sex. He had in the past been turned off by otherwise attractive women by quite minor physical flaws and he was suddenly afraid that he wouldn't be capable of making love to a woman who was so much older than him.

Completely naked now, she stood waiting expectantly by the

bed, looking at him. There was no hint of coyness in her stance, nor did it contain any hint of deliberate eroticism; it was so matter-of-fact she could have stripped off for a swim or a shower rather than a bout of love-making. 'Well?' she said, 'What are you waiting for?'

He gave a helpless shrug. 'Sorry. It's just that . . . well, you're moving a little faster than I'm used to. I normally do this a little differently . . .'

She raised her eyebrow again. He would become very familiar with this gesture. It made her look imperious. 'Really? In what way?'

'Well,' he said hesitantly, 'I rather like undressing the woman myself.'

For the first time since they'd entered the room she smiled. 'How charmingly adolescent. Perhaps next time . . .' He picked up the unspoken finish to the sentence: *If* there is a next time.

Uncomfortable under her direct, interested gaze he began to undress hurriedly. He was relieved that by the time he'd removed his underpants he at least was semi-erect. His desire was returning.

'You have a nice body,' she told him approvingly, but in the same tone she probably used to tell someone they played a good game of tennis. He felt like a piece of meat. The feeling irritated him but the same time it was strangely arousing. Now what, he wondered. He wouldn't have been surprised if she'd put on a pair of riding boots and produced a whip.

They continued to stand there facing each other. Pascal felt himself hardening until he became fully erect.

'I don't normally do this, you know,' she said, unexpectedly.

'You don't?' He was unable to keep the disbelief out of his voice.

'Oh, I don't mean *this*.' She made a dismissive gesture at the room. 'I mean I don't usually get involved with anyone from Warchester. A matter of policy. In fact you're the first.'

'Why the change in policy?'

'I don't know,' she said frowning. 'You are very attractive but it was a foolish thing to do. Let's hope I don't have to regret it . . .' She opened her arms to him. He crossed the five feet or so that separated them and embraced her. She pushed her body against his with urgent hunger. She was nearly as tall as him and strong; he could feel the almost masculine strength of her arms . . .

For the first few minutes it was more like a wrestling match than love-making. Lady Jane writhed and twisted around him as if she was trying to forcibly merge their flesh together. He felt obliged to try to match her passion but as he struggled with her on the bed – and struggle was the most appropriate word – he felt curiously detached. It was all so different from his love-making with Jenny. That had been a much gentler, slower thing. And more intimate too. He and Lady Jane might be naked together on a bed but there was no real sense of closeness yet.

She rolled on top of him, her mouth pressing down on his, her tongue thrusting an amazingly long distance into his mouth. Just when he thought he was going to gag she suddenly raised herself from him and slid down the length of his body. He felt the touch of her lips on his penis, then her tongue. A shiver of pleasure ran through him.

It soon became obvious that Lady Jane was an expert at this and before long Pascal was close to losing control. 'Oh hell, you'd better stop,' he moaned. He was in danger of coming and he knew that if he did so soon the 'audition' would be abruptly over.

She took her mouth away and he felt her shift on the bed. Then something else slid down his painfully erect penis, enfolding it in warm, silky wetness. He opened his eyes and looked. She was straddling him now, her back arched as she continued to push down on him in order to contain as much of him within her as she could.

Then she leaned forward until the tips of her breasts were brushing against his chest. Her face was damp with sweat, her eyes hooded and almost cruel. 'Try and push me off,' she said hoarsely. 'As hard as you can.'

Obeying her, he began to thrust violently with his pelvis.

Through grunts of pleasure she gasped, 'Harder . . . *harder* . . .'

He pushed upwards even more violently, lifting his buttocks clear of the bed with each thrust. She rocked back and forth over him, clutching at her breasts and squeezing them viciously.

Pascal realized he was too excited and again in danger of losing control. Desperately he tried the usual tricks to distract himself. The one that invariably worked best was visualising columns of figures and adding them up. He'd jokingly mentioned this to Jenny once: 'You women have it easy in bed; while you're having fun *trying* to come I'm busy doing arithmetic . . .'

The thought of Jenny brought back the memory of her on the office floor with Chilton. Anger flooded through him, and with it a renewed burst of sexual energy. He imagined it was Jenny on top of him instead of Lady Jane and he was determined to show her he could fuck just as well as Chilton. Hell, he would fuck her damn *brains* out . . .

The bed began to creak and strain alarmingly as Pascal redoubled his efforts. 'Oh yes!' she cried, *'Yes!'*

He became lost in a private universe of explosive, all-consuming lust. He lost all track of time until suddenly her groans became a full-throated cry and he felt her body shudder convulsively as she reached orgasm.

He let go and joined her in that sweet, all-too brief world of total pleasure . . .

Afterwards they lay there side by side, their bodies limp with exhaustion. 'God, that was *good* . . .' murmured Pascal, almost with surprise. He felt pleased with himself. He had come through okay. He'd forgotten about her age and performed well. Impulsively he raised his head, leaned over and gave her an affectionate kiss on the lips. Her reaction was to look startled.

'Why did you do that?' she asked curtly.

'Because I wanted to,' he replied. 'And because I think you're great.'

'Listen, let's get one thing straight right off. We're here together tonight for one thing and for one thing only. Don't think there's any more to it than that because there isn't. Understand?' Her tone was harsh. Bitter even.

Taken aback, Pascal said quickly, 'Yes, I understand.'

'Good,' she said, relaxing again. 'I don't want you getting any romantic illusions about me. I don't want to hurt you. I also don't want you putting pressure on me. I've got enough of that as it is right now.'

'Don't worry,' he said, a little coldly. Secretly he was rather amused at her egotism. She didn't seem to realize that he was doing *her* a favour and not vice versa.

She was silent after that and Pascal dozed off. He woke to find that she was gently licking him, her tongue caressing his testicles. He felt a stab of dismay. Surely she didn't expect him to repeat the performance? And so *soon?* But then, to his pleasant amazement, he began to harden. Lady Jane then took him in her mouth and started to move her lips rigorously up and down the length of his penis.

A couple of minutes later Pascal, his body on fire, gasped a warning that he would come in her mouth unless she stopped. She didn't.

Fifteen minutes later they were making love again. This time it was much slower and seemed to go on forever. Pascal was again surprised by this hitherto unsuspected reserve of sexual stamina. He had never lasted this long before. Lady Jane was undoubtedly having an extraordinary effect on him in spite of his reservations about her age and appearance.

After the third soul-shaking orgasm of the night he fell into a deep sleep. When he woke it was getting light. Lady Jane was already dressed. She was leaning by the window, staring down at him with an unreadable expression. He wondered how long she'd been there like that.

When she saw that he was awake she said crisply, 'I have to go now. There's a card on the bedside table with a number you can reach me with. Call me this afternoon between four and five.'

Then she was gone.

Pascal lay there smiling to himself. He had passed the audition. But then his elation was replaced by a vague feeling of disquiet. What the hell was he getting himself into?

10

'You look exhausted. Haven't you been sleeping properly?'

Pascal gave Jenny a suspicious look, wondering if she had found out about his affair with Lady Jane, but her face was a picture of innocence. 'No, it's the hot weather,' he said.

She seemed to accept this and returned to her typing. But then, a few moments later, she said, 'I haven't seen you around much at night recently. You haven't been in The Green Man for ages.'

He was instantly on guard. 'I'm surprised you noticed.'

She frowned. 'What do you mean?'

'You must be kept pretty busy by our friend Chilton.'

A slight flush appeared on her cheeks. 'I've told you before it's no big thing with us. We don't live in each other's pockets.'

Pascal bit back a sarcastic comment. Instead he said, 'But you like him a lot.'

'Yes. I do. He's a lot of fun. He makes me laugh.'

'Laugh?' Once again the memory of Jenny and Chilton making love in Brownlowe's office flashed into his mind. He felt the familiar constriction around his chest as the jealousy flared through him. But with an effort he said calmly, 'I think we'd better change the subject.'

'Fine by me. Let's get back to you and your whereabouts these last couple of weeks. What have you been up to?'

'What's it to you?' he asked brusquely.

She contrived to look even more innocent. 'I'm curious.'

He considered his answer carefully before saying, 'I've been working at home on something. A personal writing project . . .' He paused. 'A book, actually.'

'A book? How marvellous! What's it about?'

'About?' His mind went blank. He couldn't think of a thing.

'It's not about dinosaurs, is it?' she asked, with a smile of exaggerated sweetness.

'What the hell are you talking about?'

'Oh, come on, David. Stop playing games. You're not writing any book. I know what you've been doing.'

'You do?' His heart sank.

'You're following up leads on your Penward animal story. You haven't mentioned it again since that awful day but I know you well enough to know how your mind works. You're still convinced that whatever got out of the zoo wasn't a tiger . . .'

'No, you're wrong,' he protested. 'I gave up on all that ages ago.' He felt relieved that at least she didn't seem to know about Lady Jane.

'I don't believe you,' she said firmly. 'Your mother told me you had all the dinosaur books out of the library.'

He felt too tired to argue with her. He sighed and said, 'What about you? Why did *you* want those books?'

She looked round the office. It was early and they were alone apart from Mrs Fleming but she was too far away to hear what they were saying. 'Okay, I admit it. The more I thought about what you said the more it seemed to make sense. There *was* something odd about that day – the way Penward's men acted, the haste with which the animal was taken away, and the way Penward managed to avoid an official investigation afterwards . . .'

Pascal gave a tired smile. 'And now you believe it was a dinosaur?' He shook his head. 'Sorry, Jen, but those books from the library did convince me of one thing. Dinosaurs are extinct. It's scientifically impossible that one of them is still alive and kicking.'

Her response was to open one of her desk drawers and take two photocopies out. She handed them to him. The top one was a press report from four years ago. It was about an anthropologist who, while visiting some remote part of the Congo, had been told by natives about a local animal that bore a resemblance to a dinosaur. The other item was dated three months later and came from the *Warchester Times*. It was about an expedition to capture wild animals that Sir Penward was going to lead later that year. His destination was the Congo.

Pascal gave the copies back to her. 'Interesting.'

'Is that all you can say? I think it's more than interesting. I think he *did* find what he went there to look for. And he brought it back here.'

'A dinosaur?' His smile grew patronising.

A small crease of annoyance appeared on her forehead. 'Remember what *you* said that day – it might be something that *looks* like a dinosaur.'

'Perhaps it's the Loch Ness Monster.'

'Don't play dense with me. You know I'm on the right track. Now tell me what *you've* found out since we last spoke about this.'

'I told you Jenny, I've dropped it. I got nowhere and it all started to seem very absurd.'

She stared hard at him. 'I don't believe you. What have been doing at night recently?'

'Writing a book, like I said. A novel. It's about the sex life of the Warchester middle classes. Bank managers, journalists, people like that.' He stood up. 'I'm going down to the station for some coffee. See you later . . .'

He walked hurriedly out of the office before she could say anything else.

He felt more than exhausted; he felt shattered. It was as if he'd been run over by a juggernaut lorry. And in a sense he had – a sexual juggernaut. Lady Jane.

They had made love every night since their first rendezvous at the inn nearly two weeks ago. Her sexual appetite could only be described as voracious and the strain of trying to keep pace with her was wearing him out. The strain was emotional as well as physical; despite her initial declaration that her interest in him was purely sexual it soon became apparent this wasn't the case.

It was during their third consecutive night together that her guard began to drop and he soon discovered that her image as a tough-skinned sexual adventuress was a pose. She wasn't a woman in control of both her life and her emotions as he'd thought, but the exact opposite . . .

First she'd quizzed him about his love life and was too obviously relieved when he told her there was no other woman at the moment. Then she'd begun to talk about herself, telling him how unhappy she was and what a mess her life was in. Before long he realized she was desperately hungry for something. A proper love affair, he guessed, instead of her customary one-night stands.

He also guessed her growing desperation was bred out of fear; fear of growing old. She was two months away from turning forty. She wanted to hold on to – to confirm – her youth by having a serious relationship with a younger man. And it seemed he was being considered as a suitable candidate.

By the end of their fifth night together it was plain she'd come to a decision. After they'd made love she'd asked him point-blank, 'Do you think you could love me?'

Without a second's hesitation he lied: 'Yes, of course. I think I already do.' Then, to his horror, she had started crying. He held onto her as she wept and listened to her beg him that they would always be together and that he would never leave her. He assured they would and he wouldn't. Inwardly he was feeling alarmed and guilty. It suited his plans to have her fall in love with him but he was aware he was getting into a dangerous situation. Getting free of her when the time came might prove difficult. He was worried about how she would react. In the short time he'd known her he'd come to the conclusion she was more than just an emotional disaster area – he suspected she was a borderline psychotic.

'My husband's insane.'

Pascal had immediately tensed. This had been on the third night, after she'd cross-examined him about his love-life. They were staying at a small hotel near St Ives – another of her regular venues, he presumed. Lady Jane was lying on her stomach across the two single beds they'd pushed together to make a double.

'What do you mean?' asked Pascal, trying to keep any suggestion of eagerness out of his voice. This was the first time she'd mentioned her husband.

'He's mad. Totally bonkers. Deranged.' She had her face to the wall. Her tone was matter-of-fact.

'In what way?'

'He's obsessed with his damn animals. Completely. He puts them above everything else. And I mean *everything*. People mean nothing to him. He'd be happy to see every person in the world dead if it meant saving just *one* of his precious animals . . .'

Pascal could hardly contain his excitement. Was it going to be this easy? Was she going to simply and calmly tell him what he wanted to know? 'But he shot that tiger. The one that escaped,' he said carefully.

'Yes,' she said bitterly. 'It was the hardest thing he's ever had to do in his life. He'd rather have shot me.' She turned over on the bed and faced him. 'You have no idea what hell it is being married to him.'

Pascal wanted to keep on the subject of the animals but was forced to follow her into the area of her marriage. 'I'm sorry to hear it. In what way is it so bad?'

'In *every* way. It's not a marriage – it's a sick joke. Darren's incapable of love, or of *making* love ...' Her face twisted into a grimace. 'Not like a normal person at any rate.'

Intrigued in spite of himself, Pascal said, 'What do you mean?'

'He's a sado-masochist, with the emphasis on the masochism.' She gave a bitter laugh. 'You know what attracted him to me in the first place? It's very amusing – he thought I looked *domineering.*'

Pascal almost said, *But you do,* but decided it might be best not to.

'He didn't want a wife,' she continued, 'He wanted a *maîtresse,* someone to chastise him. A nanny with a whip. And unfortunately I looked perfect for the part.'

Pascal couldn't help nodding. He remembered how he'd half-expected her to produce riding boots and a whip on the first night he was with her. She *did* look like something out of *The Story of O* – it was her face with those high cheek-bones, the intense eyes and the imperious sweep of her eyebrows. 'But you're not into that sort of thing?' he asked.

'Of course not,' she said quickly. 'I don't like hurting people. Or being hurt.'

'He hurt you?'

'Occasionally, yes. But most times I was the one who had to dish it out to him. He liked being whipped. On the bottom.'

Pascal had to struggle not to laugh. The idea of Sir Penward – the ever-so-dignified aristocrat – having his rear end smacked while tied to a bed or whatever was hilarious. If only he could print this!

'It's all connected to his obsession with wild animals. That's my theory anyway.'

He frowned. 'I don't follow.'

'Well, he worships *powerful* things. All his animals are dangerous ones; lions, tigers, panthers, bears, crocodiles and so on ... He admires animals that can kill, that are capable of ferocity and ruthlessness.'

'You mean he gets a sexual buzz from being afraid?' asked Pascal, wishing he knew what kind of animals her words 'and so on' referred to.

'Not exactly,' she said, 'the buzz comes from their *power.* Perhaps it's a form of envy on his part; he collects dangerous animals because that way he can assume their power by proxy and compensate for his own sense of inadequacy.' She shrugged. 'Who knows? I've been trying to work him out for years and now I'm tired of trying.'

'Why don't you leave him?'

'I can't. He won't let me.'

'Won't *let* you? How could he possibly stop you?'

'Let's say he could make life very, *very* inconvenient for me,' she said drily.

'But why should he still care one way or the other? You give the impression your relationship with him ended ages ago.'

'It did. We lead separate lives now apart from the odd public occasion. I have the freedom to do what I want, *providing* I'm careful about it. He knows about my sexual habits and doesn't give a damn, but he would if it got into the gossip columns. It's all to do with his pride. That's why he will never give me a divorce. The break-up of our marriage would, he feels, reflect badly on him. That sense of inadequacy again. There must be no chink in that perfect image he presents to the world.' The corners of her mouth turned down in disgust. 'I wish he was dead. I wish he would make a mistake with one of his damn animals and get his damn head bitten off. It's the only way I'll ever get truly free of him.'

After that she'd talked about how lonely she was and how occasionally she considered committing suicide. Pascal, in between making sympathetic sounds, tried to nudge her back onto the subject of her husband and his animals, but without success. Since then she'd talked often about Sir Penward, repeating her complaints about him, but never returned to the topic of the animals.

Pascal didn't dare ask her straight out about the zoo. He knew that she would be instantly alert to any hint that he had ulterior motives for seeing her. She was like a human minefield; he had to step incredibly carefully. But nearly two weeks of her company had gained Pascal nothing but a feeling of total exhaustion; though he had to admit his sexual education had taken a quantum leap forward.

Despairingly, he saw the situation continuing indefinitely – an

endless succession of strenuous bouts of love-making in remote
hotels around the countryside – until he dropped dead from
sheer fatigue without ever learning a thing about the secrets of
Penward's zoo.

Jenny wasn't in the office when he returned from the police station. Relieved, he picked up the phone and dialled Lady Jane's private number at Penward Hall. He had come to a decision while
chatting with Driscoll and the others at the station.

'Hi, it's me,' he said when he heard her familiar voice on the
line. 'Look, I'm awfully sorry but I can't make it tonight. I've got
to work late and I don't really fancy a long drive afterwards.' They
had arranged to meet at a hotel near Huntingdon.

There was a silence at the other end. Then, in a strained voice,
she said, 'What's the real reason you can't see me?'

'I told you. I have to work late. And I'm tired. All the driving
I've been doing lately. I need an early night.'

'If you loved me you wouldn't mind how far you had to drive.'
Her tone was accusing now.

'I *do* love you,' he protested wearily, 'but that has nothing to do
with it. Look, I'll see you tomorrow night. Okay?'

'When will you finish work?'

Oh hell, he thought. She was going to make it as difficult as
possible. 'Around ten,' he said, grabbing the figure out of thin air.

More silence. When she spoke again her voice was hesitant.
'You could come here for the night. Darren is in London.'

Pascal tensed up. 'Stay at Penward Hall? I couldn't ...' *Easy,
easy!* he cautioned himself. At last the opportunity he'd been
waiting for! Don't blow it!

'Yes you could. I told you I have a separate flat. With its own
entrance. No one has to know.'

'But what if one of the staff should see me?' he asked, trying to
sound unenthusiastic.

'There'll be someone at the gate, that's all. You just keep low
as I drive in. There won't be anyone around the main house at
that time. I'll park right by my door. No one will see you go in.'

'Well, I don't know ...' he said slowly. 'What about tomorrow
morning? I'm certain to be spotted leaving.'

She gave a sigh of exasperation. 'So what? If someone *does* see you I'll make up a story.'

'Your husband won't like it if he finds out,' said Pascal. But it wasn't Sir Penward he was thinking of; he was wondering what would happen if he was seen by one of the keepers who knew him.

'Let me worry about him,' she said impatiently. 'Are you coming or not?'

After a pause he said, 'Well, okay . . .'

'Good. Let's see, how about if I meet you in the car park of one of the local pubs? Do you know the Phoenix Arms?'

Pascal almost dropped the phone. Recovering swiftly he said, 'Yes, I do but I'd rather avoid the place if you don't mind. Had a run-in with the manager there some time ago and got myself barred.'

She named another pub a couple of miles further down the road and he agreed to meet her in its car park at 10.30 p.m.

His heart was thudding as he put the phone down. At long last he was in reach of his goal. It was going to be risky – dangerous even – but by this time tomorrow he would have the evidence he needed. *If* it existed, of course.

He went over to where Henry Wates maintained a small kingdom of untidiness in a corner of the office. Wates was at his desk reading the *Sun*. The desk, as usual, was covered with empty coffee cups, pieces of camera equipment and the debris from long-gone meals and snacks.

'Henry, I have a great favour to ask of you,' said Pascal.

Wates looked up at him suspiciously. 'What is it?'

'I want to borrow one of your cameras and a flash. Just until tomorrow morning. And I'll pay you £15 for the privilege.'

Wates' expression grew even more suspicious. 'What do you need it for?'

Pascal grinned triumphantly. 'I'm going hunting.'

11

Penward Hall had a long history. Where the main house now stood there had once been a castle. It had been built in 1107 but was destroyed by a fire in 1438. All that remained of it today were some of the foundations. A magnificent Tudor mansion occupied the site for over 300 years but this too fell victim to a fire – in 1847. Two years later the Victorian monstrosity that was the present Penward Hall was built – a grey, sprawling edifice with no redeeming architectural feature.

Almost as ugly were the more recent buildings attached to its rear. A haphazard jumble of styles, these had been erected over the years by Sir Penward to house the members of his ever-increasing menagerie. The overall effect was a depressing one – and made more so by the contrasting beauty of the surrounding countryside with its low hills and woods.

It had been many years since Pascal had been inside the estate. The last occasion, he dimly remembered, had been a visit to the public section of the zoo with a girlfriend when he was in his late teens. It would have been beyond the wildest flight of his younger self's imagination to think that one day he would be entering the place hidden under a blanket in Lady Penward's car . . .

'Okay,' he heard her say, 'we're a long way from the gatehouse now. They won't see you.'

He pulled the blanket away and got up from the floor. His legs were stiff. He stretched as he sat down on the seat and looked around. Ahead of them, about a quarter of a mile away, loomed the grey bulk of Penward Hall. Batteries of security lights illuminated the exteriors of the main house and the zoo buildings – much too brightly for Pascal's comfort – and in the harsh glare the place had a distinctly ominous look about it. Pascal was beginning to wonder, now that he was so close to success, if he had the necessary courage to do what had to be done. He remembered the night outside the Phoenix Arms – the boot thudding into the side of his head. They were dangerous people. If they caught him inside the estate they might do more than simply beat him, especially if they *did* have something to hide.

The still night air was suddenly disturbed by the powerful cry of an animal. A big one by the sound of it. Pascal glanced at Lady Jane. 'What on earth was that?'

She shrugged. 'A jaguar, I think.' He'd noticed she'd been acting a little nervously since picking him up outside the pub and guessed she was having second thoughts about bringing him to Penward Hall.

Pascal saw no one as she drove past the wide front of the mansion and then turned into a driveway leading down the side of the building. She parked quickly and hurried across the gravel to a small, grotesque portico. Pascal followed, feeling naked in the bright lights that lined the drive, carrying his overnight bag. Usually it held nothing but a change of socks, underwear and toiletries but on this occasion it also contained a camera, torch and crowbar.

Lady Jane led the way up a flight of stairs that smelt musty and old, and then into her flat. To his surprise it was a modern, cheerful-looking apartment that seemed totally out of place in such a grim building. When he commented on this she nodded and said, 'In here I can pretend I'm not in Penward Hall. Darren hates it, of course. You should see the rooms he lives in. Full of boring bric-à-brac, dreadful paintings of his ancestors, and weapons. As you'd expect he's the type who collects swords, guns and all those other deadly toys that men like him get such a thrill from.'

'I suppose he's an expert swordsman and a crack shot,' said Pascal drily.

'He's a good shot, yes,' she replied, taking him seriously. 'But he's never done any fencing as far as I know.'

He made another attempt at humour. 'Are you *sure* he's away in London? I don't want to come face to face with an angry husband wielding a shotgun.'

She looked at him with one eyebrow raised. Then said, 'Don't worry, darling. I'd protect you.' She went to the bedside table, opened a drawer and took out a chrome-plated automatic pistol. 'I'm a good shot too.'

Pascal smiled weakly. He hoped she was making a joke but suspected she wasn't.

Pascal didn't perform well that night. He knew it but was too preoccupied with other things to give Lady Jane his full attention. Finally she said with annoyance, 'What is the matter with you today?'

'I'm sorry. It's like I told you on the phone; I'm very tired. I need to catch up on my sleep. I'll be fine in the morning. Let's continue this then . . .'

She gave him a long searching look before nodding and saying, 'All right, darling. I must admit I'm feeling rather tired myself tonight.' She reached over and switched off the light. In the darkness he mouthed a silent prayer of thanks.

'Jane?' he whispered. There was no answer. Her breathing was deep and regular. He was certain she was asleep. As gently as possible he lifted her arm from across his chest and slid slowly out of the bed. If she woke up he'd tell her he was on his way to the bathroom.

He dressed quickly. He'd taken the precaution of wearing all dark clothes; black trousers, a dark grey cord jacket and a dark blue shirt. Then he opened his overnight bag and took out the camera, torch and crowbar. He slung the camera round his neck, hooked the crowbar into his belt and, holding the torch, crept quietly out of the bedroom.

In the hallway he used the torch to search through Lady Jane's shoulder bag until he found her door keys. After checking to make sure he had the right ones he left the flat and went downstairs.

Outside he felt terribly exposed in the glare of the security lights and hurriedly crossed the driveway to get behind them. Then, taking advantage of the cover provided by the hedges and shrubs in the garden alongside the driveway, he moved cautiously towards the zoo . . .

First he had to negotiate a wire mesh fence. He found a gate but it was padlocked. Deciding not to use the crowbar unless it was absolutely necessary, he climbed over the gate instead. There was a strand of barbed wire running along the top but he got past it without much difficulty.

He was now in the section of the estate that used to be open to the public. He passed a large aviary in which a pair of eagles, perched on the top branches of a tree, watched him with cruel eyes.

He came to the first big cat compounds. A concrete structure opened out into a spacious run some forty feet long. It was surrounded by a double fence over twelve feet high. Pascal saw a dark shape sprawled out beside a log. He switched on his torch and the beam illuminated the body of a massive tiger. The tiger, its eyes glowing with the reflected light, stared back at him incuriously. Pascal guessed this was John Smith, the mate of the dead Siberian tiger Pocahontas. He switched off the torch and continued on.

The next compound was even bigger and he saw that it contained several lions. Though it was early September the weather was still warm and the big cats were lying outside their concrete shelters. All of them turned their heads to watch him as he went by, but like the tiger made no other response to his presence.

He came to another fence – it marked the boundary of the public section. Beyond it lay a number of featureless buildings, stark and uninviting in the harsh lighting. From one of them came a muffled sound, like the roar of some animal a long distance away. It didn't sound like one of the big cats.

As he stared at the bleak structures his pulse began to quicken. He also felt a cold ball of fear form in the pit of his stomach. For a few moments he seriously contemplated turning round and going straight back to Lady Jane's bed.

But instead he began climbing the wire fence. It was higher than the other one and had three strands of barbed wire on its top. Pascal had cut his hand open and torn a hole in his trousers before he was able to start down the other side.

Panting from the exertion he hurried over to the first of the buildings. The only way in appeared to be through a pair of large, sliding wooden doors on the side of the building. As he feared, they were chained and padlocked together. He took out the crowbar. It was the point of no return. From here on he could be accused of breaking and entering if they caught him.

It took a great deal of effort to break the chain. The doors were heavy and the one that Pascal managed to shift on its runners made a screeching noise he was sure could be heard throughout the estate.

He slipped through the gap and pulled the door shut behind him. Then he switched on the torch. To his surprise he was standing in a three-foot space between the outer doors and a second pair of inner doors. This must mean that the walls of the building were incredibly thick. The inner doors were unlocked. He slid one open and stepped through into the darkness beyond.

The first thing that hit him was the heat. It was like a steam room in there and immediately the sweat began to trickle down his face and neck. Then he noticed the smell – a strong, pungent aroma that he didn't recognise and yet filled him with atavistic unease.

He shone the weak beam of the small torch into the darkness. He could hear the sound of running water and moved cautiously towards it. The torch revealed some kind of barrier ahead of him. It was constructed of thick steel bars that rose up out of the concrete floor and then curved out towards him to form an overhead screen. He went to the bars and looked through. Beyond them the floor abruptly disappeared and Pascal found himself staring down onto the surface of a large expanse of black water some ten feet below. He shone the torch around and began to realize that he was on the edge of a huge, apparently circular tank set in the floor of the building.

He walked along the barrier, still playing the beam down onto the dark water. What was in there? Fish? An animal of some kind? Polar bears perhaps. No, it was too hot in here for polar bears. Then he remembered Lady Jane saying that Penward kept crocodiles . . .

He heard a splash. It was distinct from the sound made by the water continually pouring into the tank from some inlet pipe and came from the centre of the tank.

He stopped and pointed the torch in the direction of the sound but the beam wasn't powerful enough. The tank must have been at least fifty feet in diameter.

He continued on around the edge. He was about a third of the way around it when the barrier came to an end. He hesitated for a moment then proceeded on past it. He didn't feel in any danger. The surface of the water was too far away for anything to be able to leap out or scale the sheer sides of the tank to reach him. The barrier was probably more to stop people walking in to the tank than for any other reason, though if that was the case it was odd it didn't extend all the way around.

He heard another splash. Frowning, he put the torch down on the edge of the tank and unslung the camera from his neck. The next time he heard anything out there he was going to take a flash picture – he was certain the flash gun would reveal more than the torch.

He waited, the camera ready.

There was another splash, louder and closer this time. He pressed the shutter button.

This action saved his life.

The brief burst of illumination revealed a terrifying sight. Starkly outlined was a huge head on a long, snake-like neck. And the head, its impossibly wide jaws displaying rows of needle teeth, was rushing straight towards him with the speed of an express train.

As the darkness closed in again he flung himself backwards in a pure reflex action. At the same time as he sprawled on the concrete he heard the *snap* of the now-invisible jaws closing shut mere feet away; they were so near he felt a hot breeze on his face from them.

More terrified than he could remember ever being before, he frantically pushed himself away from the edge of the tank, scuttling backwards on his heels and the palms of his hands.

He felt another movement of air on his face followed by a swishing sound as the head made a second dart towards him. Again came the *snap* of unimaginably powerful jaws, but again they closed on nothing . . .

Pascal's shoulders collided with something immovable. It was the wall. He could go no further.

He huddled there, his back against the wall, his feet drawn up under him, not daring to move. It was then he realized he was making a low moaning sound.

There was a splash from the direction of the tank. How far had he come, he wondered? Was he out of range of that thing? He could see the feeble glow of the torch but it was impossible to tell how far away it was.

Trembling violently he started to edge along the wall on his hands and knees, keeping as close to it as he could. Then he stopped.

Where was the camera?

Oh God, he thought. He retraced his steps and began to feel around for it in the dark. He tried to remember when he'd let go of it, praying he hadn't left it too near the edge.

More than anything he wanted to leave the damn camera wherever it lay and get the hell out of the place. But he couldn't. He *had* to find it.

His heart thumping with fear and his every nerve sickeningly taut he crawled slowly back towards the edge of the tank, feeling around desperately as he moved.

There was a noise from the water that sounded like a whale coming up for air. God, the thing must be *huge.* He wondered how long the creature's neck was . . . it had to be at least fifteen feet to have reached over the edge of the tank.

In the weak beam of the torch lying on the concrete he caught a brief glimpse of the snake-like neck moving past. The thing was still looking for him. Or perhaps it could sense exactly where he was and was waiting for him to get closer.

That made up Pascal's mind. Screw the camera. He was getting out of there. But then, as he started to back away, his right hand touched something. It was the camera strap.

He carefully pulled the camera towards him and picked it up, then retreated back to the wall. There he examined the camera as best he could in the darkness. It seemed to be undamaged.

He felt his way along the wall, ears straining for any sound from the tank . . .

Finally he reached the doors. Once inside the space between the inner and outer pair he paused to gather himself together and to consider what to do next. It occurred to him that the one photograph he'd taken might not be sufficient. He didn't even know if he'd got a good shot of the creature. He'd look a fool if the only visual evidence he could produce to accompany his story was a blurry outline that could be anything.

He swore under his breath. He definitely wasn't going to risk taking another photograph of the thing in the tank. He would have to find another creature – a safer one. He was positive there *was* more than one of them. It was unlikely that the creature in the tank – obviously an aquatic animal – had been the one that escaped back in July. Besides, it was much too big to have been the thing in the net that Pascal had seen being carried away by the helicopter.

He wondered what the hell it was. And how Penward had possibly managed to smuggle it into the country.

Cautiously he pushed open one of the outer doors and looked out. There was no one in sight. He slid the door shut behind him and hurried away towards the next building.

This time it took much longer to break the chain on the doors. He felt weak and his hands were still trembling. He glanced at his watch. It was now 2.40 a.m. He was going to have to get this finished with quickly and head back to the house. If Lady Jane woke and found him missing . . .

The interior of this building was similarly hot and also filled with the odd smell that made his skin crawl. He stood just inside the doors, listening. He wished he still had the torch.

Something moved in the darkness. Then came a snorting sound like a horse might make. Pascal hoped he hadn't picked an ordinary stable to break into. It would be just too ironic if he'd taken all these risks just to get a photograph of a horse.

He decided to risk turning on the lights – if he could find the switch. With the doors closed, and the lack of windows, he doubted if the light would be seen from the outside.

He felt around beside the doors and eventually located a bank of switches. He pulled one down and was rewarded by lights coming on overhead. Then he gasped.

He was standing in a room about forty feet long and thirty feet wide. Cutting the room in half was a row of thick metal bars that stretched from the floor to the ceiling. Beyond the bars stood an animal. It was watching Pascal, its head cocked to one side like that of a giant bird.

Filled with awe Pascal walked closer to the bars.

It stood on two powerful hind legs. It was six foot tall and its scaly hide was a dirty red colour.

Pascal had never seen anything like it before in his life, but he knew what it was.

It was a living, breathing dinosaur.

Unexpectedly the creature opened its vicious-looking mouth and shrieked at him. He recoiled in fright. The noise was awful. But in spite of his fear he raised the camera. He couldn't help feeling a rush of triumph. This was going to be the story of the century, and it was *his* . . .

There came a muffled *pop* sound from behind him and simultaneously he felt something thud into his back between his shoulder-blades. Pascal was sent staggering forward. He fell onto his knees. The camera shattered on the concrete. *Christ, I've been shot!* was his last thought as the concrete floor rushed to meet his face.

12

A hand slapped him hard across the face.

Pascal opened his eyes. He felt vaguely surprised at still being alive. He tried to speak but his throat was painfully dry and all he could manage was a weak croak. He found himself staring into a bright light – so bright it hurt his eyes. He closed them.

The hand slapped him again. Harder this time.

'Wake up, Mr Pascal!' commanded a deep voice. Pascal recognised it. He also recognised the face that swam into focus when he opened his eyes again.

Sir Darren Penward.

Pascal groaned and tried to sit up. A strong hand pushed him back down. He realized he was lying on a hard bed. He looked around and saw he was in a small, windowless room. The bed was the only item of furniture in the place. Then he became aware of a sharp pain in his back.

'Shot . . .' Pascal gasped. 'Someone . . . shot . . . me.'

Penward shook his head. 'Only with an anaesthetic dart, Mr Pascal. You'll be sore for a while and hungover from the effects of the drug, but there'll be no lasting damage.'

As Pascal absorbed this information he began to remember everything that had happened – and his relief at still being alive and unhurt began to fade. He stared anxiously up at Sir Penward, trying to read his expression. But Penward's hawklike face was giving nothing away – it was a blank mask of indifference.

'They'll be looking for me,' Pascal said hurriedly. 'They'll trace me here . . .'

'Who are *they?*' asked Penward coolly.

'The police. I'll have been reported missing by now.'

'Possibly, but there's no reason for them to think you came here. As far as I can tell your affair with my wife has been kept a secret between the two of you . . .' His thin lips creased briefly into an unpleasant smile. 'Yes, I know all about it. Jane has told me, albeit reluctantly, everything. For a typically dull, provincial young man you have displayed remarkable persistence in this matter. Using my wife to get in here was almost ingenious . . .'

Pascal opened his mouth to protest but Penward held up his hand. 'Don't bother denying it. I told you I know everything. But I must warn you Jane is somewhat distressed by the discovery that she has been exploited by you. In fact I don't think she really accepts it yet. An obtuse woman, my wife.' He sighed. 'She has the looks of a thoroughbred but somewhere along the line her family must have indulged in a little genetic slumming. A pity.'

There was a momentary silence. Then Pascal said, 'Do you mind if I sit up? I don't feel comfortable talking this way.'

'Of course,' said Penward, 'but don't attempt anything reckless. You are in no condition to overpower me and I have men within calling distance.'

'Don't worry,' said Pascal as he eased himself upright on the bed, 'I don't think I have the strength to walk, much less run anywhere.' He was telling the truth. He felt weak and dizzy.

'I'm curious, Mr Pascal. What made you suspicious of this establishment?'

'Why should I tell you? Why should I tell you anything?' asked

Pascal, displaying a good deal more defiance than he actually felt. In reality he was feeling completely powerless and very afraid.

'Because, quite frankly, it is in your best interest to cooperate with me. Also if you answer my questions I will answer yours. I'm sure you have several.'

'Yes, of course I do. Like where you got those . . . those *creatures* from.' He couldn't bring himself to use the word 'dinosaurs'.

'As soon as you tell me what I want to know,' said Penward. 'What aroused your suspicions?'

Pascal told him what he'd seen and heard the day the 'tiger' escaped, concluding with young Simon Smythe-Graves' matter-of-fact announcement that it was a dinosaur.

Penward nodded thoughtfully. 'It was a mistake not to have disposed of the boy. A moment's weakness on my part, I admit. And with predictable results.'

These words sent a chill through Pascal. Penward was calmly talking about murdering an eight-year-old boy . . .

'Still, the situation is salvageable,' continued Penward easily. 'No real harm done.' He gave Pascal a thin, patronising smile as if to say that he presented the very smallest of irritations. 'Now, what can I tell you about my zoo?'

'Are those animals really dinosaurs?'

Penward inclined his head. 'Yes. Well, actually the amphibious one is a plesiosaur, not dinosaur, but the one you saw in the cage is definitely a dinosaur. A *Deinonychus* to be exact. A superb specimen too.'

'Where did you find them? In Africa?'

'Africa?' Penward looked amused. 'Is that what you think? That I stumbled on some Conan Doyle-like lost world in Africa? Perhaps you're even less intelligent than I give you credit for. Dinosaurs are extinct, Mr Pascal. Or rather they *were . . .*'

Confused, Pascal said, 'Then where did those things you've got out there come from?'

'They came from right here,' said Penward, clearly enjoying himself. 'I made them.'

'You *made* them?' Pascal presumed he was making some kind of joke at his expense, but failed to see the point of it.

'Not personally, I admit. I had expert assistance. But the idea was mine and I provided the means to execute it. It cost me a fortune.'

Pascal frowned. 'You mean they're not real? They're mechanical? Like robots?'

'Don't be ridiculous, Mr Pascal. Of course they're not mechanical. They are living organisms. Organisms that we created here at Penward Hall from the fossil remnants of their long-dead original selves.'

'I'm sorry, but you've lost me.'

'I will try and explain. You know what a fossil is, don't you?'

'Yes. It's the petrified remains of an animal or a plant.'

'You're half right. It's true that most dinosaur bones, for example, are petrified. The skeleton undergoes a process of mineralization over the years it's buried in the ground. Water seeps into the bones and the minerals in the water slowly collect in the skeleton turning it into stone. But not all dinosaur fossils are petrified. Occasionally an original bone will be found, or a tooth or a claw. Very, very rarely a *mummified* dinosaur turns up. Some years ago two duck-bill dinosaurs of the *Corythosaurus* species were discovered in a mummified condition in western Canada. Since then other such discoveries have been made. You appreciate the significance, of course?'

Pascal thought for a moment. 'No,' he said truthfully.

'The significance is,' said Penward wearily, 'that it is possible to obtain the original cellular material of a dinosaur with all its genetic information intact.'

Pascal made a quantum leap. 'You're *cloning* them!' he exclaimed. 'You're cloning them out of fossil cells. But ...' he frowned, '... but the cells are dead. How do you bring them to life?'

'I fear there's much more to it than a simple case of cloning,' said Penward with pride. 'What we have done is decode all the genetic information in the dinosaur cell and then transfer it on to a living cell from a contemporary animal. Needless to say it's an infinitely complicated and delicate process. There are thousands of genes in each chromosome.'

'You transfer it? How?' asked Pascal.

'First we establish the detailed structure of each gene in the dinosaur cell nucleus. To do this we use a technique pioneered at the California Institute of Technology. It involves using radio-active tracer atoms as probes. With an electron microscope we can then determine the chemical make-up of each gene's 'codon'. Codons are Nature's equivalent of the binary code in a computer program. They consist of different combinations of the four chemical subunits of deoxyribonucleic acid, DNA, the substance that genes are made of. Each gene, as you are probably well aware, is responsible for programming the manufacture in the cell of a particular protein.

'As we decode each gene the information is fed into a com-puter until we end up with a computer profile containing all the genetic information in the dinosaur cell. This is compared with a similar computer 'map' of the genetic makeup of the living animal whose cell we intend to modify, which enables us to see which codons have to be altered.'

'What animal do you use?'

'In all cases to date our dinosaurs have been grown from chicken cells.'

'*Chicken cells?*' Pascal almost burst out laughing. 'Why on earth did you choose chickens?'

'The choice is not so absurd as you seem to think,' said Pen-ward coldly. 'Any bird species would have been just as suitable, but as there had already been a great deal of work done by micro-biologists on the genetic structure of chickens for agricultural purposes, it made our mapping task easier.'

Pascal frowned. 'But why birds in the first place?'

'Because birds evolved from dinosaurs, Mr Pascal,' said Pen-ward with a sigh. 'Or rather from a specific dinosaur species – *Archaeopteryx* – and therefore share a common genetic heritage. As a result there is still a certain amount of genetic overlap between the two which means we don't have to modify every gene in every chromosome. This saves us an enormous amount of time.'

'How do you actually modify the bird genes to match those of the dinosaur?

'By using standard gene-splicing techniques – recombining the DNA and so on. But in some cases we are obliged to build the gene from scratch. We synthesize the entire gene from its basic chemical building blocks, rearranging the four chemical sub-units of the codons until we hit upon the right combination. A painstaking process, to say the least.

'Then, when the nucleus of the chicken cell is completely modified, a chicken ovum is enucleated and the doctored nucleus is implanted in its place. What *you* would call cloning. The egg cell is then carefully nurtured in an artificial oviduct until it reaches maturity and is then placed in an incubator. And finally, if all goes well, it hatches a baby dinosaur.'

'Incredible . . .' Pascal shook his head in amazement. 'Chickens into dinosaurs.'

'Genes are genes. A few changes in the chemical code within them is all that determines the difference between a chicken, a dinosaur and *you*, Mr Pascal. The basic materials are all the same, it's simply how they're arranged that determines the outcome.'

'How many animals have you hatched so far?'

'We have hatched ten dinosaurs to date – eleven if you include the plesiosaur which, of course, is not technically a dinosaur,' said Penward. 'And we have a further twelve eggs in the incubators.'

'All right. The sixty-four thousand dollar question,' said Pascal. '*Why?* What's the reason for all this?'

Penward looked surprised, as if the answer should be self-evident to any rational person. Then he seemed to come to some decision. 'Do you feel well enough to walk yet, Mr Pascal?'

'Yes, I think so. Why?' he asked suspiciously.

Penward didn't reply. Instead he went to the door and rapped sharply on it three times. It was immediately opened by one of the keepers. He was wearing the inevitable white overalls and carried a double-barrelled shotgun.

'Miles, I'm taking our guest upstairs for a short tour. Please accompany us,' Penward told him, then turned back to Pascal. 'I trust you will behave yourself, Mr Pascal. *That* gun doesn't fire harmless anaesthetic darts. Try to run and Miles will shoot you in the legs. Understand?'

'Yes,' answered Pascal weakly. He got down from the bed and leaned against it while he waited for the room to stop spinning. His stomach churned and his mouth seemed to be full of cotton wool that had been soaked in something foul.

'Come on,' ordered Penward. Unsteadily, Pascal followed him out of the room. The keeper brought up the rear. Outside was a narrow concrete corridor and instinctively Pascal knew he was underground. They passed several closed doors, all made of steel, before coming to a spiral staircase at the end of the passageway. As they climbed Penward said, 'This was all part of the dungeon area of the old castle. I had it converted into my laboratory complex.' The staircase ended in a small, bare chamber. Penward pressed a button on the wall and a section of it slid to one side. He beckoned Pascal through the opening. Beyond lay a large and gloomy library that smelt very musty. Penward pressed another button and the movable bookshelf that served to conceal the entrance slid back into place.

Penward then led him out of the library and into a large hall with a high ceiling. It was like stepping into a museum. It was filled with dinosaur exhibits. Full skeletons, parts of skeletons and individual bones were on display in glass cases. Penward held out his arms. 'All this was the work of my grandfather. Many of the fossils you see here he found locally. It's probably the most remarkable collection in private hands in the world. I spent much of my childhood in here. I became fascinated with dinosaurs. Obsessed, if you like. I came to realize that nature had reached its peak with these magnificent creatures and I was filled with a profound regret that they were now all gone. Extinct; irretrievably lost in time . . .

'I transferred my obsession onto the animals living today that were the nearest to the dinosaurs in terms of power and strength. The big cats, bears, alligators, etc . . . I took steps to protect the endangered species among them, making sure they didn't follow the dinosaurs into extinction. I tried to protect them from their most dangerous enemy – Man. I enjoyed some success in my endeavours: Penward Zoo is a testament to that, but all along, in the back of my mind, my obsession with the great dinosaurs remained.

'And then it happened. Six years ago I was attending a fund-raising dinner at the London Zoo in aid of some wildlife preservation scheme, I forget which now. I was seated next to a biologist who casually remarked that at the rate the science of genetic engineering was progressing we would one day be able to restore a living specimen of any extinct species, providing its genetic blueprint could be obtained.

'No doubt that biologist was just trying to make amusing table-talk but his words exploded like a bomb in my mind. From that moment on I could think of only one thing – that it might be possible to bring the dinosaurs back to life again. I poured a fortune into setting up the laboratory and securing the services of several top microbiologists. All were sworn to secrecy; an expensive manoeuvre, but a successful one. It's amazing what, and who, money can buy. A great deal of money, that is . . .'

Penward gave a dry chuckle and continued. 'And so after two years of frustration and repeated failures, we had our first breakthrough. We proved it *could* be done. The final results are now living and breathing in my zoo outside, an incontrovertible reality. You saw two of them last night; come and see the others.'

As Pascal followed Penward out of the dinosaur hall he reflected uneasily on the way the situation was developing. The more Penward told him the more worried he grew, the implication being that Penward was confident he wasn't going to be repeating this information to anyone. Which meant Penward intended to keep him a prisoner here indefinitely or that he intended to kill him.

13

Pascal was surprised to see that it was daylight when they went outside. He glanced at his watch. It was nearly 11 a.m. He'd been unconscious for at least seven hours.

They crossed a courtyard at the rear of the manor house and entered the private section of the zoo. Pascal saw only one other person on the way – a keeper carrying the bloody carcass of a sheep – who gave him a contemptuous glance as he went by. Pascal wondered where Lady Jane was. Would she try and help him? Would she *want* to try and help him now? Probably not, he realized grimly.

Penward first took him into the building where he'd been

caught last night. A part of the ceiling had been rolled back and the cage was bathed in sunshine, but even in daylight the red-coloured dinosaur was an awesome sight. It was munching on something as they entered and turned to face them with an angry warning snarl. Its long teeth were bloodstained and its tail began to swish back and forth over the concrete floor. It was plainly not pleased to see them.

It strutted towards them on disturbingly man-like legs, leaving a pile of shattered bones behind it – all that remained of its meal – and thrust a clawed forearm between the bars. Its snarl grew louder.

'*Deinonychus,*' said Penward proudly, 'from the Cretaceous period. It belongs to a class of dinosaurs known as deinonchysaurs. It's a relatively 'new' dinosaur in that it was only discovered in 1964. In Montana. You'll notice it has a couple of unusual features. See the second toes on its hind feet? They extend upwards like natural scythes. Amazing, aren't they?'

'Very,' said Pascal without enthusiasm.

'They're what give it its name; Deinonychus means "terrible claw".'

Pascal stared nervously at the six-foot-tall creature. 'Is it fully grown?'

'Yes. But remains have been found of a close relative of Deinonychus that must have been enormous. Only the shoulder bones and forelimbs were discovered, unfortunately, in the Gobi Desert. And no other remains have turned up since them. But the forearms were over seven feet long, which suggests a very large dinosaur indeed. It has been given the name *Deinocheirus,* "terrible hand".'

'I hope you're not in the process of making one,' muttered Pascal.

Penward laughed. 'If I ever obtain the necessary cells I will, just to see what it looks like. But I do have dinosaurs of a more impressive size than Deinonychus here. Come . . .'

They went through a double pair of connecting doors, all heavily sound-proofed, and entered another large concrete enclosure. As Pascal stepped through he was met by a deafening bellow that made him recoil.

'I should have warned you,' said Penward when it was possible to be heard. 'Our *Megalosaurus* is in a very bad mood. Has been for weeks. We suspect sexual frustration may be the cause as we can detect nothing organically wrong with it.'

Pascal flinched as the huge, green-skinned dinosaur charged at the bars. The floor vibrated as it hit them. Again came the awful bellow.

Like the Deinonychus this one also stood on its hind legs but it was much more heavily built and about ten feet tall. Its head was particularly big, and *very* ugly.

'He's a local,' said Penward. 'The cells that provided the basis for his creation came from a well-preserved fossil that my grandfather dug out of one of our claypits. Impressive, isn't he?'

'Very,' said Pascal. He was thinking how unlike the dinosaurs he'd seen in movies these things were. Hollywood dinosaurs were either lumbering creatures or moved with artificial jerkiness, due to the stop-motion photography system used to animate the models, but the Megalosaurus, despite its size, possessed an awesome speed and agility in its movements. It certainly didn't have the sluggish demeanour of conventional reptiles, such as snakes, lizards or even crocodiles.

He voiced this observation to Penward who nodded. 'That's because the dinosaurs were – are – warm blooded. It was long suspected that they were, of course, but our work here has proved it. I must admit I wasn't surprised to have the theory verified. It explains why, apart from their superior skeletal structure, the dinosaurs were dominant over competing reptile species for so long. The mammals achieved warm-bloodedness too during the dinosaur reign but had no opportunity to grow into a serious threat.'

'Is this one full-grown too?'

'Almost, but not quite. Let's say he's an adolescent. And now come and see the star of my menagerie . . .'

'A *Tyrannosaurus Rex!*' gasped Pascal, recognising the giant form behind the bars from the set of plastic dinosaurs he'd owned as a boy.

'You're close. Actually it's a *Tarbosaurus,* a close relative of Tyrannosaurus and physically very similar.'

The fifteen-foot-high dinosaur was supported on two massive hind legs but its forelimbs were disproportionately short; withered-looking little things with only two fingers on each hand. Not that they detracted from its overall fearsomeness. Most disturbing was its huge head – at least four feet in length and apparently all mouth. From head to tail it appeared to be about thirty feet long.

'Watch this. You'll find it interesting,' said Penward.

A keeper had appeared through a side door carrying a calf with its legs tied. The keeper took the calf into an enclosure beside the main cage, removed the rope from its legs then pushed it into a small pen attached to the bars. He then pulled up a section of the bars and prodded the frightened animal into the dinosaur's cage.

The Tarbosaurus had been watching all this with deceptive calmness. It had been standing almost motionlessly at the opposite end of the big cage, its head cocked to one side. But when the calf, bleating with terror, came skittering across the floor the dinosaur suddenly came to life.

Moving at a speed that was frightening for its huge bulk it covered the distance to the calf in two thunderous strides and pinned the animal to the floor with one of its big hind-claws. Then the great head darted downwards to the struggling animal and the jaws closed with a snap of breaking bones.

Pascal was reminded of some giant bird of prey, like a hawk or eagle, in the way the dinosaur tore at the now bloody flesh under its claw. He looked away in disgust.

'Did it have to be *alive*?' he asked.

'It keeps them alert,' said Penward bluntly. 'It's better for them that way. More natural.'

'Not for the calf though,' he muttered. He felt ill.

'Now do you begin to understand why I've gone to all the effort to bring such creatures back to life? When you see such a magnificent animal isn't it a crime that it should have disappeared from the face of the earth?' demanded Penward.

'It's called evolution, Sir Penward,' said Pascal. 'They had a good run but they became obsolete. A more superior, adaptable animal came along – the mammal – and took over. And we've been here ever since.'

Penward turned on him, eyes flashing with anger. 'Idiot! Is that what you really think?'

'It's true,' said Pascal apprehensively. He didn't like the look on Penward's face. It occurred to him that *he* might end up in the dinosaur cage if he wasn't careful.

'It is *not* true!' exploded Penward. 'The dinosaurs represent the *peak* of evolution. They ruled the world for over 140 *million* years. Do you have any conception of just how long a period that is? Compared to that achievement Man's reign on earth has been but the blink of an eye . . .'

'But the mammals . . .'

'The mammals evolved almost at the same time as the dinosaurs but they couldn't compete. They remained small, inconsequential creatures scuttling about underfoot all those millions of years. And that's where they'd be *today* if a terrible accident of fate hadn't destroyed the dinosaurs . . .

'The dinosaurs didn't become *obsolete,* as you so stupidly put it, Mr Pascal, they were cruelly *obliterated.* Not by any animal competitor but by a cosmic disaster that even they couldn't withstand. It was a meteor, an asteroid perhaps, which hit the world sixty-five million years ago and brought about the complete death of all the dinosaurs.'

Pascal nodded. He'd read about this. 'It's only a theory,' he ventured.

'It's more than a theory. It's the only possible explanation, and there is a great amount of evidence to support it, such as the iridium-rich band of clay that separates the Cretaceous from the Palaecene strata. The iridium could only have come from a large meteor. And that narrow band of clay marks the point in time where a whole range of species disappeared, not just the dinosaurs. A sure sign that the earth underwent a major cataclysm.'

'Yes, but some animal species obviously survived – even reptiles. Why is it that only the dinosaurs got completely wiped out by this meteor collision?'

'The explosion killed off most of the plant life. The debris blotted out the sun for years; ash rained down and coated the leaves, preventing photosynthesis. This meant there was a tremendous shortage of food. Warm-blooded animals need a lot of food – the only warm-blooded ones to survive were the small, burrowing ones. The mammals. All the bigger warm-blooded animals – the dinosaurs – died. First the herbivorous dinosaurs, then the carnosaurs. Only the cold-blooded reptiles survived – the turtles, the crocodiles and so on. And so the mammals inherited the earth – by *default.*'

Pascal sighed. 'All that may be true, but it's rather academic now. Whatever the reason, the dinosaurs were the losers. All right, they're very impressive beasts, I admit, and you've achieved something incredible in bringing them back to life; but I still don't understand what you hope to get out of all this. And I don't understand why you've kept them a secret. You could make a fortune if you exhibited them.'

'I don't *need* a fortune, Mr Pascal,' said Penward contemptuously. 'And I didn't resurrect my dinosaurs in order to display them to the brainless, gawking masses. On the contrary . . .'

He gestured for Pascal to follow him. As they left the enclosure Pascal glanced back at the Tarbosaurus. Having finished its meal it was staring at them sideways through the bars, its head cocked in that unnervingly bird-like manner.

Outside, Pascal realized that they were heading back towards the manor house. 'Aren't you going to show me the rest of them?'

'You've seen the more interesting specimens. Now I have something else to show you.'

They returned to the library and descended the staircase to the secret laboratory. Penward then took him into a room full of medical equipment. There was a strip of glass along one wall through which an eerie violet light was shining. 'One of our incubators,' explained Penward. 'Look.'

Pascal peered in and saw four large eggs resting on a bed of plastic fibre. There were several wires taped to each egg, which were about twice the size of those laid by ostriches.

'We clone four eggs at a time,' said Penward. 'Usually only one survives to the hatching stage, often none at all. But as our techniques have improved, so our success rate has become higher. On this occasion our monitors show that all four specimens are in perfect condition and should hatch within twenty-four to forty-eight hours.'

'Congratulations,' muttered Pascal sarcastically, wondering what the significance of all this was.

'What will emerge from those eggs are four healthy young Tyrannosauri. Two male, two female. For the first time we will have male and female specimens of the same species. We will be capable of *breeding* dinosaurs.'

'Your zoo is going to get awfully crowded, Sir Penward. How much longer do you think you'll be able to keep these things a secret?'

'Long enough. But these particular specimens won't be raised here. They will be flown to one of my properties in Kenya. I have farms throughout Africa, Mr Pascal, which I have managed to retain despite the various regional political upheavals. Again it's been a case of paying money in the right places. Most of the newer African governments consider me to be a friend and benefactor.'

Pascal frowned. 'I don't understand . . .'

'I also have property interests in Australia, Canada, and New Zealand. Many of them are in very remote areas. And therefore ideal for my purposes.'

'Your purposes?'

'I intend to re-establish the dinosaur on earth, Mr Pascal. I intend to release dinosaurs into the wild in each of those countries I mentioned. I am giving the greatest animals that ever lived a second chance. And then we will see who is the rightful victor in the struggle between mammals and dinosaurs.'

Pascal regarded him with horror. 'You're going to let them loose? You're *mad!*'

'Careful, Mr Pascal. Don't provoke me into doing something *you* might regret.'

'But you can't just release those things all over the world like that! Think of the number of people who'll get killed!'

Penward's mouth twisted into a sneer. 'People don't interest me, Mr Pascal. There are too many of them on this planet as it is. They are the least appetising specimens of the animal kingdom – they are like some awful vermin that has spread out over the world, leaving filth and pollution everywhere. As far as I'm concerned they are one of nature's failed experiments. It is time they went.'

His mouth dry with fear Pascal said, 'Surely you don't think your dinosaurs are going to destroy the human race? As big and powerful as they are they won't stand up to cannons and guided missiles. There's no way they can win against Man's technology...'

'Man's technology is about to run amok, Mr Pascal,' sneered Penward. 'Any fool can see that it is only a matter of time before mankind destroys itself. I predict an atomic war, either by accident or design, within a few years. It is inevitable. And when the pieces settle my dinosaurs, by then well established in the remote areas of the world, will be free to thrive and multiply. What remains of the human race will be helpless against them. We have already had one demonstration to date of the carnage a dinosaur can wreak in Man's world...'

'The one that escaped,' said Pascal grimly. 'The one that you pretended was a tiger...'

Penward nodded. 'Deinonychus – the small, orange-coloured one with the upturned claws. It's still a mystery how it got out of its cage. It was apparently left unlocked by one of the keepers though I find that hard to accept. All my men are one hundred percent trustworthy. Anyway, it then clawed its way through the outer fence. We were lucky to recapture it before it was seen. But enough of this. I have work to do.' He turned to the keeper. 'Miles, escort Mr Pascal back to his quarters...'

'Wait!' cried Pascal as the man took hold of his arm. 'What's going to happen to me? How long do you intend keeping me a prisoner?'

'Not long,' said Penward with a thin smile. 'Not long at all. We are waiting for the anaesthetic to pass through your system, Mr Pascal. We don't want any traces to be found in your body.'

'My body?' repeated Pascal. His worst fears were being realized. Penward was going to murder him.

'Your remains will be discovered in one of the big cat compounds tomorrow morning. It will appear that you, an overly-inquisitive reporter, had sneaked onto the premises during the night. Apparently you wanted to write some sensationalist story about my zoo and when I turned down your application for an interview – and when your attempt to quiz my employees at the

Phoenix Arms failed – you decided on more reckless tactics. With unfortunately fatal results.'

Pascal lunged at Penward. His intention was to get his hands around Penward's neck and throttle the life out of him. But he didn't even reach him. The keeper pulled him backwards, swung him round and slammed the butt of the shotgun into his stomach.

As Pascal fell gasping to the floor he heard Penward say, 'Careful, Miles. The less bruising the better.'

14

Pascal had occasionally wondered what it would feel like to be a condemned man on Death Row. Now he knew.

It's possible to cope with the inevitability of one's death when it remains a shadowy, abstract event in the barely imagined distant future. The usual method is just to ignore it – but when it suddenly looms into immediate proximity one can ignore it no longer; one is forced to accept its terrible reality . . .

Pascal's reaction to the undeniable fact that in the space of a few hours he was going to be killed in a particularly unpleasant way was one of sheer panic. He couldn't stop trembling and had suffered several attacks of severe diarrhoea during the three hours since being returned to the cell. The bucket – the nearest thing to toilet facilities available – was already half full and smelling very bad.

Not that he noticed. All he could think about was somehow getting away, but the more ideas he came up with the more futile they seemed. The only way out was through the door and it was locked. There was no chance of breaking it down and even less chance of overpowering one of the keepers and grabbing his gun. There was nothing in the cell that he could use as a weapon. He thought of setting fire to the mattress, but he had no matches or lighter. And even if by some miracle he did get out, he would still have to get past all of Penward's men and scale an electrified fence.

So he paced impotently up and down the small room, wondering how long he had left and how painful it would be when –

He staggered over to the bucket again, this time to throw up in it. He was still retching when he heard someone at the door. *Oh no,* he thought, *it's time . . . !*

The door opened and Pascal almost collapsed with relief. It was Lady Jane. Then he felt ashamed that she should see him this way. He got up, wiping his mouth with the back of his hand. 'Christ, am I glad to see you,' he told her.

She remained by the door, her expression unreadable as she stared at him. He couldn't tell if there was accusation or pity in her eyes. Finally she spoke. 'Darren said I could see you for a few moments. It amuses him. Us, I mean.'

Pascal noticed a purple bruise on her left cheek. 'He hit you?'

'I refused to answer his questions. At first.'

'You weren't exaggerating when you said he was insane. He's bloody crazy! Dropping his marbles all over the floor.' Pascal gave a strained laugh. 'He plans to let his dinosaurs loose across the world. In the Australian outback, Africa, places like that, so they'll be ready to take over the planet again after the Third World War. Did you know about all this?'

She nodded. 'But I couldn't tell anyone. Darren would have killed me.'

'A lot of people are going to die if he actually does start distributing those monsters around the globe, World War Three or no World War Three. And the first on the list is *me*. He's going to throw me to the lions, literally. And I'm not even a practising Christian . . .' Pascal tried to grin. '. . . though I am thinking seriously of re-enlisting.'

'Is it true?' she said grimly. 'What he told me about you?'

'It depends on what he told you,' he said, stalling desperately.

'You know what I'm talking about.'

He had no choice to admit the truth. Or at least *part* of the truth. 'Yes, I guess I do. It's true I was suspicious about this place. I'd found out it wasn't really a tiger that escaped that day. I wanted to find out what your husband was hiding here. But you *knew* I was a reporter all along . . .'

'Is that all I was to you? Just a way of getting in here?' Her face was stony; her gaze coldly penetrating. Pascal was struck again at how closely she resembled Penward physically. She was like a female version of him. Had Penward chosen her, either consciously or unconsciously, because of this resemblance? Had it been his way of marrying his ideal – himself?

He took a deep breath. His life depended on her believing the lie he was about to utter. 'At first, yes, you were. But not for long. I was telling the truth when I told you I loved you. I fell in love with you in spite of myself. Please believe me, Jane. I *do* love you.'

She stared at him silently, her face as stony as before. He waited anxiously, praying that she would give him the benefit of the doubt. She was his one small chance of escaping. If she turned her back on him he was finished for sure.

Suddenly her face softened. She came nearer to him. There were tears in her eyes. 'I *want* to believe you. Desperately. I'd give my soul if it were true.'

'It *is* true!' he cried. 'If only I could prove it to you!'

'You can prove it. Promise me you'll come away with me for good. We'll leave the country. Hide where Darren will never find us. I have money. Secret accounts he doesn't know about. Do you promise? Do you promise to stay with me forever?' Her eyes sucked at him like hungry black holes in space.

'I promise,' he said quickly. 'I promise I'll stay with you forever.' The twinge of guilt was nothing to the relief he felt. He could indulge his conscience later – right now survival was all that mattered.

'I believe you,' she said, slowly and deliberately. 'Pray to God I never learn I'm making a mistake or . . .' She didn't finish. The meaning – or rather the threat – was clear. Then she hugged him hard, her mouth finding his. It occurred to him that he must taste pretty foul but she gave no indication of it; instead the kiss went on for a long time.

Finally she released him and said, 'We've got to get you out of here.'

'Can't you just call the police?'

'No. There's no way I can phone out. Darren has closed down the switchboard. I'm forbidden to leave the estate as well. I'm just as much a prisoner as you.'

'Except *you're* not on the big cats' menu. Have you any idea when he plans to . . . to . . .' He couldn't bring himself to say the words 'kill me'.

'No. But I don't think it will be until late tonight. Which gives us at least nine hours . . .'

'Have you anything in mind?'

'Nothing specific yet. Only a vague plan.'

'Let's hear it.'

'I'll create a diversion. The ideal target is the generator. We have our own separate electricity supply here for the zoo lighting and heating, the security lights, the electric fence and so on. If I can sabotage that somehow it might give us enough time to get to my car . . .'

'How will you get me out of *here?'* he gestured at the walls.

'That gun I showed you. Darren doesn't know about it. There's only one man on guard out there.'

'And what about getting through the main gate?'

She gave a casual shrug of her shoulders. 'The gun again.'

Pascal was thoughtful. It all sounded very haphazard, but it was the only hope he had. 'I'll leave it up to you. Just make sure you don't arrive too late.'

'I'll find out from Darren when he intends . . .' She couldn't say it either.

Without warning the door opened. One of the keepers stood there, shotgun in hand. 'Time's up, Lady Jane,' he said, looking a little embarrassed.

'Thank you, Farson,' she said haughtily. She turned back to Pascal and gave him a reassuring smile. 'I'll talk to Darren again. See if I can't get him to forget all this nonsense. Chin up, darling.' She gave him a quick kiss and strode out of the room, ignoring the guard. But when she had gone the man smirked at Pascal and said in a low voice, 'Don't get your hopes up.' Then he slammed the door shut.

Pascal felt better after Lady Jane's visit but the next nine hours were still hell to endure. Even though there was now hope where none had existed before, he had strong doubts about her ability to get him off the estate. There were just too many things that could go wrong with her plan; it depended too much on pure luck. There was also the grim possibility that Penward and his men would come for him before Lady Jane could put her plan into operation.

This fear grew ever bigger as the hours wore on. By eleven o'clock his nerves were strained to the breaking point. He wanted to scream and beat his fists against the walls – anything to release the agonising tension within him.

Then, at 11.15 p.m. he heard the distant ringing of bells. A short time later he heard movements in the corridor outside. A long pause, then the sound of the key in the lock. His bowels seemed to fill with ice cold water. Was it Lady Jane or his executioners?

'Oh, thank God . . .' he whispered as Lady Jane came in. She was dressed in a black tracksuit and was carrying the chrome-plated pistol he'd seen before.

'Come on, we've got to hurry. I've got my car parked right by one of the side doors. If we can only make it . . .'

He followed her out into the corridor. A guard lay on the floor, face down. Blood seeped from the side of his head. 'Your diversion worked?' he asked her as they hurried along the passageway.

'Not mine, someone else's,' she told him over her shoulder. 'I was on my way to the generator when the alarm bells started ringing. Means an intruder, or intruders, must have set off the heat sensors on the fence. Darren and a lot of his men went off to investigate, so the coast is clear, temporarily.'

They raced up the spiral staircase and emerged warily into the musty library. The lights were on and it was empty. But as Lady Jane approached one of the doors leading out she held up her hand in a silent warning, then signalled urgently for him to get out of sight.

He ducked behind a large leather chair just as the door began to open. Lady Jane, right by the doorway, raised the pistol like a club. One of the keepers entered. He was obviously on security patrol, as he carried a high-powered rifle under his arm. As he came into the library Lady Jane stepped out from the door, which had shielded her from him, and hit him very hard on the back of the head with the butt of the gun.

He gave a grunt of pain and dropped the rifle but didn't fall. Instead he stood there, swaying, and began to turn. Lady Jane hit him again. The butt of the gun made an unpleasant *thonk* sound as it slammed into the side of his head. He fell to his hands and knees, shaking his head as if trying to clear it. She hit him a third time, putting all her strength into the downward blow. He fell on to his face and lay still.

Pascal stood up from behind the chair, feeling shaken. Now he knew what had happened to the guard outside his cell.

Lady Jane, unperturbed, picked up the rifle and handed it to Pascal. 'Take this. Do you know how to use it?'

'Yes.' He nodded towards the guard. 'I think you killed him.' He could see a definite indentation on the back of the man's head. It was full of blood. She shrugged. 'One less of Darren's devoted slaves to worry about. But there are plenty of others. Let's go.'

Pascal followed her down what seemed an endless series of long, gloomy passageways. The rifle felt heavy in his hands and he hoped he wouldn't have to use it. He wasn't sure if he'd be *able* to use it. All he'd ever shot before were targets; he'd never fired a gun at a living thing, not even a rabbit . . .

But they made it outside without encountering anyone else. The car, an Alfa Romeo, was there waiting as she'd said. They scrambled into it and she started the engine. *We're halfway there!* thought Pascal. *All we have to do now is get through the gate . . .*

As the car began to move he expected to hear shouts, or even shots, from the house but there was nothing. He began to relax a little as Lady Jane turned onto the main drive. She had her lights off but obviously knew the road well enough to handle it in the dark.

'I'll slow down before we get to the gatehouse and you'll get out with the rifle,' she told him. 'They'll stop me at the gate – they've got orders to – and I'll start arguing with them. Then I'll say that Darren has given the okay for me to leave. One of them will ring the house, and while all that's going on you'll take them by surprise . . .'

'And do what?' asked Pascal nervously.

'Just cover them with the rifle. There'll only be two of them. When you pop up I'll produce the pistol. I'll have it under the seat. Then we'll force them to open the gates, tie them up and away we go. To freedom. To a new life . . .'

'I hope so,' he muttered. The sick feeling in the pit of his stomach was back again.

'Shit!' Unexpectedly she swerved the car off the road, just missing one of the trees that line the driveway. The car bumped over the grass and then ploughed through a row of shrubs.

'What's wrong?' cried Pascal in alarm as she braked to a stop.

'Darren's coming back already, damn it!' she cursed.

Pascal then saw three sets of headlights coming towards them along the driveway. 'Do you think they saw us?'

'No, but keep low . . .'

The car was about thirty feet from the road and partly concealed by the shrubs. There was a good chance it wouldn't be spotted in the darkness but Pascal's heart began to pound alarmingly as the three vehicles approached at high speed.

Peering over the edge of the door he saw three Land Rovers rush by their hiding place. Then suddenly they were receding into the distance, their speed unchanged.

But Pascal felt too shocked to experience any relief. In the second vehicle he'd seen someone he recognised. He'd only got a brief glimpse but there was no mistake – the lights from the Land Rover behind had illuminated all the faces.

And one of them had been Jenny's.

'Thank God, they missed us,' said Lady Jane. She reached forward to switch on the ignition but Pascal grabbed her arm. 'Wait,' he said urgently. 'We've got to go back.'

'What?'

'I saw Jenny in one of those vehicles. We've got to go back for her.'

'Who – is – *Jenny?*' Lady Jane's tone was icy.

'A girl I work with. A friend of mine. She knew I wanted to get into the zoo. She must have figured out where I was and followed me. How are we going to get her out of there?'

'You've never mentioned her before. Just how *much* of a friend is she to you?'

'Hell, she's a friend, that's all!' he cried. 'What does it matter? What's important is working out a way of rescuing her.'

'She's *more* than a friend,' Lady Jane accused him, her voice becoming a snarl. 'I can tell by the way you're talking about her.

You've slept with her, haven't you . . . you *bastard* . . .'

'For Christ's sake, let's discuss all this later!' he cried. 'Jenny's life's in danger! Are you going to help me or not?'

'Go on, tell me, just what *is* she to you?' demanded Lady Jane, ignoring his question.

Pascal could barely make out her face in the darkness – it was ugly, contorted with rage and jealousy. Suddenly Pascal could take no more. He snapped.

'You want to know about Jenny?' he yelled. 'Okay, I'll tell you. I *love* her! I've been lying to you all along. I lied to you this afternoon. I don't love you. Hell, I don't even *like* you very much. You're an arrogant, crazy, self-obsessed, raving nymphomaniac! You don't need a lover, you need a stud farm! If I had to screw you just one more time I think I'd throw up with self-disgust!'

He yelled the last few sentences at the top of his voice. The deathly silence that followed was unsettling. A long moment passed and then Lady Jane came to life. Her hand darted into the glove box . . .

Pascal knew what was in there. Her pistol. He reacted fast. He'd been holding the rifle ever since getting into the car. The butt rested on the floor between his feet and the end of the barrel leaned against the top of the windshield. Instinctively he slammed the barrel towards her: it hit on the side of her temple. She grunted, then slumped forward over the wheel.

He felt her pulse. It was strong, to his relief. He doubted if he'd done her any serious damage. Not physically at least. He was already regretting his outburst. He should have handled things better than that, but he guessed the pressure of the day's events had pushed him over the edge. And he was also relieved that the big lie he'd been living was definitely over . . .

He took the pistol out of the glove box and flung it into the bushes. Then, after settling Lady Jane into a more comfortable position, he got out and started back in the direction of the manor house, which was at least a half a mile away.

He had no idea what he was going to do when he arrived there. All he knew was that somehow he had to sneak into the building and find Jenny. And then . . .

He'd been walking for about ten minutes when he saw the

lights of one of the Land Rovers coming back along the road. He ducked behind the bushes until it had gone by. He guessed that his escape had been discovered and they were now looking for him, and Lady Jane as well.

He continued on. The house was getting close now. He would have to make a wide detour and approach it from the side.

Suddenly a loud, familiar sound filled the air. He looked up and saw a dark shape moving towards him through the sky. It was Penward's damned helicopter. And ahead of it, sweeping back and forth over the ground, was a circle of bright white light.

Pascal tried to run but almost immediately he found himself caught in the spotlight's ruthless glare. Then an amplified voice boomed from the sky: 'Drop the gun and stand still!'

His response was to raise the rifle and fire three shots at the blinding light and the dark shape behind it. Then, without waiting to see if his bullets had any effect, he turned and ran as fast as he could, zig-zagging as he went.

But the white circle of light soon found him again and this time there was the distinctive pneumatic drill-like sound of a heavy calibre machine gun. Chunks of lawn were blown into the air only feet away from him. Pascal stopped running. He dropped the rifle and raised his hands. The noise of the helicopter grew deafening as it touched down nearby. Then he heard someone running towards him. Dazzled by the spotlight, he didn't see the rifle butt until it hit him in the side of his face.

15

Pascal was still stunned when they pulled him out of the Sikorsky. It had landed in the rear courtyard between the zoo buildings and the manor house. He tried to get his footing as he was dragged roughly over the gravel but the muscles in his legs refused to obey his commands.

He was taken into the library. Penward was there, and so was Jenny. She was sitting dejectedly in a chair. When she saw Pascal she gave a cry of alarm and tried to rise to go to him but was pushed back down by one of the keepers. She was very pale and had a bruise on her right cheek but otherwise seemed unhurt. So far.

Pascal was dragged upright by the two keepers holding his arms. Penward strode up to him, eyes flashing with anger. 'Apparently, Mr Pascal, I underestimated your power over Jane. Where is my dear wife, by the way?'

'I don't know,' said Pascal, with difficulty.

'If *you're* here then she must be nearby. She certainly hasn't left the estate. The gatehouse hasn't seen her and there's been no indication of her trying to get over any of the fences. Which brings us to Miss Stamper here.' He swung round to face Jenny. 'I understand this beautiful young lady is a colleague of yours. Correct?'

Pascal nodded. Then he gave her a weak smile and said, 'Hi, Jen. Are you all right?'

'I'm fine . . .'

'Yes, she's fine, Mr Pascal,' cut in Penward, 'though she shouldn't be. She narrowly avoided electrocuting herself on the inner fence. Her method of entry was alarmingly amateur, involving two aluminium ladders and a rubber sheet. She's very lucky to be alive. You should feel flattered, Mr Pascal. She took all those risks for your benefit. The big question is: how did she know you were here? Well, Miss Stamper?'

Jenny gave Pascal a worried glance, obviously wondering how much she should tell Penward. Then she said slowly: 'When David didn't turn up for work yesterday, and didn't call the office, I rang his mother. She didn't know where he was but wasn't too worried because he hadn't been at home much during the last couple of weeks . . .'

'And we know why,' interrupted Penward drily, turning to Pascal. 'He was fully occupied with my darling wife. Isn't that so, Mr Pascal?'

Pascal said nothing. He avoided looking at Jenny.

'Continue, Miss Stamper,' ordered Penward.

'Well, I didn't think anything more about it until lunchtime when Henry – he's our photographer – came and asked me if I knew why David had wanted to borrow the camera the night before, and what he'd been so excited about. All he knew was that

David had said something about "going hunting". I knew David was obsessed with getting in here so I guessed this was where he must be . . .'

'And so you organised a lone rescue attempt?' asked Penward.

'Yes . . .well, no . . .' She realized her mistake too late. 'I did tell a couple of people where I was going,' she said hurriedly.

Penward raised a supercilious eyebrow. 'Really? *Who*, exactly?' It was plain he didn't believe her.

'Uh, Henry . . . and I told Johnny MacGibbon. He's another reporter on the paper . . .'

Penward shook his head. 'No, I don't think you did.' He walked over to a table and picked up a camera. He showed it to Pascal. 'I fear Miss Stamper's motives for rescuing you were not purely altruistic. She had this with her. Like you, her journalistic instincts got the better of her. She wanted to keep this potentially big story to herself. I sincerely doubt if she told anyone on the paper about it. Or anyone else at all. Isn't that correct, Miss Stamper?'

She stared back at him defiantly. 'I *did* tell them where I was going. If I'm not at work tomorrow they'll come here looking for me.'

'I'm afraid I must call your bluff, Miss Stamper,' said Penward, a little wearily. 'Not that it matters either way. Tomorrow morning a great many people will know your whereabouts, but it won't be of any benefit to you.'

Jenny frowned. 'What do you mean?'

But Penward was no longer paying her any attention. He was staring thoughtfully at the camera he was holding. Then he said to the keeper behind Jenny's chair, 'We can still use our original plan – with some modifications. We'll have to devise an explanation as to how *both* of them entered the lion compound . . .'

Pascal saw Jenny go pale. 'What are you talking about?' she demanded.

But Penward continued to ignore her. It was as if he no longer regarded her as a living entity. In his mind she was already dead meat. He rubbed his long chin thoughtfully. 'It *is* feasible. The lion compound resembles just another section of parkland. In the dark, especially, it would be easy for someone not to realize what it contained. We will leave one of Ms Stamper's ladders against the fence. It will look as if the two inquisitive young reporters were making their way towards the manor house, climbing fences as they went – and by mistake entered the lion compound...'

Jenny had gone completely white now. She looked imploringly at Pascal, hoping that he might give her some reassuring sign that it was all a joke. All he could manage was a brave smile. It had the effect of increasing the fear in her eyes.

'Perhaps we can embellish the scenario a little,' mused Penward. 'It might be a good idea if the girl's body is found with a broken leg. It will appear that she broke it falling from the fence. The young man went to her assistance and refused to leave her even when it became evident there were lions in the compound. That way we can explain why the lions succeeded in getting both of them...'

As Penward talked Jenny seemed to grow smaller and younger until, in her dark blue tee-shirt and jeans, she looked like a frightened teenager. Pascal felt a rush of overwhelming compassion for her. He *had* to save her somehow. He no longer gave a damn about his own life. She was all that mattered.

The door suddenly opened and another of Penward's men hurried in. 'We found Lady Jane's car, Sir Penward. It was hidden in some bushes just off the main driveway about half a mile from the house. No sign of Lady Jane though.'

'Keep looking,' said Penward, annoyed. 'I want her found and locked up in her flat within the hour.'

As the man left, the keeper behind Jenny said, 'Should we break it now?'

'What? Break what?' asked Penward distractedly.

'Her leg,' said the keeper blandly, indicating Jenny.

'No. Not here. Outside,' answered Penward with equal blandness. 'We'll do it now. Bring them along.'

The two men holding Pascal's arms immediately tightened their grip and there was nothing he could do to prevent himself from being dragged backwards. At the same time the other keeper reached down and hauled Jenny out of her chair. She struggled, but he was much too strong for her.

Soon both she and Pascal were being hustled along the gloomy passageways towards the rear of the building. And in the distance he could hear a chilling sound – the roar of lions.

It wasn't just the lions roaring. As Pascal was dragged out into the courtyard it seemed as if *all* the big cats were screeching and snarling. The night air was filled with a cacophony of feral sounds that even the wildest section of African jungle wouldn't be able to equal.

Penward came to an abrupt halt. 'What the hell's the matter with them?' he cried.

'Something's spooking them,' said one of the keepers who had hold of Pascal.

'Yes, but what?' demanded Penward irritably.

He soon got his answer. From around the corner of the nearest of the big zoo buildings that contained the dinosaurs a keeper appeared. He was sprinting as fast as he could and when he spotted Penward and the others he started to yell a warning. His words were unintelligible; but that didn't matter, for the purpose of his warning immediately became apparent.

From around the same corner stepped the Tarbosaurus.

Out of its enclosure the thirty-foot-long, seven-ton creature looked even bigger. It paused at the corner of the building, searching for its prey. It spotted the running man almost at once and began to bound after him.

The keeper was running across the courtyard straight towards Penward and his party, all of whom were frozen to the spot. The keeper only made it halfway. The Tarbosaurus, demonstrating the same frightening speed that Pascal had seen when it was in its cage, caught up with him and pinned him under one huge clawed foot. The keeper screamed shrilly, then the great head with its rows of long teeth darted downwards and he was suddenly nothing but shredded rawness between its tearing jaws. Again Pascal was reminded of some giant, featherless hawk or eagle in the way the dinosaur looked and moved.

Jenny was screaming. Slowly, as if underwater, Penward and his men began to act. Penward started to run towards the dinosaur but then, obviously realizing the foolishness of such an action, came to an abrupt halt.

The two keepers on either side of Pascal let go of him and ran to join Penward. One of them had a rifle slung over his shoulder and he began to unsling it as he ran. 'What should we do, Sir?' he cried to Penward. 'Shoot it?'

Penward wavered with uncertainty. The dinosaur meanwhile ignored them as it finished consuming its victim. Then, with a final crunch of bones, it lifted its head, cocked it to one side and stared at them.

Penward came to a decision. 'Hell, yes!' he cried angrily, 'we'll have to! Aim for the eye!'

The keeper dropped to one knee and raised the rifle to his shoulder. The Tarbosaurus continued to watch them, presumably wondering which one to choose as its next victim. Its right eye presented a perfect target to the man with the rifle. The dinosaur was less than ten yards away – he couldn't miss.

But at that moment one of the Land Rovers entered the courtyard, returning from the search for Lady Jane. When the driver saw the dinosaur he braked sharply and the vehicle skidded over the gravel.

As the startled Tarbosaurus turned to look at this new distraction, the rifle went off. The bullet struck its upper neck, burying itself in the thick muscle and causing no serious damage to the animal. But the dinosaur reacted as if it had – it let out a tremendously loud, high-pitched shriek of pain and rage and spun round to charge the Land Rover. Its reptile brain had mistakenly connected the vehicle with the sudden blaze of pain in its neck, and as it turned, its long, massive tail whipped across the gravel – straight toward Penward and his two men . . .

Penward and one of the keepers flung themselves backward just in time, but the one with the rifle, who was still in a kneeling position, couldn't move fast enough. It was like being hit with the trunk of a tree. He was sent sailing through the air to land fifteen feet away in an agony of shattered bones. He lay there writhing, unable to get up.

The Tarbosaurus now sprang at the stalled Land Rover. Its four occupants jumped clear as one of the great hind feet was lifted high and then brought down on the vehicle's roof like a clawed pile driver. The windshield vaporized as the roof caved inward with a screech of tearing metal.

One of the men from the vehicle was carrying a shotgun. He fired both barrels at the dinosaur, but the pellets rattled harmlessly off its leathery scales. The huge foot came down for a second time on top of the Land Rover, reducing it to a total wreck, before the dinosaur turned its attention back to the humans . . .

Pascal, meanwhile, was seizing his chance. The keeper who'd been holding Jenny had let her go and was staring transfixed at the raging dinosaur. Pascal stepped up close behind him and hit him as hard as he could on the back of his neck with the edge of his hand. The impact jarred every bone in his hand and wrist and made him grunt with pain, but he had the satisfaction of seeing the keeper topple over.

He grabbed Jenny by the arm and pulled her back toward the doorway they'd come out of. Neither Penward nor any of his men noticed as Pascal opened the door and thrust her inside – all eyes were on the dinosaur . . .

They ran down the passageways. Pascal had no idea where they were going or what they were going to do next. He had some vague notion of finding the switchboard that Lady Jane had mentioned and phoning for help; but mainly all he could think about was that he and Jenny had been granted a reprieve from a horrible death.

Suddenly they found themselves in a dimly-lit billiard room. It was empty apart from four dejected-looking suits of armour that stood against each of the walls facing the billiard table. 'Let's stop – get our breath,' he gasped at Jenny, who was already leaning against the table and panting heavily. 'We should be safe here for a time. Penward and his merry men are going to be too busy with that thing outside to worry about us.'

She turned a tear-streaked face to him. 'David, what *was* that horrible thing? Where did it come from?'

Pascal grinned at her. He felt light-headed with relief. Euphoric even. 'Horrible? That's no way to speak about the creature that saved your life. *Both* our lives . . .'

'But what *was* it?'

'A dinosaur, of course. The place is full of them,' he said cheerily. 'But God knows how that one got out.'

'A *real* dinosaur?' said Jenny in wonder. 'Where did it come from? Africa?'

'No. Not Africa. It's a long, complicated story which I'll tell you later. In the meantime let's figure out what we're going to do next.'

She covered her face in her hands. 'I don't believe this is happening. It's like a nightmare. First Sir Penward was actually going to *kill* us and then that monster appearing and tearing that man to *pieces* . . .'

He went over and gently pulled her hands away from her face. He kissed her lightly on the lips. 'It *was* a nightmare, but now we're together and we're going to get out of here. By the way, thanks for coming after me. I only wish you hadn't come alone . . .'

She looked slightly abashed. 'I wasn't absolutely sure you were in trouble. When I decided you were probably here, I thought you might be a guest . . .'

'A *guest*? Why on earth would you think that?'

'Henry Wates didn't just tell me about the camera you borrowed; he also told me he was pretty sure you were having an affair with Lady Penward.'

'Good old Henry,' muttered Pascal.

'I laughed at first, then I remembered you hadn't been around for weeks. It's true, isn't it? Sir Penward said it too, about you and his wife . . .'

He sighed. 'Yes, it's true, but . . .'

'Do you love her?' she asked anxiously.

'No! I don't!' he cried, 'I love *you*!'

Her eyes widened. 'Do you mean that?'

'Of course I do. I finally realized how much this afternoon when I was locked up downstairs. I knew I only had hours to live and I was scared shitless. I was thinking of all the things I would never do, never see again . . . the most painful thing was the thought I'd never see *you* again.'

'Oh, David . . .' She flung her arms around him and buried her face against his neck.

He hugged her just as tightly. He knew they were still in great danger, but he couldn't help feeling enormously happy. The happiest he'd been for a long time.

There was a loud crash in the distance, followed by the sound of glass shattering. Someone screamed, then came the roar of some animal.

Jenny stiffened and looked up, startled. 'The dinosaur . . .'

Pascal frowned. 'That sounded as if it came from *inside* the house, and from the front – it can't be the same dinosaur.'

'You mean there might be *two* of them loose?'

Before he could say yes they heard it roar again. Closer this time. Whatever was making the sound was coming their way.

16

The Tarbosaurus shrieked its annoyance to the night sky, then whirled round to confront the newest source of irritation. Three more keepers had entered the courtyard. Two of them had tranquilliser guns and were firing darts into the huge animal, but with little effect other than to enrage it further.

'It's no good!' cried Penward as his men scattered before the creature. 'Its skin has become too tough for the darts!' He had picked up the rifle dropped by the man hit by the creature's tail, but the barrel had been bent by the impact. Penward cursed and flung it away. Then he remembered the heavy calibre machine gun in the helicopter.

'Miles!' he yelled across the courtyard, 'the *gun*!' He pointed at the Sikorsky parked in the far corner. Miles, the nearest to it, gave a thumbs-up sign and ran towards the aircraft. The Tarbosaurus, meanwhile, had turned its attention to Penward, having failed to catch any of the running men.

Penward realized his danger almost too late as the dinosaur came bounding across the courtyard towards him – he had underestimated the thing's speed . . .

He turned and ran for the cover of the open doorway. He made it just in time. No sooner had he slammed the door shut behind him and flung himself flat on the passageway floor than the door splintered to pieces as the great hind foot smashed through it.

Penward scrambled further down the passageway as the claws ripped up the floor, searching for him. But the dinosaur soon tired of this game and went off in search of easier prey. Warily

Penward peered out through the shambles of the door. The dinosaur was moving towards the helicopter. 'Miles, you bloody fool!' cried Penward angrily. The keeper had switched on the aircraft's interior lights, presumably to see to operate the gun, but they had attracted the animal . . .

What happened next had an awful inevitability about it. The dinosaur arrived at the machine before Miles had a chance to bring the heavy machine gun into play. The great hind foot rose again and lashed out – the fragile fuselage crumpled under that terrible force. From the wreckage came a long, wailing scream.

Again the dinosaur sent its hind claw crashing into the aircraft. It fell over on its side and a smell of petrol immediately filled the air. Then there was a flash and suddenly flames were shooting out of the wrecked Sikorsky.

Alarmed, the Tarbosaurus backed away from the fire, then turned and began to stride briskly out of the courtyard towards the zoo. Penward ran from the cover of the doorway shouting orders to his men. 'Get that fire out! We don't want the damned fire brigade out here!' The flames from the burning helicopter were now leaping high into the air. Miles could no longer be heard . . .

Penward surveyed the scene with a sinking heart. A valuable aircraft destroyed, two men dead, possibly three – the one that had been hit by the creature's tail looked in a bad way. And the Tarbosaurus was still loose. It had to be stopped before it made its presence known to the outside world. He would not tolerate the ruination of his grand dream at this late stage of the game. It was *unthinkable.*

'Come with me!' he commanded one of the keepers who was watching the burning helicopter with a dazed expression. 'We can't let the bloody animal out of our sight!'

They caught up with it outside the lion enclosure. The big cats were rushing back and forth behind the wire in a frenzy of fear and anger while the dinosaur looked down on them from over the top of the 12 ½-foot high fence. Whether it regarded them as prey or natural enemies it was impossible to tell, but suddenly it gave a loud snarl and began to kick at the fence.

Penward, watching from around the corner of a nearby

building, cursed with rage. Then he pointed at the walkie-talkie hanging from the keeper's belt and said, 'Call the security room. Tell them I want every available man here immediately. And I want them all armed with rifles!' Then he turned back to the lion compound. The fence was beginning to buckle inwards under the force of the dinosaur's kicks. The wire mesh started to rip, while inside the lions – two males and five females – grew even more frenzied.

'There's no answer from the security room!' cried the keeper.

'Idiot!' snapped Penward and tore the crackling radio out of the man's hand. It was his strictest order that the security room – the hub of the estate's network of alarms, sensors and cameras as well as the centre of the internal communication system – be manned twenty-four hours a day. He pressed down on the CALL button savagely, but the keeper was right – all he got was static.

The fence caved in with a ringing crash. Penward saw the dinosaur step over the tangle of shredded wire mesh and enter the compound. The lions, displaying their customary feline intelligence, exited at speed. They spilled out around the advancing Tarbosaurus, running with their bodies close to the ground like frightened house cats. All but one, that is. A lioness. It found its way blocked by the dinosaur and so, with coughing snarl, launched itself at the bigger animal. Its leap took it all the way up to the dinosaur's shoulder and it clung there, claws dug deep into the scaly hide and its teeth buried in the dinosaur's neck. The Tarbosaurus screamed with pain as it tried to dislodge the lion.

Penward didn't see the outcome of the uneven struggle between these two carnivores from different eras; he had more pressing things to worry about. Two of the panic-stricken lions were rushing straight towards where he and the keeper were standing. Normally Penward had no fears of lions – he was an expert at handling them – but these two were in such a frenzied state he knew they'd kill anything that got in their way without even pausing.

So he turned and ran . . .

He had no idea what happened to the keeper. As Penward raced down an alley he threw a glance over his shoulder, but there was no sign of either the man or the lions. Penward hoped sincerely that both of the cats were after the keeper.

Penward slowed down and frowned. There was a hell of a commotion coming from the direction of the stock pens. The herds of sheep and cows that provided the food for the zoo's meat eaters grazed on the hundred acres or so of open land on the southern side of the estate but some stock was kept penned up at the rear of the zoo complex so as to be conveniently to hand. Also kept in the pens were a number of bulls and rams used for breeding purposes.

He emerged from the narrow alley that ran between two of the dinosaur enclosures and tried to interpret the sounds that were coming from the pens. The animals sounded terrified – had one of the escaped lions got there already? But no, those lions would still be too frightened to think about food. Then he heard the sound of wood splintering and a familiar snarl. His blood went cold. It was the Megalosaurus! It was out too! But how?

As he ran towards the pens he realized he was still holding the radio. He again pressed the CALL button. Again all he got was static. Then suddenly something appeared out of the shadows ahead of him. It was running straight towards him. He jumped to one side out of its way before he recognised what it was.

It was about the size of a baby elephant but had a long neck, like a swan's, and ridiculously small head. It was a young Brachiosaurus, so far the only herbivorous dinosaur that Penward had cloned. Fully grown it would be taller than a four-storey building and weigh over eighty tonnes.

As the frightened young dinosaur ran bleating past him, Penward was forced to accept the unpleasant truth – someone was *deliberately* letting loose all the dinosaurs.

And he had a good idea who.

His face twisted into a mask of fury. He raised the walkie-talkie and stabbed at the CALL button. This time he got a reaction. 'Security,' answered a shaky voice. 'Who . . . ?'

'Penward here. Why the hell weren't you at your post?'

'Uh, Sir Penward, you'd better come quickly. We've got trouble here. Deinonychus is loose in the house . . .'

'Has anyone seen Lady Jane?' snapped Penward.

'Lady Jane . . . ?' The voice was surprised. 'I don't think so. But Sir Penward – Deinonychus – what shall we – '

Penward didn't hear the end of the sentence. He'd flung the radio against a concrete wall. Fuming with rage he began to run back towards the house. He had to get hold of a weapon. *Any* kind of weapon. That bitch! She'd ruined everything . . . !

He was only dimly aware of the sound of hoofbeats behind him. By the time he turned it was too late. A large, dark bulk slammed into him, knocking him off his feet. At the same time there was a searing pain across his groin and inside his left thigh.

It was only when he managed to struggle into a sitting position that he saw what had hit him. Disappearing into the darkness he saw the rear of a black bull. It had obviously escaped from the stock pens . . .

He looked down at himself. His injuries were serious – possibly fatal. His left groin and inner thigh had been ripped open. There was already a sizeable puddle of blood beneath him. Even so, the bizarre irony of what had happened made him smile bitterly. A number of the most dangerous flesh-eaters that had ever existed on earth were loose on the estate and *he* had been gored by an ordinary bull . . .

Pascal went to one of the suits of armour and prised loose the handle of a battle-axe from the pair of steel gauntlets that gripped it. He hefted the axe and winced. It was too heavy. He needed a lighter weapon.

'David!' cried Jenny.

He heard it too. Footsteps coming towards them. Fast. Then one of the doors was flung open and a man staggered into the billiard room. He wore some sort of dark uniform and Pascal guessed he was one of Penward's servants. A butler, perhaps, or a valet. If so he was going to have to consider a new profession – he now only had one arm. Where his right arm had been was a six-inch long bloody stump hanging down from his shoulder. Blood from it dripped onto the polished wooden floor as he lurched towards them, his face grey as lead. 'Help me,' he gasped. 'It's after me . . .'

More sounds. Louder ones. Something bigger and heavier

than a man was coming along the same passageway behind the
injured servant. 'Jenny!' he screamed. 'This way. Hurry!'

Jenny had been moving to assist the man; now she backed
away quickly and ran to join Pascal on the other side of the billiard table. She was just in time. The dinosaur leapt through the
doorway and landed with a floor-shaking thud mere feet from
the servant. He gave a choked scream and tried to duck to one
side but the dinosaur kicked out with its hind-claw like a prehistoric exponent of Kung-Fu. The scythe-like middle claw opened
up a gash down the man's side that extended from his armpit to
below his waist. His body was propelled into the billiard table,
bounced off a corner and slid across the floor.

The dinosaur showed no further interest in its victim – its
attention was now fixed on Pascal and Jenny. Food was obviously
not the foremost thing on its mind; its blood-lust was up. It was
after enemies, not prey . . .

Pascal had seen this one before, in one of the cages. It was the
small, rust-coloured dinosaur with the grotesque claws on its
hindfeet. It had a large head and there was a disturbing look of
vicious intelligence in its green eyes. It stood there on the other
side of the billiard table watching them intently. Its chest heaved
in and out at a fast rate and it made a hoarse, rasping sound as it
breathed.

'Jenny,' said Pascal quietly, 'head for the door behind us. The
one we came in. I'll try and hold it off long enough for you to get
out.' He hefted the heavy axe with difficulty, knowing it would be
useless when the creature sprang at him. He wouldn't be able to
swing it fast enough.

'Don't be silly, David,' said Jenny, in a frightened whisper. 'I'm
not leaving you here to play the hero.'

'Jenny . . . go!' he ordered.

The dinosaur began to move around the billiard table towards
them. Pascal moved in the opposite direction. To his frustrated
annoyance Jenny came with him.

The creature stopped moving and cocked its head to one side
in the familiar bird-like manner as if trying to work out what to
do next. Out of the corner of his eye Pascal noticed he was standing next to the rack of billiard cues. It occurred to him that one

of them might make a better weapon than the axe. He came to a swift decision. He flung the axe across the table at the dinosaur, then made a grab for a cue.

The axe struck the dinosaur a glancing blow on the side of the head but didn't appear to even distract it. Instead, with an angry shriek, the six-foot-tall creature leapt *onto* the table . . .

But before it could spring down on top of them Pascal rammed it hard in the belly with the cue he'd snatched out of the rack. The dinosaur recoiled with a grunt of pain, its hind claws ripping holes in the green baize of the table top as it tried to keep its balance. Then it snarled and lunged forward again.

To Pascal's surprise another cue appeared beside his, its tip thrusting hard into the dinosaur's face below its left eye, making it flinch and again delaying its attack. 'Damn you, Jenny!' he yelled. 'Get out of here! Make for the door!'

'Not without you!' she yelled back as she thrust her cue again at the dinosaur's face.

They kept this up for about thirty seconds; Pascal repeatedly ramming it in the stomach while Jenny aimed at its eyes and snout. Then it managed to break the end of Pascal's cue with a swipe of one of its forearms. Pascal looked at the splintered wood he was holding and then the inspiration and the action came almost instantaneously. He darted forward, risking his face and arms being sliced open by the flailing foreclaws, and thrust the end of the broken cue between the creature's jaws and down deep into its throat.

The dinosaur shrieked with pain and staggered back across the billiard table. It began to shake its head violently, trying to dislodge the splintered cue from its throat.

'Come on!' Pascal pushed Jenny so hard she almost fell over. 'The *door,* hurry!'

As they reached the doorway Pascal glanced back over his shoulder. The dinosaur – which he now remembered was called Deinonychus – was still doing a bizarre dance on the billiard table, the cue protruding from its mouth. Then, to his horror, he saw the cue sent flying across the room by a violent flick of the creature's head.

'Oh shit,' he muttered, slamming the door.

'Where to now?' gasped Jenny as they ran down the corridor.

'As far away from that thing as possible,' he yelled back.

Behind them he heard the door to the billiard room shudder as something hit it. Then came the sound of splintering wood.

17

On the catwalk above the circular tank Lady Jane sighed with satisfaction as the valve wheel finally submitted to her efforts and shifted. She grinned in the darkness. She had now closed the outlet pipe, having already increased the flow of water into the tank. The level would quickly rise and the plesiosaur would be able to climb out. As an added encouragement to it she had also switched off the tank's heating.

She picked up her torch from the floor of the catwalk and turned towards the gangway leading down to the ground level. She only took one step then froze. Standing there in the beam of the torch was her husband.

'I'd guessed I'd find you here,' he said calmly. 'All the others are loose. This is the last one. You've had a busy night, my dear.'

In a voice as equally calm she said, 'Yes, I have, Darren. It's quite exhausted me.'

'You were fortunate one of them didn't catch you. You were very lucky.'

'One of them almost did. The one with the two bony ridges sticking out of its head. You know what I'm like with names . . .'

'Dilophosaurus. '

'Oh yes. That's the one, I'm sure.' She grinned maliciously. 'You, on the other hand, appear not to have been so lucky.' She had now noticed his blood-encrusted trousers. She also saw that he was using his belt as a tourniquet around his upper left thigh. 'Which of your dear little pets did the dirty deed?'

'It wasn't one of the dinosaurs; it was an escaped bull.'

She threw her head back and laughed.

'I thought you'd find that amusing,' he said, his voice still calm.

'Oh, I do Darren, I do,' she replied. From below there was a series of loud splashes. She played the beam across the water and caught a glimpse of shiny grey hide and one massive flipper. The plesiosaur was heaving its bulk over the rim of the tank onto the concrete floor. Beyond, the large double doors stood open to the night . . .

She swung the beam back to Penward, illuminating his gaunt, strained face. Somewhere in the distance a man screamed.

'I presume it was you who sabotaged the generator too,' he said tonelessly. Twenty minutes before, all the lights in the zoo and around the house had gone out.

'Yes,' she answered brightly. 'I chopped the fuel pipes open with an axe. Then I chopped holes in the fuel tanks.'

'Why?'

'To make it dark, of course. I thought your pets would appreciate the advantage it gives them. And by the sound of it they're making the most of it.'

'You know what I mean. Why have you done all this? I realize now that it must have been you who set the Deinonychus free last July as well . . .'

'It's simple, Darren. I've had enough. I wanted to expose you so that I could be free of you. I wanted to be off your leash, and now I am.'

'But you *had* your freedom,' he protested. 'All you needed. Did I ever complain that you were in the process of fucking every male – *and* some of the females – under the age of thirty in Cambridgeshire?'

'Did you ever wonder why?'

He frowned slightly. 'Not really. I presumed you had over-developed sexual appetites. The result of a hormone imbalance possibly. Or perhaps you're just plainly and simply an old fashioned slut.'

She gave a contemptuous laugh. 'If I'm a slut it's *you* who turned me into one, Darren. If I'd married a real man instead of a sick creature who can't get it up unless he's being hurt and humiliated, and even then is incapable of satisfying a woman, maybe things would have turned out differently.'

He smiled thinly. 'We could continue to exchange insults for the rest of the night, but as you can see I'm in no condition to stand here for much longer. All I want from you is your reason for what you have done tonight.'

'I've told you already. I wanted to be free of you. I wanted to end everything once and for all.'

'Yes, but why tonight? What sparked you off? I really want to know. It's important to me. Was it that young man, the reporter? Was it because he rejected you? Or because you discovered he had a girlfriend?'

'Go to hell,' she snarled.

He nodded sadly. 'Yes, that *must* be the reason. To think – all my plans ruined, my years of work wasted – simply because an ageing, ridiculous woman suffers an attack of jealousy over a young, provincial yob. How ironic . . .' He raised the barrel of the gun he'd been holding by his side.

'You're going to kill me?' she asked, almost without concern.

He bared his teeth at her. 'No. I'm not going to kill you. Not *me.*' He pulled the trigger and instantly a feathery red tuft appeared against the whiteness of her throat. Her legs folded and she collapsed face down on the catwalk. Penward gazed dispassionately at her for a few moments then scooped her up under one arm and carried her down the gangway as if she weighed nothing. But as he walked he left a thin trail of his blood on the iron stairs.

'God, what *is* this place?' cried Jenny, looking around.

'Penward's private dinosaur museum,' Pascal told her. They were in the hall containing the fossil skeletons and bones. They had put as much distance between themselves and the billiard room as possible. With luck the Deinonychus wouldn't be able to track them down. 'I can't understand how those things are getting out unless someone is releasing them deliberately.'

'But who would do such a thing? They'd have to be crazy.'

'Crazy is the right word for . . .' He paused suddenly, his face going pale. 'Oh, Jesus, I think I *do* know who's doing it. Lady Jane. And that means *I'm* responsible too . . .'

'What are you talking about?'

'Jenny, I *knew* she was mentally unstable, but what I did to her tonight has pushed her over the edge. Don't you see? She was pinning all her hopes on me – she saw me as her last chance and I more or less kicked her in the teeth . . .'

Jenny shook her head. 'No, I don't see. And I certainly don't see why you should feel responsible for whatever that woman has done.'

'But I *do*. If I hadn't . . .' He didn't finish. The sudden sound of gunfire outside made them both jump. Then they heard a man start screaming as if in terrible agony.

Jenny looked fearfully at Pascal. 'David, I want to get *away* from here.'

He put an arm around her shoulders. 'It's going to be tough. We don't know how many of those things are loose out there. And there are Penward's men to worry about too. I know they've got their hands full at the moment, but one of them might just decide to take a pot-shot at us if we're seen . . .'

'I left my car hidden in some woods by the road that runs along the north side of the estate. It was a long way from where I tried to get over the fence, so it's likely they never found it. If we could just get to it . . .'

'But how are we going to make it over the fences? Remember the inner one is electrified and we don't have the equipment you brought with you.'

'Oh Jesus . . .' she whimpered. She was looking over his shoulder and the expression on her face made the pit of his stomach give way. He turned.

At the other end of the long hall a lion was casually strolling towards them. It was male, with a large, shaggy mane, and its expression was one of total disinterest. Not that that made Pascal feel any better . . .

He looked around frantically. Behind them was a tall window of leaded glass that stretched all the way up to the vaulted ceiling of the hall. In front of it a double staircase led up to a narrow gallery that ran along both sides of the room. Pascal considered making a dash up one of the staircases, but guessed that the lion could easily overtake them before they were even half-way to the gallery.

'Don't move!' he hissed to Jenny out of the corner of his mouth. 'Stay perfectly still and don't show any fear.'

'What book did you get *that* out of?' she asked through chattering teeth.

The lion kept coming towards them at the same casual pace. It was enormous. Pascal stared into its eyes, desperately trying to penetrate its expression of apparent disinterest. Was it hungry? Angry? Or just curious?

When the lion was about twelve feet away Pascal's nerve broke. He made a lunge for a nearby high-back wooden chair and picked it up. It was heavy, but terror gave him extra strength. He swung its legs round towards the advancing lion . . .

The lion continued for another few paces then stopped, its ears flattening against its head. Its body began to sink down towards the floor and Pascal, fearfully, thought this was a prelude to it making a spring at him. But to his astonishment the lion suddenly turned and ran.

Pascal looked at the chair he was holding in amazement. 'Hell, it *works!*'

Behind him Jenny screamed. At the same moment there came a tremendous crash of breaking glass. Something hit him in the back of his right shoulder, stinging painfully. He turned in time to see the tall, church-like window burst inwards as a dinosaur came through it . . .

It was one he hadn't seen before. It was similar to Tarbosaurus but not as big – it was about eight feet tall at most – and with more powerfully developed forearms. Pascal guessed it wasn't fully grown. It certainly moved in a youthfully energetic way as it came bounding into the hall, broken glass spraying around it in all directions.

'Run!' screamed Pascal as he threw the chair in its general direction. He could have saved his breath; Jenny was already running down the centre of the hall. He followed her . . .

The floorboards shook as the dinosaur gave chase. Pascal knew they'd never make it to the door. He caught up with Jenny and pulled her to one side between two of the big glass cases containing skeletons. It was Pascal's intention to double back behind two of the showcases and escape through the broken window. But the dinosaur reacted too quickly; it skidded to a halt, turned and lunged for them *through* the case they'd ducked behind . . .

The dinosaur's lunge took it through the glass front of the case and into the fossilised skeleton of a twelve-foot tall duck-billed

Iguanodon. The skeleton, its wire and steel supports shattered, promptly collapsed – most of its heavy bones falling onto its living relative.

The dinosaur gave way under the weight of the mineralized fossils and fell heavily across the base of the showcase. When Pascal lowered the arm that he'd flung across his face to protect it from the flying glass, he saw the dinosaur, obviously stunned, struggling feebly to get out from under the pile of bones . . .

He grabbed Jenny by the hand and they ran for the door at the end of the hall.

Sir Darren Penward carried his unconscious wife into the garage. He dropped her unceremoniously on to the floor beside his dark blue Bentley and fished in his coat pocket for his keys. When he found them he opened the rear door, picked up Lady Jane and flung her across the back seat. Then he slammed the door.

As he was leaving the garage he came face to face with one of his keepers. The young man, whose name he remembered was Charles, looked immensely relieved to see him. 'Thank God, Sir Penward – we've been searching everywhere for you! *All* the dinosaurs seem to be loose, sir, and a lot of the big cats as well . . . what are your instructions?'

Penward smiled humourlessly at him. 'Instructions? I have no instructions. It's all over. Finished. I suggest you leave while you can. Tell the others – if any of them are still alive.' Then he walked past the man, leaving him standing there open-mouthed.

Penward entered the house through a side door, ignoring the headless corpse he had to step over in front of the doorway. He went straight to the library and down the spiral staircase to the laboratory complex. A white-faced technician hurried up to him in the corridor. 'Sir Penward, what are we going to do? How are we going to get out? Those damn things are everywhere up there! I saw one of them kill Baxter!'

'Get out of my way,' said Penward curtly, trying to push past the man. 'I don't have the time to waste with you. How you escape is your concern.'

'But Sir Penward!' cried the technician, seizing him by the arm, 'You've *got* to help me!'

Penward reached into his pocket and drew out the .45 automatic he'd recovered from his study earlier and shot the man twice in the face. Then, without even pausing to watch the man fall, he hurried along the corridor to the incubator room.

Inside he unsealed the door to the incubator chamber, entered and picked up two of the large eggs. Cradling them carefully in his arms he carried them outside . . .

It was as he climbed the spiral staircase that he realized how weak he was becoming. Then a wave of blackness passed over him and he almost passed out. He hoped he would have sufficient strength to do what had to be done.

As he walked through the library he heard a tremendous noise coming from another part of the house. He wondered, almost indifferently, which of the dinosaurs it was.

When he reached the grounds again one of the security guards, his face covered in blood, came running up to him in a state of near hysterics. Penward ignored him and continued past him towards the garage.

He placed the two eggs carefully on the front passenger seat of the Bentley, covering them with his jacket, then, after checking that Lady Jane was still unconscious, started the engine and drove the big car out of the garage.

The security man was still outside and tried to stop the car by getting in front of it, but Penward simply pressed his foot down on the accelerator and the man was forced to jump to one side to avoid being run over.

Penward drove round to the front of the house. On the way he didn't see any of the dinosaurs but did pass a tiger sitting nonchalantly beside the driveway. He recognised it as the male Siberian, John Smith, the mate of the one he'd been forced to shoot. Thanks to Lady Jane. He tightened his grip on the steering wheel. The bitch was going to pay for that as well.

At the front gate the two security men on duty approached his car with worried expressions. 'Sir Penward, what in the world's going on back there? Sounds like every animal in the zoo's going berserk. We've been trying for ages to raise the house on the phone but no one answers . . .'

Penward was in great pain now and the seat was wet with his

blood, but he forced himself to say calmly, 'I don't have the time to explain but we have a serious problem. There is nothing you can do about it. I suggest you get in your own vehicle ...' He indicated the Land Rover parked by the gatehouse. 'And leave the area immediately. But don't shut the gates when you go. I want them left open, understand?'

They plainly *didn't* understand and stared at him blankly.

'Remember,' he said, 'Leave the gates *open*.' Then he drove away into the darkness. He was leaving Penward Hall forever. And so was Lady Jane.

'Are you all right?' asked Pascal anxiously, examining Jenny. There were several cuts on her face caused by the flying glass, but thankfully they all appeared to be minor ones.

'I think so,' she said grimly, 'but I'm not sure about you. Hold still a moment. This going to hurt ...'

'What ... ?' he began as she walked behind him. Then he yelped with pain as she pulled something from his right shoulder. She held up a triangular piece of glass about four inches long. The end was bloodstained. 'You've had that sticking in you ever since the dinosaur came in through the window.'

'Hell,' he muttered, wincing. He reached behind and gingerly felt the wound. When he looked at his hand his fingers were covered with blood. Jenny was extracting Kleenex from her pockets and making a wad out of them. 'This will have to do until we get to a doctor,' she said as she inserted the tissues under his shirt against the wound. 'It's not bleeding *too* badly.'

'For some reason I don't believe you,' he said with a weak smile.

They had taken refuge in a small dining room which looked as if it was for the use of staff members rather than the Penward family. They had pushed a heavy table against the door and were now wondering what to do next.

Pascal went to one of the windows and peered out into the blackness. 'All the lights are off out there. The generator can't be working, which means the electric fence isn't getting any juice either.'

'We can climb over it!' cried Jenny.

'Yeah. All we have to do is *get* there, and that's not going to be easy.' Outside, the night air was full of animal sounds – screeches, roars, bellows. It was as if every demon from hell was loose in the grounds around Penward Hall.

'But if we stay here, sooner or later something is going to come and *eat* us,' said Jenny. 'I'd prefer to take my chances outside.'

Pascal sighed. 'Yes, so would I.' He opened the window. The cacophony of feral cries became much louder. He looked at her questioningly. She gave him what she probably thought was a brave smile. Again he was struck by how much he loved her. Why hadn't he realized it before, he wondered?

'Okay, let's go,' he said.

18

Arthur Nicholls was fifty-five years old and a poacher. He'd been a poacher for forty of those fifty-five years – having been apprenticed into the craft by his father – and he made a good living at it.

On this particular September night he was planning to poach trout from the Warchester River, a tributary of the Great Ouse. This section of the river was owned by the Penward family, and had been for many centuries, even though it ran outside the estate's perimeter fence. Nicholls was proceeding warily through the woods because it was Penward's habit to have the river patrolled by either one or two of his game-keepers.

Nicholls felt uncomfortable. Attuned as he was to the wood's nocturnal atmosphere, he was more than aware that there was something wrong tonight. Part of the reason was easy to determine; there was a godawful racket coming from Penward's zoo. Every animal in the place seemed to be roaring its lungs out, which made Nicholls feel he was making his way through an African jungle rather than a quiet wood in Cambridgeshire.

Out of curiosity he decided to veer towards the fence, though he doubted if he'd be able to see anything this far from the zoo – but who knows, perhaps the place was on fire. *Something* serious had to be going on for the animals to sound so spooked.

He came to the edge of the woods and peered through the

double row of fences in the direction of Penward hall and the zoo. But he could see nothing – there was no tell-tale red glow in the sky or anything else to indicate what might be happening over there.

With a puzzled shake of his head he continued along the fence, intending to follow it for about a hundred yards to the spot where the river curved near to it. He'd gone about thirty yards when he came across a surprising sight. A large section of both the inner and outer wire fences had been flattened as if a steam-roller had driven through them. Curious, he went closer to the fifteen-foot gap in the fence, expecting to see the tracks of some heavy vehicle, but there were none.

The fences, he noted, had been pushed *outward,* which meant that whatever had done it had come from the estate. But if it wasn't a vehicle, what could have caused such damage? An elephant? As far as he knew there were no elephants in Penward's zoo – and in any case he could find no trace of animal tracks in the churned-up ground. There *were* signs that something big had been dragged over it, and there were strange marks on either side of the main furrow that he didn't recognize . . .

He looked into the woods, and despite the darkness his expert eyes could easily detect the path through the bushes that the object, whatever it was, had made. Cautiously he began to follow it.

The trail led straight to the river bank and disappeared. Nicholls scratched his head and frowned. *It* had gone into the water. Which meant it had to be some kind of animal. An aquatic animal? Or had it been an elephant, after all, trying to cross the river? He gazed out over the black expanse of water to the far bank. If so it almost certainly wouldn't have made it. The river was much too deep at this point.

But no, it *couldn't* have been an elephant, he decided, as he knelt down and examined the ground. No animal tracks at all. On the contrary the weeds along the bank had been smoothed flat, though there were more of the odd scuff marks on either side of the smooth section. It was very perplexing.

Something huge broke the surface of the river. Startled, Nicholls looked up to see a great bulk moving through the water towards him. Outlined in the moonlight was a long neck with a large head on the end of it. He saw the glint of teeth . . .

Nicholls got to his feet and ran, leaving his fish traps and other gear on the river bank. He ran as hard as he could, ignoring the branches that whipped his face as he raced between the trees. He didn't look back for fear of seeing the dreadful apparition following him through the woods . . .

Eventually he could run no further and fell panting to the ground. His heart thumped alarmingly in his chest and he feared he was going to have a heart attack. He had no idea how long he'd been running or even where he was. For the first time in his life Nicholls was lost.

He looked up as the nearby bushes rustled. 'Jesus Christ,' he whispered as a large tiger came walking out of them straight towards him. He was beyond surprise now. He didn't even try and get away as the tiger, with a deep growl, sprang at him and removed his face with one terrible blow of its paw.

The seemingly endless run across the Penward estate was the stuff of nightmares. With all the exterior lighting gone the darkness was almost palpable and very quickly both Pascal and Jenny lost all sense of direction. They just had to trust to luck that they were still heading towards the north fence and not running in circles. And with every step they took there was the continual fear that one of the dinosaurs would materialize out of the blackness . . .

But their luck held and it was the fence that finally loomed out of the darkness ahead of them. 'Thank God,' gasped Pascal as they reached it. Beyond the double fence, mere yards away, lay the real world. Sanity. Freedom. Once they reached it they'd be safe. The nightmare would be finished.

Pascal warily touched the inner fence with the back of his knuckles, half expecting that the power had been switched back on and he would see a blue spark and experience a numbing pain up his arm. But there was no spark, and no pain. The fence was dead. 'You go first,' he told Jenny. 'Watch out for the barbed wire on the top.'

Jenny was half-way up the twelve-foot high inner fence when

he heard a rhythmic drumming sound behind them in the darkness. Some large animal was running across the park, and appeared to be heading in their direction.

'Quick!' Pascal hissed to Jenny, who had stopped when she heard the approaching animal. 'Keep going!' He jumped at the fence and began to scramble up after her.

They'd almost reached the top when the animal came charging out of the darkness. Both of them laughed with relief when they saw what it was. It was a cow. An ordinary cow.

It veered sharply to the right when it saw the fence, its eyes showing their whites in a look of terror, and very quickly the night swallowed it up again.

Pascal and Jenny then applied themselves to the problem of getting over the strands of barbed wire without getting hooked on it. Both felt a little foolish at being so frightened by a cow. Already the dangers they'd faced that night were receding into memory and beginning to seem unreal.

But then they were jolted back into the nightmare . . .

For there came another sound in the darkness: a heavy *thump, thump* of something big that was running on two legs. And they suddenly realized why the cow had looked so terrified. It was being *chased* . . .

Its pursuer soon came into sight, emerging from the shadows like a prehistoric ghost, but a ghost made of all-too-real flesh and blood. It was the Tarbosaurus.

The barbed wire immediately became an inconsequential obstacle. They crawled over the strands in panicky haste, oblivious to the cuts and jabs they received, and began to slither down the other side.

The Tarbosaurus had come to a halt by the fence, regarding them with apparent indecision. It was obviously torn between following the cow or turning its attention to them.

It chose them.

'Jump!' screamed Jenny as the dinosaur lunged forward. They both let go of the wire and dropped the remaining six or so feet to the ground. The fence shook with a loud clanging noise as the dinosaur struck it with its head.

There was a ten foot gap between the inner and outer fences.

Pascal and Jenny covered it in micro-seconds and flung themselves at the second fence. They scaled it like circus acrobats as, behind them, the sounds of destruction made it obvious that the Tarbosaurus was making short work of the inner fence.

At the top of the fence Pascal risked a look back and saw that the dinosaur was ripping at the fence with one of his hindclaws and already the wire mesh was tearing apart. Soon it would be coming through . . .

'David!' cried Jenny. She had hooked her upper arm on a piece of barbed wire and couldn't get free. Maintaining a precarious balance on the top of the fence with only one hand he reached across and tried to pull her arm loose from the wire. She screamed with pain. The barbs had penetrated deep into the soft flesh of the underside of her upper right arm . . .

Pascal heard the inner fence give way with a metallic shriek. There was no time left to be gentle. He pulled her arm with all his strength, shutting his ears to her cry. Her arm came free but a small lump of flesh glistened redly on the wire . . .

Then he and Jenny were through the wires and scrambling down the fifteen-foot high fence.

The Tarbosaurus was already in the gap between the two fences. The great head with the unbelievably huge jaws darted forward, trying to get at them through the fence. The impact of its head against the wire caused them both to lose their grips and fall backwards. It was an eight-foot drop to the ground and both landed heavily. Pascal felt a lightning bolt of pain shoot up his leg from his left ankle and when he got to his feet he found it almost impossible to walk.

Jenny had landed flat on her back. She sat up, struggling to breathe. She had been badly winded by the fall but otherwise seemed unharmed. Pascal staggered over to her, gritting his teeth against the agony of his ankle, and helped her up.

Not far away the Tarbosaurus was attacking the second fence in a frustrated rage. The outer fence was both higher and more strongly constructed than the inner one, but Pascal could see it wouldn't last long against the dinosaur's onslaught.

'Where's your car? Is it near here?' he asked her anxiously. She looked around, dazed. 'I'm not sure where we are,' she gasped.

Then she frowned and lifted an arm. 'I *think* it's in that direction,' she said, pointing up the road.

'Come on then . . .'

They made painfully slow progress. Pascal was forced to lean on her for support; he could hardly bear to put his left foot down. And behind them came a sound like giant tortured bedsprings as the dinosaur inexorably kicked his way through the wire fence . . .

They'd got about fifty yards up the road when Jenny gave a happy cry. 'That clump of trees ahead on the left – I think I recognize them!'

'Great,' wheezed Pascal. He glanced back over his shoulder. The fence was collapsing outwards and already the Tarbosaurus was stepping over the wreckage.

'You run on ahead,' he told her. 'Find the car and start the engine – I'll catch up.'

'I'm not leaving you,' she protested.

'*Please* Jenny, don't argue. Go! It may be our only chance!' He gave her a shove in the back. She hesitated for a moment, then did what he said.

As she disappeared into the trees by the side of the road he looked back again. The dinosaur had spotted them now and was coming up the road after them. Pascal tried to run faster but the pain was almost unbearable.

It was the fag-end of the party; the time of the morning when even the best champagne tastes foul. When alcoholic euphoria has turned into grey depression, that final stage before the onset of the inevitable hang-over. And no matter how much you drank from now on it was impossible to bring back the elation; all that happened was you felt worse . . .

'And *God* do I feel bad,' reflected Anthony King as he tried to swallow the remains of a glass of red wine. He made a promise to himself that he would never again mix booze and dope – a promise he'd made before. It was a guaranteed formula for prolonged nausea.

His only consolation was that his girlfriend, Melissa Forbes-Richardson, was obviously feeling a good deal worse. She was bending over the stern of the boat, groaning and trying to be sick. Serves her right, he thought maliciously, she'd been a pain in the arse all night.

The boat they were on was a large, converted canal boat. It had been turned in to a restaurant and was owned by the father of Dickie Radford, the host of the party. Dickie had invited twenty of his fellow students for a weekend binge on the boat – a floating party down the river and back. But already the idea had palled for Anthony. It was only Saturday morning – 2 a.m. to be exact – but he'd had enough. The prospect of spending another two days of heavy drinking on the boat was simply awful.

Melissa continued to make disgusting noises from over the side of the boat. Anthony stood indecisively behind her, holding her handbag. He never knew what to do when people got sick, especially girls. He wondered whether he should do something like pat her on the back or perhaps just hold her arm. If she leaned any further over the side she'd be in danger of falling in. But he didn't move. His own stomach was getting pretty queasy too and if he had to watch her throw up he'd be joining her over the side . . .

'Feeling any better yet?' he asked, a little impatiently.

'Oh piss off and leave me alone,' she groaned. 'I'm dying . . .'

What happened next was simply unbelievable. And it happened so fast that Anthony *couldn't* believe he'd seen it.

For suddenly, behind the boat, a great reptilian head rose up out of the water. Then it darted forward and seized Melissa in its jaws. One second she was there, bending over the side; the next second the top third of her body was inside this huge mouth. Anthony saw the top row of needle-like teeth sinking into the back of her white cardigan just below her shoulders, then he had a brief glimpse of her thin, pale legs kicking convulsively as she was pulled swiftly head-first over the side. Then both she and the reptilian head were gone.

Anthony took a step backwards, his mouth dropping open. His alcohol-fogged brain was incapable of dealing with what he'd just witnessed. His first response was to regard it as some kind of elaborate joke. He turned, half-expecting to see all the others laughing at him. But they weren't. Apparently no one else had seen what had happened. Apart from three couples reclining on blankets on the roof all the others were in the long, narrow cabin. Those who were still conscious were engaged in what used to be termed 'heavy petting' but now could be more accurately described as intense foreplay. Each couple appeared oblivious to everyone, and everything, else . . .

Still clutching Melissa's black handbag Anthony finally found his voice. 'Hey!' he cried to the six people on the cabin roof, 'Did you *see* that?'

The nearest couple broke off from what they were doing and turned towards him. The girl, whose name was Charlotte, said in a slurred voice, 'See *what*, Tony?'

Anthony gestured weakly at the stern. 'Something just grabbed Melissa . . . Some kind of sea monster. It pulled her over the side. Just then. You *must* have seen it.'

'You're drunk,' said Charlotte dismissively.

'Or you've been dropping acid,' added her boyfriend, Julian.

Anthony looked at them helplessly. How could he convince them of what he'd seen when he couldn't believe it himself? But something *had* happened to Melissa. That much was definite. So someone had to do something . . .

He held up her handbag as if offering them conclusive proof of what he said he'd seen. 'I'm not joking!' he cried. 'Melissa's gone! She's back there in the water, I swear it! We've got to go back for her . . . !'

All six on the cabin roof were staring at him now. He could tell from their expressions they thought he was either joking or out of his head.

Then Charlotte said, almost gently, 'Where *is* Melissa, Tony?'

'I told you!' he yelled in exasperation. 'Something grabbed . . .'

He didn't finish. All of a sudden their faces had changed. Their eyes had widened in horror. Then he realized they weren't looking at him but at something behind him . . .

'What . . . ?' he began. Then he felt the breath knocked out of his body as something powerful slammed into it. He didn't understand what was happening even as he was lifted into the air, his arms clamped to his sides as if seized in a giant vice.

It was only as the cold water closed over him that he began to comprehend what had happened to him; what *was* happening to him. It didn't even hurt. Not at first.

Ahead of him Pascal heard a car engine turning over. Then he saw the red glow of a tail light. He wanted to cry tears of pure joy. Jenny had found the car! But already he could hear the Tarbosaurus crashing through the branches behind him. It was going to be a close thing.

He put on speed, trying to ignore the agony in his ankle. When he reached the MG Jenny had the passenger door open ready for him. He jumped in and slammed it. 'Go! Go!' he screamed. But the car didn't go. Instead its rear wheels spun impotently on the carpet of newly fallen leaves that covered the ground between the trees.

Then the car shuddered and jolted forward without warning. Something had hit it from behind – the dinosaur! There was a ripping noise above their heads, and the tip of a claw came through the roof of the MG. But the beast had unwittingly freed its prey. Revving madly, the MG cleared the leaves and leapt forward. Jenny skilfully swerved it through the clump of trees ahead of them and onto the road. Then, with a squeal of burning rubber, the sports car was hurtling down the road towards Warchester.

At that moment Pascal knew without a shadow of a doubt that he *did* love Jenny. Absolutely and totally. He would have cut off his right arm and given it to her there and then.

'Jesus, you're terrific!' he cried, then leaned over and kissed her on the cheek. 'We made it!'

She let out a long sigh. 'Thank God. But what now? Where do we go?'

'The police station. We've got to let people know what's going on back at Penward Hall before more of those damn things get out.'

'Shouldn't we stop at the first house we come to and ask to use their phone?'

Pascal considered this and shook his head. 'You fancy the idea of trying to convince Sergeant Monroe or Keith Driscoll over the phone that there are dinosaurs running around loose in Warchester? No, we'd better do it in person.'

'You think they'll even believe us in person?'

'Well, the way we *look* should convince them we're not playing games.' He twisted in his seat and peered out through the rear window. 'Oh shit,' he groaned.

'What's the matter?' she asked anxiously.

'It's *following* us!' he cried. 'The fucking thing is chasing us!' In the moonlight he could make out the Tarbosaurus's bulk about a hundred yards behind them. It was running like the wind, covering some fifteen feet with every one of its giant strides. The gap between it and the car continued to widen as he watched, but the sight was no less alarming. He turned and glanced at the speedometer. They were doing forty miles an hour which meant the dinosaur was doing at least thirty-five mph. He made a mental note to write to one of the authors of the dinosaur books he'd read and inform them that a young but almost fully grown Tarbosaurus was capable of such speeds. He might end up as a footnote. If he lived that long.

As Jenny pushed down on the accelerator the dinosaur began to recede in the distance. 'Persistent bugger,' muttered Pascal, feeling better again.

'You don't think he'll follow us all the way into town, do you?' she asked.

'No. He'll lose interest once we get out of sight.' *Or encounters easier victims,* he added to himself. God knows how many people that thing would kill before the authorities managed to destroy it. Perhaps Jenny was right: perhaps they should stop and find a phone right now. But no – he glanced at his watch – at this speed they would be at the station in less than ten minutes.

Exactly three minutes later the engine coughed. Once, twice, three times. Then it cut altogether. The MG coasted to a halt.

They had run out of petrol.

19

It was the fact that the dogs had finally *stopped* barking that made Lee Hagen leave his comfortable bed for the second time that night. When they'd started barking hours before he'd gone downstairs to the yard for a look around but found nothing. So he put the cause of it down to the unusual ruckus coming from Penward's zoo tonight. His farm worker, Bernie, who had also got up because of the dogs, agreed with him. Hagen's farm lay adjacent to the Penward estate and the sounds made by Penward's animals often carried to it, especially if the wind was blowing in the right direction – as it was tonight.

But neither he nor his employee had ever heard as much noise from the zoo before. And what was odd was that the loudest of the animal cries was totally unfamiliar. Not only that but they sent prickles of unease up the back of Hagen's neck. 'Now what the hell kind of animal makes a sound like that?' he had asked Bernie as the two of them stood listening in the yard.

'Beats me, Mr Hagen,' Bernie had replied, shaking his head. 'Thought I knew every cry those different types of big cats make, but I never heard anything like this before.'

Hagen considered giving them a call at Penward Hall to see what the problem was, but decided against it. Penward would probably interpret the call as a complaint and the farmer had no wish to get on the wrong side of his powerful neighbour.

As he'd been turning to go back to the house Bernie added, thoughtfully, 'That young feller a while ago – *he* asked if I ever heard unusual noises from the zoo . . .'

Hagen looked questioningly at him. 'What? Who did?'

'Young feller from town a couple of weeks ago. Asked me if I heard animal sounds I didn't recognize . . . I thought he was a brick short of a full load.' Bernie frowned at Hagen. 'What do you think he was getting at, Mr Hagen?'

Hagen had no idea and said so. 'Come on, let's get back to bed. We've got a lot to do tomorrow.'

But now, three hours later, he recalled Bernie's words and pondered on their significance. Why should anyone be asking about strange noises from Penward's zoo? And what *had* been making those weird sounds earlier tonight?

Well, whatever it was had stopped now. He couldn't hear a thing as he crossed his bedroom to the window. And that worried him. Just a short time ago the dogs' barking had become even more frantic and now it had suddenly ceased.

He looked out of the window and frowned. The lights were on in Bernie's small bungalow on the other side of the yard. Bernie must have been puzzled by the silence too. Hagen decided to go down and have another look. Sighing, he put on his dressing-gown and shoes.

When he opened the back door he got a surprise. One of the farm cats rushed in past him and disappeared under a cupboard. This was very strange behaviour. The cats *never* came in the house. They were practically feral. He didn't even feed them – they lived on rats and mice in the various barns and sheds.

It was going to be a hell of a chore getting that cat out, he thought irritably as he walked out into the yard. He'd have to get Bernie to help.

He couldn't see Bernie anywhere so he headed for the bungalow. There were only the two of them on the farm. Neither man had a wife. Hagen's had died four years back, of cancer, and Bernie had never married. Bernie's interest in women seemed to be non-existent, which was fortunate because no woman had ever displayed the slightest interest in him either.

Surprise Number Two occurred halfway across the yard. He tripped over one of the dogs. Or rather the *remains* of one of the dogs. All that lay there on the cobblestones was the hind-quarters and the head. The bits between were just bones with strips of flesh attached . . .

He experienced a flicker of sick fear. He remembered what had happened back in July. The tiger that escaped from Penward's zoo. Something like that must have happened again. It would explain the commotion he and Bernie had heard from the zoo tonight.

After casting a quick, nervous look around the perimeter of the shadowy yard he hurried on towards Bernie's bungalow. The kitchen door, he saw, was open. Good. Bernie had a .303 rifle. *And* he was a crack shot.

Surprise Number Three came as he stepped through the doorway of the bungalow. Lying on the kitchen floor was Bernie. He looked like he'd fallen into the threshing machine. And crouching beside him was some kind of animal the likes of which Lee Hagen had never seen before. It was gnawing on Bernie's right thigh.

He froze. The animal raised its head and looked at him.

Hagen didn't hesitate. He turned and ran.

If he could make it to his back door he would be safe. Then he would ring the police. *God damn Penward!* he thought as he ran . . .

He was only a few feet from his back door when the Deinony-chus caught up with him.

'I don't believe it!' cried Pascal, punching the dashboard with his fist. 'You came out last night without checking the petrol?' How *could* you?'

'Don't be horrible! I just *forgot*, that's all. I was in a rush, what more can I say?' She sounded close to tears. *'I'm sorry.'*

'You had time to get a camera, a rubber sheet and two fold-ing ladders, but you forgot to fill the damn car with petrol. Jesus Christ! You *woman driver!*'

It was the worst thing he could think of to call her. Especially since they were both well aware that she was a far superior driver to him.

'I said I'm sorry,' she cried, looking anxiously into the car mirror. Pascal turned and looked down the road himself. There was no sign of the dinosaur.

'We left it far behind us,' he said, as much to reassure himself as her. 'I'm sure it's not still following us . . .' He opened the door. 'Come on, I guess we walk the rest of the way.'

'Wait,' she said, pointing ahead. 'There's a pub over there. With two cars in its car park. I've got my siphoning tube in the boot. We can get some petrol from one of them . . .'

Pascal recognised the pub. It was the Phoenix Arms. After a brief pause he nodded. 'All right, but let's hurry.'

As he got out of the car the pain in his ankle hit him again. He'd almost forgotten about it. The pain in his shoulder also flared up. The wound was still bleeding too – the whole back of his shirt was sticky with blood.

Hobbling painfully, he followed Jenny into the pub's car park. She was already at work at the rear of a Jaguar XJ6 by the time he arrived. 'Looks as if you've done this sort of thing before,' he whispered to her. He saw the white flash of her teeth in the darkness. 'I have. One of these days I'll fill you in on my shady past . . .'

He waited nervously while she filled the can she'd brought. It gave him a strange feeling to be back in this car park again. He winced at the memory of that night weeks ago.

To distract himself he peered into the interior of the Jaguar – and gave a start of surprise. *'Jen,'* he said, 'the keys are in the dashboard.' He tried the door. It was unlocked. 'We could take it. It would save time.'

Jenny came round. 'Do you think that's a good idea?' she asked dubiously. 'I've got the petrol.' She held up the can. 'I don't really want to leave my car sitting back there on the road.'

'No,' he said firmly, his mind made up. 'Get in. The sooner we get to the station the better. We can come back for the MG later.'

But as he opened the door a voice suddenly said, 'Caught you in the act, you bastards!'

Pascal whirled round. Standing there was the publican. He couldn't mistake that handlebar moustache even in the darkness. Nor could he mistake the double-barrelled shotgun the publican was holding. And on either side of him stood two younger-looking men, his bar staff probably. They were carrying what appeared to be police batons.

'I thought the bait would be too good for you to resist,' said the moon-faced publican in an ugly voice. 'After you bastards failed to steal it last week, I knew you'd be back. We've been waiting for you.'

'Look, this isn't what it seems,' protested Pascal weakly. 'We weren't . . . well . . . we weren't *stealing* this car, we were just going to . . .'

'*Borrow* it, right?' sneered the publican.

'It's an emergency,' said Jenny. 'We've got to get to the police station.'

'Oh, don't worry, Miss. We'll get you to the police station all right. *Eventually.* After we've taught you two a lesson you'll never forget. Right boys?' The two young men sniggered in reply. One of them slapped the baton he was holding against the palm of his other hand. The meaning was clear.

'We're not the car thieves!' cried Pascal. 'She's telling the truth, there is an emergency. A serious one. We're all in great danger . . .'

The publican laughed. 'Come off it, lad. We're not idiots. The only ones in danger around here are you.'

Pascal took a step forward. 'Look, you must remember me! Look at my face. Back in August I was in your pub trying to talk to some of Sir Penward's keepers and you practically barred me from the place. I'm a reporter. My name's David Pascal. I work for the *Warchester Times*. So does she. Her name is Jenny Stamper. Ring the police! They'll confirm it!'

'Yeah, I *do* remember you,' said the publican slowly. 'But it makes no difference where you work. You were trying to steal my car and that's a fact.'

'Oh shit!' Pascal exploded, 'fuck your bloody car! This is literally a matter of life and death! We've just come from Penward Hall. A lot of dangerous animals have got loose over there. And at least one of them is on the rampage *outside* the estate! We've got to warn people! That's why we've got to tell the police!'

'Animals? What kind of animals?' asked the publican suspiciously. 'And what were you doing trespassing on the estate at this time of night?'

'Look, we don't have the time to explain,' cried Jenny. 'Just believe us, will you? Call the police!'

The publican rubbed his chin for a maddeningly long time. 'I think I'd better give the Manor House a call,' he finally told his two employees. 'These two might have got up to some mischief over there that Sir Penward should know about. Stay here with them. If they move an inch whack 'em as hard as you like.'

'Don't call Sir Penward, call the police!' pleaded Jenny as the publican turned to go. Pascal tried to follow him but as he moved one of the men lashed out with his club and gave him a sickening blow across his right arm. Pascal staggered backwards with a cry of pain. The man had raised the club for a second blow but was distracted by a yell from the publican.

'Bloody hell! What in God's name is *that?*'

'That' was the Tarbosaurus. It was walking quickly along the road, its chest heaving from the exertion of its run. At the sound of the publican's cry it stopped and looked in towards the car park. Then the sixteen-foot-tall creature strode towards them, its great jaws opening in anticipation . . .

The publican and his two men were rooted to the spot, too stunned by the incredible form approaching them to move. Pascal and Jenny, on the other hand, didn't waste any time. Accustomed by now to the sight of a dinosaur, they both acted immediately;

without having to exchange any words they each opened a door and jumped into the Jaguar. Pascal, in the driving seat, started the engine.

Something went *bang*. The publican had recovered his wits enough to use the shotgun. But it didn't even slow the Tarbosaurus down. As the car started to move Pascal saw the publican disappear beneath one of the giant hind-claws.

The dinosaur was blocking the exit from the car park. Pascal had to swerve round it and as he did so the dinosaur turned sideways with alarming speed and lashed out with the same claw that had just crushed the publican. There was a brief rattle of claw on glass before the passenger window on Jenny's side shattered, but Pascal kept control of the vehicle. The next thing they knew they were out on the road again.

'You okay?' Pascal asked her as he sped the car on towards the centre of town.

'I think so,' she said shakily.

He glanced in the rear mirror. He couldn't see the dinosaur. Perhaps it was busy chasing the two other men. Pascal realized, with a slight shock, that the thought didn't bother him too much.

'Not much further,' he told her, 'then it's all out of our hands. We can relax . . .'

'Want to bet?' said Jenny grimly.

Dickie Radford was well aware that he wasn't a very attractive person. 'Colourless' was the word he would have used to describe himself. He had a colourless personality and he knew he was physically colourless too. So to compensate he spent money – or rather his father's money. He gave lavish parties and soon became well known for them at university. The ploy worked; he acquired a wide circle of friends. They were bought friends, true, but he comforted himself with the thought that his money was the equivalent of someone else's good looks or vivacious personality. Attractive people bought their friends as well, they just used a different currency.

During the last hour and a half, however, Radford's expensively acquired circle of friends had been drastically reduced in number. Of the original twenty-five people on the converted canal boat only sixteen remained. The rest had been picked off by the creature outside . . .

The boat was stuck firm on a sandbar; in the panic to reach the shore they'd run aground. The bow of the vessel was only a tantalising ten feet from the river bank but those ten feet might as well been a hundred miles. No one who had tried to cross the gap had made it.

Radford, like most of the others, was cowering under one of the restaurant tables. The floor was covered with broken glass from the shattered windows. On several occasions the thing's head had come through the windows like a bulldozer and pulled people right out of the cabin. They'd turned all the lights off now and were trying to keep as quiet as possible in the hope that the creature would give up and go away. For the last few minutes there'd been no sound from outside and Radford was beginning to dare hope that it *had* gone.

Somewhere in the darkness a girl was whimpering. It was getting on Radford's nerves. Finally, in a hoarse whisper, he said, 'Shut up, whoever that is! We've got to keep quiet!'

'I can't help it,' the girl wailed. 'I'm *scared*. I have to get *out of here! Now!'*

'Don't be stupid,' hissed Radford unpleasantly. 'You go out there and you'll end up in the same place as Melissa, Tony, Isabelle and all the others.'

'Maybe it's gone now,' suggested one of the men. 'I haven't heard anything for a while. What do you think, Roger?'

'Roger' was Roger Harmsworth. He was a zoology student and after the first attacks everyone had naturally turned to him for advice. He'd confessed he had absolutely no idea what the creature was but they continued to expect information from him. 'I wouldn't risk it,' he replied worriedly. 'I say we should stay here until help arrives. It'll be daybreak in a few hours. Someone will spot the boat then.'

'Yes, but will any of us still be alive?' murmured another girl. Radford recognised the voice of Charlotte Foster. Her boyfriend Julian had been one of the early victims. She had narrowly escaped being grabbed herself. 'Someone else should try and make it to shore before it gets us all.'

'Are you volunteering, Charlotte?' asked Radford. 'You saw what happened to Mark ...' Mark Fraser had been the last one to try to wade the ten feet to the river bank. The creature had got him while he was still on the boat, crawling towards the bow.

'Yes, I *am,* if none of you so-called men are willing to have a go!' Charlotte replied angrily.

Radford sighed. 'Stay where you are, Charlotte. I'm going to take a look around.' He felt depressingly responsible for the night's events. It had been his party, after all. But how the hell could he have known Warchester had its own version of the Loch Ness Monster?

Cautiously he emerged from under the table and raised his head until he could see out of the windows on either side. There was sufficient moonlight to see a fair distance in all directions. The surface of the water was undisturbed. 'Looks all-clear out there,' he told the others.

'Don't risk it,' advised Harmsworth. 'That thing – whatever it is – is *cunning.*'

'Look, what we should do is create a distraction,' said Radford. 'One of you go to the stern and start chucking bottles as far out into the river as you can. If the thing's still around it should head for the splashes.'

There was a lengthy silence in the dark cabin and then Harmsworth said unenthusiastically, 'All right, I'll throw the bottles ...'

Charlotte had to see what happened. She couldn't resist leaving the shelter of the table and standing up. Harmsworth was already at the stern, a shadowy outline in the moonlight. As she watched he threw the first of the champagne bottles into the air. There was a distant splash. Harmsworth crouched, ready to scramble back into the cabin, but nothing happened. He waited thirty seconds then threw a second bottle. 'No sign of movement,' he announced. 'I don't think the thing is out there any more.'

'I hope you're right,' said Radford. 'Here I go! I'll be back with the cavalry as soon as I can, folks. Hang on in here ...' He stepped out through one of the forward hatchways onto the narrow deck.

Charlotte had no intention of staying in that death-trap a moment longer if she could help it. Ignoring the queries of the others she hurried along the cabin to the hatchway Radford had just gone through and looked out. If he made it to the shore she was determined to follow him.

She saw Radford's thin figure jump from the bow into the water. It came up to his shoulders. He began to head towards the bank. She held her breath. Six feet, four . . . *Ah,* he'd made it! He was climbing up the muddy, reed-covered bank. Then she gasped as, from out of the darkness, a long neck whipped through the air above the water beside the boat. Before she could even comprehend what she was seeing the thing had Radford by the left foot. It was dragging him backwards off the bank. He screamed and clawed frantically for a handhold but it was useless.

The next thing she knew Radford was hanging upside-down from the creature's mouth as the long neck rose back into the air. He was still screaming. Then the huge head plunged back down into the deeper water, taking him with it.

Charlotte, shaking with fear, retreated into the cabin.

After a long, stunned silence a man's voice said, with an edge of hysteria to it, 'Well, you've got to say one thing for good old Dickie; he sure throws a hell of a party . . .'

20

Stanley Pitt, MP for Warchester, was woken by an incessant buzzing sound. When he opened his eyes he saw that there was a red light flashing on the console beside his bed. He sat up quickly, switched on the light and leaned over the console. On the display screen there was an illuminated map of his house and grounds. A small animated arrow was pointing at a spot inside the east wall.

He snatched up the phone beside the console and punched two numbers. He didn't have to wait long for a reply. 'Steve, we've got ourselves a prowler,' he said rapidly. 'He just set off one of the pressure pads alongside the east wall.' He continued to stare at the display screen. Another arrow appeared. 'Hello! *Now* he's broken one of the photo beams in the orchard. Meet me downstairs right away! We'll give this character a surprise he'll never forget.'

Pitt dressed hurriedly, took a shotgun down from the wall, loaded it, and went outside. In the hallway a door opened and his wife appeared, looking anxious. They had slept in separate bedrooms for years now. 'What is it, Stanley?' she asked.

'Nothing,' he told her irritably. 'Go back to bed.'

'But you've got a gun.'

'I told you it was nothing, Cynthia.' He rushed past her towards the stairway.

Steve was already waiting at the foot of the stairs. He too carried a shotgun, and also had a powerful torch. He was theoretically Pitt's chauffeur but he also acted as his bodyguard. He was an ex-Royal Marine.

'Have you called the police, Mr Pitt?' he asked as Pitt hurried down the stairs.

'Not yet. We can handle this ourselves, don't you think, Steve?'

Steve, a heavily-built man in his early forties, frowned. 'If you say so, sir,' he said doubtfully. 'But to be on the safe side we should –'

'No,' Pitt cut him off. 'Let's see what we've netted first.' He was already hurrying out of the hallway, his round, bald head flushed with excitement.

Steve, looking unhappy, followed his employer into the east wing of the house. In the spacious living room Pitt stopped by a console similar to the one in his bedroom and examined it. 'He hasn't tripped any other sensors yet. He's still in the orchard.' He couldn't keep the boyish eagerness out of his voice. Here was a rare chance to use the expensive toys his company manufactured.

He took a bulky-looking device that resembled a handheld hair dryer out of a drawer beneath the console and flourished it proudly. It was another of his security company's products – a portable infra-red detector. Then he gestured towards the patio doors.

Steve hesitated. 'Shouldn't we switch on the outside lights?' All of the grounds were studded with concealed security lights. One touch of a button and the whole place would be as brightly lit as the Blackpool Tower.

'No,' said Pitt curtly, 'that might frighten him off.'

'I thought that was the whole idea,' muttered Steve as he

opened the doors and, stepped out onto the patio. It was then, beyond the insulation of the double-glazing, that he heard the dogs.

Pitt was the Master of the Hounds for the local Hunt and bred and raised his own foxhounds. There were seventeen of them in a row of kennels near the orchard and by the sound of it every last one of them was barking its head off.

'Listen to those dogs!' said Pitt. 'They've obviously got wind of the fellow.'

'Or *fellows*,' said Steve ominously. He wasn't a coward but he prided himself on being a careful man. In his experience people who took needless risks were the ones who didn't get to collect their old age pension. He intended to be around to collect his.

But Pitt was not prepared to be cautioned. He hurried off across the lawn and Steve was obliged, reluctantly, to follow.

When they got to the kennels they saw that the dogs were in a frenzy of excitement, leaping and jumping behind the wire of their kennel runs.

Observing their state Steve peered worriedly towards the orchard. He didn't like this situation one bit. The dogs wouldn't get this crazy over a single prowler. They could smell something else, but what? Steve sniffed the air himself. Was it his imagination or could he detect an odd scent on the breeze?

Pitt, meanwhile, was pointing his infra-red device at the rows of trees and staring at the little illuminated dial on the back of it. 'Nothing,' he announced, disappointed. 'Let's go further in.'

They walked quietly into the orchard, Steve scanning the surrounding trees warily while Pitt kept his attention on his device which he kept waving back and forth.

A short time later Pitt gave a strangled cry of alarm.

'What's the matter?' Steve asked urgently, raising his gun.

Pitt was looking down at his feet. 'I've *stepped* in something. A great *turd* . . .'

Steve bent down. It *was* a turd. A big one. Huge, in fact. And it was very fresh. He straightened quickly and looked around nervously. 'That's an animal dropping and I don't want to meet the animal that dropped it.'

'An animal?' gasped Pitt. 'What kind of animal?'

'No idea. But it's big, whatever it is. Too big.'

'But there are no wild animals around here,' protested Pitt, obviously unwilling to relinquish the idea of a human prowler.

Steve hesitated, then said, 'Don't forget Sir Penward's zoo.' It was a taboo subject in the Pitt household ever since the death of their son. 'It happened once, it could happen again.'

'Never!' snapped Pitt. 'My own company constructed those new fences around the estate. *Nothing* could ever escape from there again!'

Steve sighed. 'All right then, perhaps something has escaped from a circus, but wherever it's come from and whatever it is I'm certain it's too big for us to deal with. Let's get back to the house, switch on all the lights and call the police.'

'No,' said Pitt after a moment's thought. 'I'll tell you what we'll do – we'll let the dogs out. We'll let them take care of it!'

'I don't think that's a good idea, sir,' Steve told him. 'If it's another big cat . . .'

'It's *not* a big cat!' snapped Pitt. 'I told you – no big cat could ever get out of Penward's zoo again. I guarantee it! Now come on . . .'

His feeling of foreboding increasing rapidly, Steve followed his employer back to the dog kennels – glancing back over his shoulders the whole way.

Pitt opened the door at the end of the kennel run and the hounds rushed through it, climbing over each other in their eagerness to get out. Then, to the surprise of the two men, the pack of dogs raced off into the darkness *away* from the orchard.

Neither man said anything for a time until Steve broke the silence. 'Well, at least we know it's not a fox in there.' He turned and looked back at the orchard, his gun raised and ready.

'I don't understand it,' muttered Pitt, 'those are the best hunting dogs in the county.'

'Maybe they're clever enough to realize something we don't,' said Steve. 'So I say we get back to the house – *now.*'

'No, wait a minute . . .' Pitt raised the infra-red detector again. He peered at the dial and then cried, 'Hey, I've got a reading here! It's over in that direction!' He pointed at a row of trees to their right. Steve looked but could see nothing moving.

'Good lord,' said Pitt, 'It's registering over eight times the body heat of a man.'

Steve did a quick mental calculation. It had to be a big cat; a Siberian tiger perhaps, like the last time.

But he was wrong. The thing that emerged from the apple trees was no Siberian tiger. It stood on two legs and was about seven feet tall. It had a long tail and there were two bony crests running parallel along the top of its big, reptilian head. It cocked the head on one side and looked at them.

Steve gaped. Pitt hadn't seen it yet; he was still peering at the dial on his infra-red device. 'Mr Pitt . . .' began Steve in a strangled voice.

'I think it's coming in this direction – the needle's moving up the scale . . .' Then he looked up. *'Good God!'*

Steve fired both barrels of his shotgun, aiming at the thing's head. The creature shrieked with pain and began clawing at its head with its forearms. The pellets had apparently hit it in the eye.

'Run!' yelled Steve, giving Pitt's shoulder a jerk. But instead of running Pitt simply began to back away slowly, his eyes fixed on the thing. 'What *is* it?' he asked with amazement.

'Who gives a fuck, you silly old bastard! *Run*, damn you!' yelled Steve at the top of his voice. Then, to his horror, he saw it was too late. The creature had caught sight of them again with its remaining good eye. It gave a bellow of rage and began to charge . . .

'Jesus,' gasped Steve. He turned and ran, not bothering to see if Pitt was following. He knew he had no chance of reaching the house so he headed for the kennels. The kennels were made of concrete, though the roofs were wooden.

He scrambled through the gate and fell flat on his stomach in the kennel run. Something heavy landed on the back of his legs. He gave a start of terror but it was only Pitt crawling in through the kennel gate after him.

'It's right behind me!' cried Pitt.

'Shhh! Shut up!' hissed Steve as he saw the legs of the thing approaching the kennel run. The huge clawed feet went right past the run, then came to a hesitant stop. As Steve hoped, the half-blinded beast had lost sight of them in the darkness. It had vision like a bird's – peripheral only – and with one eye gone it was at a real disadvantage. If they lay absolutely still it might miss them completely.

The long seconds dragged on as Steve lay there in the dog run with his employer, panting with fear, lying almost on top of him. Steve realized, with a grimace, that his face was resting in dog shit. It was certainly a night for turds, he thought wryly.

Out of the corner of his eye he saw the clawed feet, followed by the enormous tail, begin to move off. The thing was giving up!

Then, unbelievably, all the lights came on. It had suddenly become as bright as day. 'Oh Christ!' yelped Pitt. Steve knew, with a sick anger, what had happened. Mrs Pitt, wondering where they were, had come downstairs and decided to switch on the security lights. *What bloody perfect timing!*

Startled by the lights the thing stopped abruptly and began to look nervously around. Steve could see it clearly now – it was huge, at least fifteen feet long from nose to tail. Its skin was a mottled grey and brown, hard-looking and scaly. With a shock of recognition Steve suddenly knew what it was. It was a *dinosaur.* But where . . . *how?*

There was no time to ponder the mystery. Pitt was struggling to his feet. 'He's seen us!' he cried.

'You fool,' cursed Steve as the creature turned and cocked its good eye in their direction. Then it began to move towards them, its mouth opening. It seemed to possess an impossibly large number of teeth.

'Quick, into the kennel!' cried Steve, crawling speedily into the nearest kennel opening. Pitt came after him and they huddled fearfully in the small, cramped space that smelled so strongly of its canine occupants.

When nothing happened for what seemed a long time Steve began to hope that the dinosaur – as he now thought of it – had lost interest in them again. But just as he started to relax slightly there was a splintering of wood above them and then the creature's snout came at them through the roof.

Before Steve had time to react the dinosaur's jaws had closed around Pitt's head and he was lifted, struggling and screaming, up out of the kennel. Steve made a grab at his kicking legs and clung on to them. For a few seconds Pitt continued to be pulled upwards but then suddenly he fell back on top of Steve.

'Are you . . . ?' Steve began as he climbed out from under Pitt, but there was no need to finish. Pitt couldn't hear him.

He had no head.

'A dinosaur? Loose in Warchester?' said Constable Keith Driscoll. He looked from one to the other and shook his head with weary amusement. 'Okay, I give in. What's the gag?'

Pascal groaned and glanced at Jenny. It was as they feared. Neither Driscoll nor the other young constable on duty believed them. He tried again. 'Keith, it's no joke. Do we *look* as if we're playing games? It's all true, I swear it! And you've got to do something about it before more people are killed!'

The other constable, Tom Hazelmere, couldn't keep his eyes off Jenny. The struggles through the barbed wire had reduced her blue tee-shirt to tatters, exposing almost all of her left breast. Pascal hadn't even noticed until now. And neither, apparently, had Jenny, but when she became aware of what Hazelmere was so interested in she quickly rearranged the torn material to try and cover more of herself. She didn't succeed and Hazelmere's eyes bulged even wider.

Driscoll, who also couldn't resist casting covert glances in the direction of her chest, said with a smirk, 'I don't know what you two have been up to tonight but you certainly look as if you've been having a wild time of it. What happened? Did you prang your car? Is that what all this is about?' He leaned towards Pascal and sniffed his breath. 'At least you haven't been drinking by the smell of it.'

Pascal resisted the urge to grab his old schoolfriend by the throat and shake him until he turned purple. Very slowly he said, in an artificially calm voice, 'As incredible as it may sound there is a very large and very dangerous animal on the rampage in Warchester. It is almost as tall as a double-decker bus but moves a damn sight faster when it wants to. It got loose from Penward's zoo. Others might be loose as well by now.'

'You mean there's more than *one* dinosaur?' asked Driscoll, the disbelief evident in his face.

'Sir Penward was breeding them secretly. Cloning them somehow from fossils. It's all too complicated to explain – just *believe* me! He's mad! Crazy! He intended turning them loose all over the world . . .'

'And he tried to kill us tonight!' interjected Jenny. 'He was going to murder us – he was going to throw us to his lions . . .'

Driscoll turned and looked at Jenny. 'Sir Penward was going to throw . . . you . . . to . . . his . . . lions?' He gave a wide grin. 'What's the matter? Doesn't he like Christians or what?'

Jenny winced. 'I know it *sounds* unbelievable, but it's true! Every word of it. All you have to do is send someone to the estate to check. When we left, the place was in chaos. There were animals everywhere, killing people. Sir Penward's probably dead himself by now.'

Still grinning, Driscoll asked, 'And how did all these animals – these *dinosaurs* and things – escape?'

'I think Lady Jane let them out on purpose,' said Pascal grimly.

'Lady Jane?' Driscoll raised his eyebrows. 'Why?'

Pascal shook his head. 'There's no time to go into that now. Look Keith, please do me a favour and *pretend* you believe us, just for a few minutes! Call up Penward Hall. See if anyone answers.'

Driscoll looked at his watch. 'It's just past 4 a.m. I'd be as popular as hell out there ringing them at this time of the morning.'

'Shit!' cried Pascal and slammed his fist down onto the desk with frustration. 'Why is there never a policeman around with a *brain* when you need one!'

Driscoll frowned. 'Easy now, Dave. I'm not putting up with that sort of stuff, even from you. Now I've been pretty patient with you two so far – it's about time you told me the truth. What happened to you two?'

'Oh God,' groaned Pascal and slumped resignedly into a nearby chair. 'It's useless. Like trying to talk to a speak-your-weight machine.'

Hazelmere, meanwhile had stopped staring at Jenny's partially exposed, breasts and walked over to the front door. 'Hey,' he said, 'Isn't that Percy Oliver's Jag out there?'

'If Percy Oliver is the landlord of the Phoenix Arms, then yes,' said Pascal.

Driscoll joined Hazelmere at the front door then turned back to Pascal. 'What are you doing with it?' he asked suspiciously.

'We stole it,' said Pascal calmly, who'd reached the point where he didn't give a damn any more. He'd done his best to deliver the warning. It was no longer his responsibility, no matter what happened.

'You *stole* it?' exclaimed Driscoll. 'Why?'

Pascal couldn't help smiling. Tell Driscoll that there were escaped dinosaurs and God knows what else loose in Warchester and he didn't bat an eye, but a stolen car certainly got his policeman's adrenalin going. 'Why? Well it was either that or stay and be eaten by a dinosaur that looks like a large mouth on two legs. The one I told you about – the one that was chasing us. Besides, good old Percy Oliver, the drinker's friend, had no further need for it. The last time I saw him he was being stepped on.' Pascal shrugged.

Driscoll looked at him silently for a time then beckoned him over to the door. Pascal got up and went. Driscoll pointed out through the glass doors of the police station. 'What do you see out there, Dave?'

'Nothing.'

Driscoll then opened one of the doors a few feet. 'Hear anything?'

'No.'

'Right. Not a thing. Now if there was an animal loose out there as tall as a double-decker bus don't you think there might be some signs of its presence by now? The odd scream for help, perhaps?' He turned and indicated the switchboard. 'Or perhaps a phone call or two from the citizens informing us of the fact they've just spotted the Son of Godzilla?'

Pascal said nothing.

'Where *is* your dinosaur, Dave?'

21

By the sheerest of coincidences Pascal's mother could have answered Constable Driscoll's question at that very moment.

Always a bad sleeper at the best of times she hadn't slept at all that night. She was too worried about Pascal. Even though he hadn't spent one night at home these past few weeks he at least kept in touch with her, but it was now over forty-eight hours since he'd phoned her.

She lay there, tossing restlessly back and forth, trying not to think of all the terrible things that might have happened to her son. She wished she knew the reason for his strange behaviour during the last weeks; she presumed his nocturnal absences meant he was involved with a new girlfriend, but why hadn't he told her? Whenever she'd tried to ask him about it he merely said it was to do with work – but she knew that couldn't be true. There was little enough to do on the *Warchester Times* during normal working hours, much less through the night. So what was he trying to hide?

A sound from outside interrupted her uncomfortable train of thought. She frowned in the darkness. It had been like a muffled grunt or snort, as if made by an animal . . .

Puzzled, she got out of bed and went to the window. Her bedroom was on the second floor and the window faced to the rear of the house. Her heart literally missed a beat when she saw *it*.

Stepping with almost dainty precision over the series of five-foot high garden walls that separated each small garden was a dinosaur. She could see it quite clearly in the fading moonlight; she even thought she recognised the species – a Tyrannosaurus Rex. (She was wrong; it was, of course, the Tarbosaurus.)

When the great beast stepped into her garden she felt a tremor run through the floorboards. Then the flat head was passing right by her window, its eye level with her own – for a nerve-chilling second it seemed to be looking right at her. She was certain the creature would stop and push the huge grinning mouth through her window . . .

But it kept moving; she saw it step carefully over the next wall into the Benfords' garden. She kept watching it until it was out of sight. She thought of opening the window and leaning out to see where it went once it reached the end of the row of houses, but decided not to. Instead she just stood there, in the grip of a terrible panic.

'I'm forty-nine years old and I'm going insane!' she told herself. 'Oh God, why . . . *why?* Why is this happening to me?'

She stood there for about five minutes, lost in her own horrifying thoughts. She didn't hear the dog start barking at the end of the street, nor did she hear its piteous yelp of pain, followed by abrupt silence.

Finally she went to her bedside table, took out the bottle of valium tablets and swallowed three of them. Then she lay back down on her bed.

The driver of the thirty-ton articulated lorry kept glancing at the girl sitting next to him. *She's hot for it,* he told himself excitedly. Why else would she be hitching at this time of the morning? True, she didn't look or speak like the usual sort he was familiar with, but these days who could tell? He'd heard lots of stories about the number of middle-class birds who'd joined the ranks of the trucker groupies. The 'rough trade brigade' they were known as . . . Well, he could be as rough as the next man.

He looked at the girl again. She was sitting right up against the door, her chin resting on her hand, and staring out at the passing countryside. She was very good looking. Blonde, in her early twenties, and with large tits. She was wearing a corduroy jacket and tight jeans. *Really* tight jeans. He felt himself start to swell . . .

'You live in Warchester?' he asked her.

'No,' she said, without looking at him. 'I've got friends there.' She didn't elaborate.

'You a student?'

'*Was,*' she said, a hint of bitterness in her voice. He noticed then that there was a puffiness around her eyes, as if she'd been crying.

After another period of silence he said, 'You in the habit of bitching so late at night?'

'Sometimes.' She continued to stare out through the window.

'It can be dangerous. You never know who might pick you up.'

'So who gives a damn.'

His hands tightened on the wheel. He was right! She *was* asking for it. Maybe she'd had an argument with her boyfriend and was getting her own back on him by going after some casual sex on the side. Maybe she was just bored and looking for a quick thrill. Or maybe she was simply a nympho who enjoyed getting her brains screwed out regularly. Well, whatever the reason she was going to get what she was after. He knew a good place a short way ahead where he could pull the truck off the road. Nice and secluded it was.

He looked at her again. Then he reached out and put his left hand on her thigh. She started to turn her head slowly towards him, but as she did so something on the road in front of them caught her attention. Her eyes widened and she yelled, 'Look out!'

He whipped his eyes back to the road but it was too late. He had a brief glimpse of some large animal in the beam of the headlights; it was green coloured and seemed to be all teeth and claws. Then came the impact.

The Megalosaurus, having satisfied its voracious appetite in the stock pens behind the zoo, had begun a quest to satisfy its equally powerful sexual appetite. It had wandered out of the Penward estate in a futile search for a female member of its species, mercifully unaware that over 130,000,000 years separated it from sexual satisfaction.

Eventually it wandered onto the main road, just in time to be struck by the thirty-ton juggernaut being driven by another male animal with nothing but sex on its mind . , .

It was an uneven encounter: the two-ton dinosaur was no match for the truck's thirty tons travelling at over forty miles an hour. It was killed instantly, its neck and back broken in several places.

The juggernaut continued on for another hundred yards,

slewing all over the road and threatening to jack-knife before the startled, panic-stricken driver managed to bring it to a skidding halt on the soft shoulder.

'Jesus,' groaned the driver. He had hit his head on the windshield and blood was trickling down his face from a cut on his scalp. He was shaking badly. The girl, though pale with fright, was unharmed. She opened her door and jumped from the cab. After taking several deep breaths she looked back along the road. Lying on one side of she could just make out the shape of whatever it was they'd hit.

The driver got out of his side of the cab and walked, or rather staggered, to the front of the vehicle. There he let out a cry of anguish. 'Oh Christ, look at it!'

She joined him and saw that the front of the truck had stoved in – even the massive front bumper had a great bend in it – and water and oil were pouring out of the engine. Even to her unpractised eye it was obvious the vehicle was no longer driveable.

'Hell, what am I going to do?' he cried. 'I got to have this load in Peterborough by noon tomorrow! My boss is going to kill me!' Then suddenly he looked at her accusingly and snarled, 'It's all *your* fault!'

'*My* fault?' she said in surprise. 'Why?'

'Because you distracted me! You deliberately distracted me, coming on so strong like you were and getting me all worked up! You damn bitch! You're all alike! Don't care what you do to get what you want! And now you've wrecked my rig!'

The girl stared at the driver – a tall, balding forty-year-old with a beer belly – in astonishment. Then she said coldly, 'Look, mister, I don't know what you're talking about. But I *do* know that what put this dent in your lorry is lying back there in the road.' She jerked her thumb in its direction. 'And it might be a good idea if we went and found out what it is that you've killed.'

Still muttering under his breath about sex-crazed nymphos and the danger they presented to married men like himself, the driver climbed back into his cab to get torch. Then they walked back a hundred yards to the dead animal ...

'Fucking hell!' exclaimed the driver as he shined the torch over the corpse. 'What *is* it?'

'A dinosaur,' said the girl dazedly. 'You've run over a dinosaur.'

'A *what?*'

'You know – like you've seen in the movies.'

'Oh . . .' he said, nodding. Then, 'Yeah, but I read where all those things died out *years* ago. They're – what's the word – *extinct.* Yeah, extinct!'

'Not in Cambridgeshire apparently,' pointed out the girl drily.

'Well, hell – you'd think the damn authorities would *warn* the public that these things are still running around about here. I mean they should put up *signs* or something.'

'You mean a sign like "Dinosaur Crossing"?' asked the girl seriously, fighting the urge to have an attack of hysterics.

'Yeah, yeah,' he said, nodding vigorously. 'I mean, look at those teeth! That thing was probably very dangerous.' He prodded the creature's foreleg warily with the toe of his boot. 'And hell, it must weigh over a ton!'

The girl glanced nervously at the surrounding trees. 'I just hope there isn't more than one of them in the vicinity . . .'

He looked at her with alarm. 'You think there might be *more* of these things around here?'

'I don't know what to think. All I know is that this creature has no right to exist. It shouldn't *be* here! Something very weird is going on. I think we should go back to your lorry and wait inside until another car comes by.'

They hurried back to the wrecked juggernaut, both of them hoping they'd see the headlights of an approaching vehicle. But the road remained eerily deserted.

The girl climbed back up into the cabin speedily, but the driver hesitated. 'I'd better go and lay out the warning lights, otherwise someone is liable to run into the back of us . . .' he said reluctantly.

She watched as he walked up the road ahead of the truck, positioning a number of battery-powered yellow lights. Then he disappeared behind the truck to put more lights at the rear.

As she waited for him to come back she hoped it wouldn't be long before another vehicle appeared. Not only was she frightened that there might be more creatures around similar to the one lying dead in the road, but she was worried she might have a problem with the driver. The shock of the accident seemed to have knocked all ideas of sex out of him for the time being, but she suspected it wouldn't be long before his thoughts turned in that direction again.

Minutes passed. What was keeping him? She leaned out of the cab window to see, but the looming bulk of the truck's freight container blocked her view. 'Hey, you okay?' she called. There was no answer. Finally she opened the door and leaned out as far as she could. In the glow of the yellow warning lights she could see his boots and part of his legs lying in the road about ten yards behind the truck. Then, as she watched, his legs and feet slowly disappeared from view. Something was *dragging* him away . . .

She ducked quickly back into the cabin, slammed the door and wound the windows shut. She was trembling. There must be another of those monsters out there, and it had got the driver . . .

The tension became unbearable as she sat there trying to keep an eye on both rear vision mirrors at once. Time passed with agonising slowness.

She screamed.

Something had suddenly leapt up onto the truck's bonnet. But it wasn't a dinosaur – it was a panther. A big, black panther.

It peered in at her through the windshield and bared its fangs in a snarl.

The girl shrunk back against the upholstery. Would it be able to shatter the glass or was the windshield thick enough to keep it out?

But then, unexpectedly, the big cat simply sat down on the bonnet, though it continued to stare at her with blatant interest. It was evidently in no hurry to get at her and she knew why – it had probably just eaten the driver.

As the staring game between them dragged on and on the girl couldn't help remembering what her friends in Warchester were always complaining: 'Warchester is the dullest place in England. *Nothing* ever happens here!'

Obviously things had changed.

'You know what I think?' asked Driscoll.

'No. What *do* you think?' asked Pascal sarcastically.

'I think you two got into some sort of trouble tonight. An accident in your car maybe. Or you were both high on something. So then you decided to take Percy Oliver's car and now you've concocted this crazy story as a cover.'

Pascal glanced at Jenny. 'What were we high on tonight, Jen? Was it coke or smack? I can't remember.'

Jenny, who was slumped in a chair with her arms folded tightly over her breast, didn't answer.

Driscoll, his expression earnest, continued. 'Look, Dave, for old times' sake I'll do all I can to help you. I'm giving you a chance to tell me your version of events before I have to ring up Percy Oliver and inform him you've stolen his car.'

'You're going to have a long wait for him to answer the phone. The last time I saw him he was being turned into a human cowpat,' said Pascal coldly. He looked at his watch. 'The more time you waste the more of those animals are getting out. It's just not those dino ... those big reptiles, it's big cats as well. We saw a lion on the loose *inside* the manor house which means their compound fence must be down. God knows how many wild animals there are wandering about the countryside by now. You've got to *do* something, Keith.'

Driscoll shook his head sadly. 'You really intend to keep this load of cock-and-bull up to the bitter end, don't you?'

'Cock-and-*dinosaur*,' corrected Pascal with a malicious grin. He was beginning to feel light-headed and strange. It occurred to him that Driscoll might be right. Perhaps he *had* invented the whole thing. Maybe he was going crazy ...

'Dave, for the last time I implore you to face the facts,' Driscoll was saying. 'If there were any wild animals running about in Warchester tonight we'd have heard about it by now. *And* McCaffrey and Nolan in the patrol car would have seen something as well; if there *was* anything out there to see.'

'Who knows?' said Pascal. 'Perhaps they already *have* seen something. Perhaps even now they're being digested by one of Penward's pets. Have you heard from them recently?'

Driscoll gave him a pained look. 'Okay, you've had your chance. I'm going to call Percy Oliver.' He reached for the phone on the front desk but before he could pick it up a light on the switchboard began to flash and the same phone rang. Frowning, Driscoll answered it.

Pascal watched his face carefully. He wasn't too surprised when the colour drained from Driscoll's face 'What . . . *what* . . . are you *sure?* Well stay right where you are, Mrs Pitt; we'll have a car there as soon as possible. Yes, yes, I promise. I've got to hang up now, Mrs Pitt. Just stay calm and keep the doors locked. Goodbye . . .'

As he put the phone down he stared at Pascal and Jenny with shocked eyes.

'What's wrong?' asked Hazelmere puzzledly.

'That was Mrs Pitt,' he said slowly. 'She was hysterical. Said there's some kind of wild animal loose in their back garden. She thinks it's already killed her husband . . .'

'So it's started,' said Pascal simply.

22

'You're seeing a rare and wondrous sight, Jen,' said Pascal with deliberate unpleasantness. 'You're watching a policeman add up two and two and get four.' He had no intention of letting Driscoll off the hook. He would never forgive him for not believing their story, or at least not allowing them the benefit of the doubt.

Driscoll was on the radio to the patrol car, directing it to the Pitt residence. When he put down the microphone he said worriedly, 'They're less than half a mile away. They should be there in a couple of minutes . . .'

'But they're not armed, are they?' asked Pascal.

'Of course they're not.'

'Then you'd better call them back and tell them not to go wandering around the Pitt's back gardens. Not that revolvers would be any use – if it's the Tarbosaurus that's paying the Pitts a visit you'd need a bazooka to take it out.'

Driscoll ran a hand nervously through his hair. 'Look, I admit there does seem to be something to this wild animal story of yours, but I'm not buying all that nonsense about *dinosaurs.*'

'Suit yourself,' replied Pascal, shrugging. 'But when all this is over and you have to write your report you might as well do it in the dustbin because that's where your career as a cop is going to end up.'

Driscoll snatched up a phone. 'I'm calling Penward Hall. I'm going to find out if any of their animals have escaped.'

'You're wasting your time,' said Pascal wearily. 'Call Inspector Bodycome instead and tell him we've got a full-scale emergency on our hands. Or rather *your* hands. Tell him to alert the emergency services throughout the county – there are probably even more casualties now than the local hospital will be able to handle. And he'd better call in the army too. You're going to need the military to take care of some of those creatures.'

But Driscoll wasn't listening. He was waiting for someone to answer the phone at Penward Hall.

While he was waiting another of the phones started to ring. Hazelmere picked it up.

As Driscoll finally hung up Hazelmere cut in urgently: 'I've got a driver of a petrol tanker on the line. He's in a call-box near the Phoenix Arms; he says the entire pub has been demolished, as if a bulldozer had gone right through it! He says he saw bodies in the wreckage and a couple of them look as if something's been *eating* them . . . !'

Driscoll went a distinct grey. He snatched up his phone again. 'I'm calling the old man,' he told Hazelmere. 'You call the Sarge and the rest of the lads and have them all report in immediately. Tell them it's a possible Code 09 emergency!'

'Hurrah,' muttered Pascal. 'The penny has at last dropped.'

Jenny got up and came over to him. 'I'm going to the office. I want to make a couple of phone calls too.'

'Who to?'

'One is to my parents. Our house is pretty isolated. I want to make sure they're okay and to warn them to stay inside if they hear any strange noises.'

'Good idea,' said Pascal, getting to his feet. The effort made him wince with pain. His ankle still hurt like hell and was now badly swollen. He thought of calling his own mother, but he felt sure she wasn't in too much danger.

Neither of the policemen noticed them leave – both were too busy talking on the phone.

Outside, on the front steps, Jenny stopped and held up her hand. 'Listen. When Keith opened the door a little while ago and asked if you could hear anything, there wasn't a sound, but now . . .'

Pascal nodded. It seemed that every dog in town was barking.

After Jenny had phoned her parents she said firmly to Pascal, 'Right, as soon as we get you cleaned up we get to work.'

'Work?' he asked her blankly.

'Have you forgotten why we got involved in all this in the first place? We were after a big story, remember? The story of the century, you called it. Well, now we've *got* it!'

Pascal stared at her with a mixture of surprise and admiration. He *had* forgotten the reason for his infiltration of the zoo. All thoughts of journalism had fled his mind. Yet Jenny, despite all she'd been through in the last few hours, was proving herself the true professional. Not long ago he would have resented this further demonstration of her superiority, but all that was past now.

As she led him into the bathroom where the first-aid box was kept she continued: 'First thing we do is call one of the press agencies and get this story onto the wires, with the promise we'll supply an exclusive background story plus all the details within a couple of hours . . . *Damn*, I wish we'd got some pictures!'

'Maybe we should call Henry,' he suggested.

'No, not yet. It's too dangerous for him to be roaming about out there.'

'He probably wouldn't even believe us. Come to think of it, the press agency won't believe us either.'

'They soon will. By now Driscoll should have got a major alert rolling through the county. All the agency will have to do is make a couple of phone calls to confirm that *something* big has happened in Warchester.'

In the bathroom he let her peel his blood-encrusted shirt off his back, an action that reawakened the pain in his gashed shoulder. 'Ugh, it's a mess,' she told him. 'But at least it's stopped bleeding.'

While she washed it clean with a solution of water and disinfectant she asked him to tell her as much as he knew about

Penward's dinosaurs. He did his best through the agonising treatment repeating Penward's description of how they'd been genetically engineered: how the genetic code contained in fossil dinosaur cells had been literally *transcribed* onto living bird cells.

'Chickens!' she exclaimed in astonishment at one stage. 'You're saying those huge monsters were created out of chicken cells?!'

'It sounds crazy, I know, that's what he told me,' Pascal, and went on to explain about birds having evolved from a dinosaur species and thus having a lot of genetic makeup in common.

As she worked on his less serious cuts and abrasions he told her about Penward's mad scheme to release breeding pairs of dinosaurs in remote places across the world. 'He saw himself as a kind of Noah – a Noah of the dinosaur kingdom. He was going to help them reinherit the earth.'

'God!' exclaimed Jenny excitedly. 'You were right, David. This *is* going to be the story of the century! And it's all ours!'

Pascal smiled, but he couldn't share in her enthusiasm just yet. Feelings of guilt were beginning to plague him again. It was thanks to his investigation of the zoo that all this was happening. Would Lady Jane have let the creatures out if he hadn't rejected her so cruelly? He doubted it, and as a result of her action a lot of people had died. And it was likely that a lot *more* people would die before all the dinosaurs were either killed or recaptured.

When Jenny had done all she could for him she stripped off the remains of her tee-shirt and her jeans so that he could do the same for her cuts. She had cuts on her face, several scratches on her legs from the barbed wire and the nasty-looking hole on the underneath of her upper right arm – but compared with him, she'd got off lightly.

He remembered the last time he'd seen her naked – it had been here in the office, the night he'd caught her with Tony Chilton. The memory still hurt badly, but at the same time it also excited him. Jealousy, he reflected, was a great aphrodisiac . . .

Jenny was sitting on the closed lid of the toilet, her long legs stretched out in front of her so that he could treat the cuts with mercurochrome. She sat hunched forward, her breasts jutting provocatively. He had forgotten how beautiful her breasts were.

As he knelt in front of her he looked up into her face and said seriously, 'I've missed you, Jen. I've missed *all* of you.'

She smiled down at him. 'I've missed you.'

'This Tony Chilton character – are you going to keep seeing him?'

'What do you mean?'

'You know what I mean.'

She pretended not to. 'I'm not going to stop talking to him just because we're back together again. He's a friend of mine.'

'*Lover*, you mean,' he said bitterly.

'Look, I only got involved with him after you suddenly dropped me. You just broke off our relationship without even giving me an explanation. I was hurt, and lonely. You can't blame me for taking up with Tony.'

'I'm sorry . . .' he muttered thickly.

'*Why* did you end it like that, David? Why wouldn't you tell me the reason?'

He shook his head. 'It's too stupid now. I'll tell you one of these days. The important thing is that we're back together again. For good. We *are*, aren't we?'

She reached down and touched the side of his face. 'We are.'

'Let's make love,' he said suddenly. 'Here. Right now. On the floor.'

Her eyes widened with surprise, then she laughed. 'We *can't*, David. We've got too much to do. Besides, you're in no condition for it.'

He put his hands on her thighs and gripped her hard. '*Please*, Jen. Please do it. It's important to me.'

She stared down at him with a look of puzzlement, then her expression softened. She slid forward off the toilet seat onto her knees in front of him, putting her arms around him. 'All right,' she said, 'But we're going to have to hurry . . .'

He kissed her and then said, his throat dry, 'For a change I'll try and be as quick as I can.'

He kissed her again, running his hands over her smooth sides. Then he hooked his thumbs under the elastic of her briefs and slid them down her thighs . . .

Jenny, now wearing a spare jacket that she kept in the office set, was on the phone to a press agency based in Cambridge. She was giving them a skilfully-edited version of the situation in Warchester, saying that the police were on a full-scale alert after a number of dangerous animals escaped from Sir Penward's private zoo. Without actually mentioning the word 'dinosaur' she told them that several of the escaped animals were believed to be specially bred monstrosities that Sir Penward had created illegally, in a secret genetic engineering facility.

Pascal was only half listening to her. He felt incredibly tired now, as well as very hungry. He realized that he hadn't eaten anything for over twenty-four hours.

'Did they buy it?' he asked when she finally hung up.

'Yes. I said we'd have the full story on offer by 7 a.m. at the latest.' She looked at her watch. 'Doesn't give us much time, I know, but by then every reporter in the country will be homing in on Warchester. So let's get cracking.'

'You start,' he told her. 'I think I'd better give my mother a call after all.'

His mother took a long time to answer the phone and when she did she sounded very drowsy.

'You okay?' he asked her anxiously. 'You sound strange.'

'David, where have you been? You've got to come home right away. I need you. I'm not well.'

'What's the matter?'

'I think I'm – I'm going mad. I'm hallucinating. I looked out of my bedroom window a little while ago and thought I saw – no, I can't tell you. It's too embarrassing . . .'

'*What did you see?*' he demanded.

'David. I don't *want* to tell you. It's so . . .'

'You saw a dinosaur, didn't you?' he told her.

'But how do *you* know I saw . . . ?'

'Answer me, Mum! This is important. Did it look like a Tyrannosaurus?'

'Yes, but . . .'

'Which way was it heading?'

'Heading? Er, west, I suppose. Yes, because it went into the Benfords' garden after ours . . .'

'Christ! Look Mum, I have to go. I'll explain everything later, but you weren't hallucinating, believe me. Now stay in the house no matter what you hear going on outside. Understand?'

'Yes, but David, what . . . ?'

He hung up on her. 'The Tarbosaurus is already in town,' he told Jenny, 'I'm going to go tell Driscoll.'

'Your mother saw it?'

'Yeah. In *our* back yard of all places,' he said as he headed for the door.

'Hang on,' she cried. 'I'm coming with you.'

They had just got outside when they heard the Tarbosaurus. There was no mistaking its distinctive shriek. The hair on the back of Pascal's neck prickled instantly. Then came a sound of glass shattering. Jenny pointed to the big new shopping centre a short distance along the high street. 'It's coming from there! Don't tell me it's *inside* – !'

Alarm bells in the centre were ringing now. Pascal saw Driscoll and Hazelmere come running out onto the footpath ahead of them. 'Keith!' he yelled, 'You're about to get your first look at something that doesn't exist!'

Driscoll wore the expression of a man who was suddenly finding life too much to cope with. He turned helplessly to Pascal as a tremendous crash from inside the shopping precinct shook the ground 'What *is* it? What's happening?'

'It's one of those mythical dinosaurs I've been telling you about! Come take a look!' cried Pascal as he crossed the road. 'Jenny, you stay where you are!' he added pompously.

But when Pascal arrived at the entrance to the mall he found Jenny right behind him. He was going to protest, but knew it wouldn't do any good. Instead he peered in through the metal security grille that covered the glass doors. He glimpsed something big moving about at the far end of the shopping mall but it was too dark inside to see clearly. 'It's the Tarbosaurus' he told Driscoll and Hazelmere, who'd joined them. 'Or another dinosaur just as large. Must have smashed its way in through the rear . . .'

Driscoll suddenly bent down and began unlocking the big padlocks that secured the metal grille. 'I've got the keys here. I'm going inside to see for myself.'

'Don't be mad!' exploded Pascal. 'You're not even armed!'

Driscoll ignored him. 'Go and get the two .32 revolvers from the Inspector's office,' he ordered Hazelmere.

Hazelmere hesitated. 'But Keith, the Inspector's got the keys to the gun locker – and besides, we have to get official permission before we can take out those guns.'

'Just do it!' snapped Driscoll. 'Break the locker open! I'll take full responsibility!' He'd unlocked all the padlocks now and was starting to raise the heavy grating. Hazelmere hesitated for a few more seconds, then ran off back towards the police station.

'I've just thought of something,' said Jenny to Pascal. 'I'll be back in a moment.'

Before he could say anything she too was running back across the street.

Hoping that what ever she'd gone to do would occupy her for a long time and thus keep her out of harm's way, Pascal continued to watch anxiously as Driscoll rolled the grating all the way up and unlocked the glass entrance door.

From inside the shopping centre the clamour of alarm bells had increased in volume. 'Sounds like that thing's set off the fire alarms too,' muttered Driscoll as he started to slide the door open. They could still hear the sounds of glass being shattered from the far end of the mall.

Driscoll stepped through the gap he'd opened and Pascal, unwillingly, followed him. He told himself that if the dinosaur took even one step in his direction he'd be back outside at the speed of sound.

'The light switches should be right here,' said Driscoll, feeling around on the wall. He found them. Suddenly, section by section, the lights in the new shopping centre – the pride and joy of the Chamber of Commerce – came on.

'Jesus,' gasped Driscoll.

The Tarbosaurus was at the opposite end of the precinct. All around it lay the debris from the damage it had wrought upon Warchester's consumer paradise; on a carpet of smashed plate glass were scattered a variety of items, from broken TV sets to stuffed toy animals.

The reason for the spectacular amount of damage immediately became clear. As the lights came on the dinosaur was in the act of tearing at something it had pinned beneath one of its giant hind claws. When it looked up, startled, Pascal saw part of an Alsatian dog dangling from between its teeth. There were three Alsatian guard dogs that were left to run free in the precinct each night as a security precaution; the Tarbosaurus had apparently been chasing them about the place, wrecking the shops as it went.

And even as Pascal and Driscoll watched, the dinosaur's tail went swinging through another shop-front window, creating an explosion of broken glass.

'It *is* a dinosaur!' cried Driscoll.

Pascal grabbed him by the arm. 'Glad to hear you finally believe me. Now let's get out of here.'

But as they backed towards the door the dinosaur, having spotted them, opened its jaws and let loose an angry shriek that echoed horribly within the lofty interior of the mall. Letting the remains of the dog fall unheeded to the floor, the giant beast started towards them.

Pascal and Driscoll ran for the door. Once through they slid it shut. 'The grille!' cried Pascal. 'For God's sake get it back down!'

The dinosaur's charge had, fortunately, been halted by a collision with the circular fountain that stood in the centre of the mall. But the delay was only a temporary one; the Tarbosaurus's seven tons quickly obliterated the concrete and plaster eyesore. The water, which had been turned off for the night, began to spray up in all directions from the fractured pipes.

They got the metal grille down just as the dinosaur reached the front door. Pascal and Driscoll sprinted for safety as slivers of glass hurtled past them.

Once on the other side of the street Pascal turned and looked back. The dinosaur, crouched low, was battering at the metal grating with its lowered head. The flexible screen of steel links was bulging outwards with each impact. It obviously wasn't going to hold for very much longer.

Someone ran past Pascal towards the central entrance. To his horror he saw it was Jenny! She was carrying a camera and he realized she must have got it out of Henry Wates' desk.

'Jenny!' he screamed, running after her. 'Come back, you idiot! It's getting out!'

23

Jenny came to a stop less than five yards in front of the mall entrance and raised the camera. By now the enraged Tarbosaurus had succeeded in breaking loose one entire side of the security grille and was trying to force its head through the gap.

'Are you crazy?' cried Pascal as he reached her. He started to pull her away but she shook loose of his grip. 'Just a couple more!' she yelled, aiming the camera at the dinosaur again. 'We've got to get it while it's still in the light!'

'If you don't move your stupid arse you'll be able to photograph it from the *inside!*' he screamed, grabbing her again. The dinosaur's head was now protruding round the side of the grille and the metal was screeching in protest as it buckled.

Then suddenly Driscoll and Hazelmere were there beside them firing their revolvers at the animal. The guns looked ridiculously small and puny to be used against such a creature but the bullets, aimed at its head, seemed to have an effect. Screeching with pain it withdrew behind the barrier.

The two policemen kept firing until their guns were empty. By then Pascal had managed to hustle Jenny back across the street. 'You stupid bitch! Don't ever do that again!'

But she merely grinned and held up the camera. 'I'm going to develop these in Henry's darkroom right away! These are going to make us *famous!*'

Pascal was about to tell her he didn't give a damn about being famous if it meant risking her life when she was interrupted by the approach of Warchester's one and only fire engine, its siren wailing.

The fire engine pulled up in front of the shopping centre and its crew spilled out onto the street. At the same moment the Tarbosaurus resumed its awesome assault on the grille and the firemen froze into postures of disbelief. In different circumstances Pascal would have enjoyed the expressions on their faces as they gazed at the dinosaur, but now it was too alarmingly clear that the grille would shortly give way completely and that the animal would be loose in the high street.

'Connect your hoses! Connect your hoses!' someone screamed. 'It's our only chance of stopping it. *Move*, damn you!' It was Driscoll, running among the firemen, yelling at the top of his voice and waving the empty gun at them. Pascal saw immediately what he had in mind and, fortunately, some of the firemen caught on too. They began to unwind the fire hoses from the appliance and connected them to nearby hydrants.

They were just in time. No sooner had two of the hoses been readied than several metal bolts exploded out of the entrance wall like rifle bullets and the whole grille collapsed onto the footpath. The dinosaur, ducking to get under the top of the entrance, emerged into the street.

It was instantly hit by two powerful jets of water from the fire hoses. The force was sufficient to knock it off balance and it fell over onto its side with a thud that made the ground shake. Struggling to rise, hind legs kicking frantically, it gave an ear-splitting shriek of rage.

'We've got to get more hoses on it!' cried Driscoll, but by now the rest of the firemen had roused themselves from their dazed state and were connecting the other two hoses.

The Tarbosaurus finally succeeded in regaining its footing. It tried to lunge forward at its frail attackers but one of the hoses was kept trained on its head, blinding it. Then the other two hoses were brought into play and the combined strength of the four jets of water was enough to force it backwards.

'Push it back into the mall!' ordered Driscoll. 'We can trap it then – block both the front and rear entrances with vehicles . . .'

Foot by foot the protesting, struggling prehistoric animal was forced back into the shopping centre. The firemen followed it inside, using the jets of water as battering rams; knocking the creature off its feet again and again.

The Tarbosaurus was by now becoming confused. The constant impact of high-pressure water in its eyes and against its sensitive ear cavities had disorientated it badly.

Finally it panicked.

Bellowing loudly it turned from its attackers and tried to escape. But instead of heading towards the opposite end of the mall where it had originally broken in, the great beast charged blindly into one of the columns supporting the mezzanine floor above.

The momentum of the animal's seven ton bulk was enough to shear the column in two. And as it collapsed it brought down a whole section of the mezzanine floor with it.

Shrieking with pain the dinosaur vanished under tons of falling debris. A great cloud of dust rose into the air and with it came silence.

The Tarbosaurus was dead.

Mrs Myra Goodwin woke to hear the sounds of her ten-year-old son Philip playing in the front garden. *What on earth is he doing up at this hour?* she asked herself irritably. She looked at the clock on her bedside table. It was only 5.50 a.m. and just getting light. Damn the boy! He was becoming a real little nuisance. It was his father's fault. He was away too much on sales trips to be a proper father to the boy, and when he *was* home he never disciplined him, just spoiled him rotten.

Philip was laughing excitedly. Vaguely she wondered what he'd found that was so entertaining at ten to six in the morning. Then she heard another sound; it was like a cross between a sheep's bleat and the honk of a goose.

Frowning, she got out of bed and went to the window. Down in the front garden she saw her son, in pyjamas and dressing gown, feeding handfuls of grass to some kind of animal. At first she thought it was a baby elephant but then saw that what she'd mistaken for a trunk was in fact the creature's neck. The head on the end of the neck, which was very long, was quite small and out of all proportion to the rest of the animal.

She opened the window and called out, 'Philip, what *is* that you've got there?'

Both boy and animal looked up at her. The animal bleated. 'It's a dinosaur, Mummy! Can I keep him, *please?*'

Mrs Myra Goodwin sighed. Another pet! 'I don't know,' she told him. 'You'll have to wait and ask your father.'

The residents of Warchester – the ones still alive – woke up to a world that was vastly different to the one they'd gone to sleep in. There were police cars moving slowly up and down the streets issuing amplified warnings to people to stay in their houses. Helicopters, most of them with military markings, were constantly flying back and forth at very low levels. Then suddenly there were armoured cars and light Scorpion tanks rolling through the streets as well. What was going on? Was it *war*?

The local radio didn't provide much information at first, except to say that a number of dangerous animals had escaped from Sir Penward's zoo and to repeat the police warning that people should not leave their homes until they were told it was safe to do so. This didn't satisfy many people. Even if several big cats had escaped from the zoo wasn't this large military presence something of an over-reaction?

Then, in a late news bulletin on *Good Morning Britain* the word *dinosaur* was mentioned for the first time . . .

Bit by bit the residents of Warchester got to know of the true situation: there were prehistoric monsters on the loose around the town and in the surrounding countryside. As incredible as it seemed, Sir Penward had actually manufactured the creatures by means of genetic engineering. And as the day wore a series of experts were paraded on radio and TV news bulletins, explaining how Sir Penward had probably achieved this. Gradually it began to seem less and less incredible and just very, very frightening.

Of course many people in the area didn't need expert confirmation on the existence of the dinosaurs – they'd already had first-hand experience of the creatures. Like Sylvia Pitt, wife of the late Stanley Pitt, MP for Warchester. She had spent several terrified hours hiding in the wine cellar after seeing, through her front window, two policemen torn to pieces by the Dilophosaurus, the same dinosaur which had earlier killed her husband.

She had tried to warn the two policemen by signalling from the window as they got out of their patrol car – she had glimpsed the creature walking round the side of the house a short time before – but they continued to walk up. The next thing she knew the huge two-legged reptile had pounced on them. One policeman died instantly – bitten almost in two – but his partner had tried to run back to the car. He almost made it, but the reptile caught up with him before he could open the door. To Sylvia Pitt, who'd quickly looked away from the window, his screaming seemed to go on for ever.

The Dilophosaurus, with its distinctive crested head, was next seen by a milkman an hour later. The dinosaur was calmly walking down the middle of a road in one of Warchester's most expensive residential areas. The milkman jumped from his still-moving float and raced to the front door of the nearest house, where he hammered and banged frantically until it was finally opened by an irate elderly man. The milkman simply pointed at the dinosaur, which was now passing directly in front of the house, and pushed past the old man. The man took one look at the animal and slammed the door. They then tried to call the police but they couldn't get through. By then many others were also trying to ring the station.

One of them was a farmer by the name of Stan Lewis who, to his amazement, had just seen a large reptile some twenty feet long, with a big spiny fin down its back, chasing his herd of milking cows across one of his fields. After trying repeatedly to call the police, without success, he got his rifle and went off to try and deal with the bizarre problem by himself – against his wife's advice.

He never came back.

Another frustrated caller was a salesman called Vincent Haye. Driving towards Warchester he had passed three incredible sights in quick succession: first was the body of some kind of giant lizard lying in the road, next had come a gory mess barely recognisable as the remains of a man, and then, as he'd driven past the stationary juggernaut, he saw a large, black panther sprawled on the bonnet of the truck. It had turned to look at him as he went by, then returned its gaze to a girl cowering in the cab.

The salesman didn't even consider stopping. Instead he put his foot down until he reached a call box a couple of miles further along the road.

One caller who did succeed in getting through was another early motorist who saw what appeared to be an entire pride of lions in a field he passed. Ironically, the big cats were to present an even bigger problem to the police and army units than the dino-saurs. For one thing there were many more of them – over sixty lions, tigers, panthers, leopards, jaguars and pumas had escaped from the zoo and most of them, frightened by the giant reptiles, had left the estate and spread across the countryside. Several members of the hastily-assembled army of inexperienced hunt-ers were to fall victim to fatal attacks by the big cats before the day was over.

The hunters scored their first dinosaur at 10.20 a.m. An army unit cornered the Dilophosaurus in the playground of the Warchester Primary School. It proved difficult to kill: after being hit repeatedly by rifle fire it was finally despatched with a cannon shell fired by one of the Scorpion tanks that had swiftly arrived on the scene.

The second dinosaur kill occurred an hour later. The crew of an Army Lynx helicopter spotted it eating a cow in a field. It was the finned dinosaur that had been seen by farmer Stan Lewis – who by then was lying dead in another field along with several of his cows. Its official name was *Altispinax* and unlike the other carnosaurs that Penward had resurrected it walked on all fours. A native of prehistoric England, it had formerly flourished in the Lower Cretaceous period.

The Lynx swooped down on it and opened fire with its 20mm AME 621 cannon. The Altispinax started to run but quickly received a number of direct hits, one of which shattered its skull. It collapsed nose-first onto the ground, its four ton mass skidding for over twenty feet before it came to a stop. Even with its brain destroyed by 20mm shell, the body continued to twitch and jerk for a half an hour.

The reptile that proved most difficult to deal with wasn't even, theoretically, a proper dinosaur – it was the plesiosaur. The canal boat containing the survivors of the late Dickie Radford's party wasn't discovered until after 9 a.m. By then there were only twelve students huddled in the cabin; a further three had been snatched by the creature after Radford had been killed.

The soldiers, once they understood what sort of animal it was, began using hand grenades as makeshift depth charges. The water in the vicinity of the canal boat was seeded with numerous grenades, but though a lot of mud was churned up and a few dead fish floated to the surface, the plesiosaur was nowhere to be seen. It eventually became clear that the amphibious reptile was no longer in that section of the river. The big question was – had it gone up or down stream?

An urgent request for an anti-submarine Westland Sea King helicopter, equipped with dipping sonar, was sent to the Navy. In the meantime soldiers in rubber boats, powered by outboard motors, proceeded in opposite directions away from the stranded canal boat and tossed grenades into the river at regular intervals.

The first clue to the creature's whereabouts came when a call was received at the police station – which had been converted into the operations nerve centre – from a hysterical woman who said that her husband, a dedicated angler, hadn't returned from his customary dawn fishing session on the river. His regular fishing spot, it was learnt, was near a traffic bridge that crossed the river almost in the centre of town.

The soldiers in the rubber boats sped to the location. Grenades were again thrown into the water. The residents of Warchester, already battered by a series of staggering surprises that morning, were now subjected to the ominous *thump, thump of* the exploding grenades. Some even suffered broken windows from the concussions.

At first it seemed that the plesiosaur had moved on – after twenty grenades had been dropped in the water near the traffic bridge the soldiers began to relax – but then suddenly the great head on its long neck reared up out of the water right beside one of the rubber boats. Taken by surprise the boat's four occupants didn't react fast enough. They were still staring at the creature in stunned amazement when the head plunged downwards – straight into the middle of their frail craft. One man was killed by the impact, another was dragged beneath the surface by the reptile. The other boats converged on the spot and quickly pulled the two survivors from the water: then more grenades were dropped.

When the beast surfaced again it was obvious it had been mortally wounded. Dark blood gushed out of its mouth and it whipped its neck about in a frenzy of pain. The soldiers opened fire with their 7.62mm automatic rifles but they needn't have bothered; the plesiosaur was as good as dead. When it finally stopped its threshing about and rolled slowly over onto its back the soldiers could see that its massive belly had been ruptured by the grenades. Soon the only sign of life was a weak movement in one of its long flippers.

At 11.13 a.m. army units had entered the Penward estate and were cautiously heading towards the manor house and zoo. Leading the way were several light Scorpion tanks, and it was one of these that became the first casualty of the clean-up operation.

Less than a quarter of a mile from the house and zoo complex the crew of the lead tank saw a large dinosaur busily munching shrubbery near the roadway. It was about twenty-five feet long and resembled a giant armadillo. It was covered with great bony plates from which protruded horns and spikes. Its most distinctive feature was its tail. Immensely thick, it ended in an enormous bony club with two giant spikes growing out of it.

The Scorpion tank turned off the road and approached the dinosaur, which immediately lowered itself flat on the ground in a clearly defensive posture. In that position the animal was a living blockhouse, invulnerable to all attack.

Inside the tank the crew debated whether a shell from their 20mm cannon would penetrate the dinosaur's natural armour or whether they should try to kill the thing at all. It was obviously herbivorous and might not present any threat to human life. The tank commander was about to suggest they wait until the scientists arrived from the Natural History Museum, when the dinosaur jumped to its feet and charged them.

Its bone-covered, beaked head ploughed straight into the side of the Scorpion, caving in the tank's light armour. Then the dinosaur delivered the *coup de grace*: it swung its tail round and sent three hundredweight of spiked, bony club crashing into the rear of the vehicle. The effect was the same as if the tank had suffered a direct hit with a 90mm shell. The Scorpion blew up.

Startled but unharmed the dinosaur – a Scolosaurus from the Upper Cretaceous era – trotted away from the blazing wreck. Brief moments later its small brain had already forgotten the incident, and it resumed feeding.

The shocked crews of the other tanks and armoured cars went swiftly into action. Keeping well clear of the animal they opened fire with cannon and heavy calibre machine-guns. It took a remarkably long time to die and they kept firing even when it no longer moved. The firing only stopped when the animal was nothing but chunks of smoking meat and bone scattered about the ground.

From then on the soldiers took no chances – they shot at everything that moved.

By 12.45 a.m. the 'battle' for Penward Hall had been won. The dinosaurs were all dead. There had been only one further casualty sustained by the military – a soldier entering one of the top floor rooms in the manor house had been surprised by Deinonychus – the Terrible Claw – and ripped open before his companions could shoot the creature.

After that it was all over.

Or so it seemed.

24

As the only two people who knew the full story behind the appearance of prehistoric animals in Warchester, Pascal and Jenny were questioned endlessly by a succession of police officers, army officers, government officials and scientists for most of the day. When it became clear that Pascal knew more about the situation than Jenny she was allowed to leave the police station, which was serving as the command post. Pascal was obliged to stay on and endure yet more interrogation.

His only respite during the day was a quick trip to the hospital where a harassed doctor examined him, stitched up the gash in his back, told him his ankle wasn't broken but badly sprained, and pronounced him relatively fit. Then it was back to the police station again.

As the day progressed and the death toll mounted, his feeling of guilt increased. He couldn't help thinking that if he hadn't meddled with Penward's secrets none of this would have happened. He tried to reassure himself with the thought that sooner or later Lady Jane might have done the same thing anyway for some other reason – and it occurred to him that she might have been the cause of the Deinonychus getting out in the first place. And if he hadn't interfered, perhaps Penward would have activated his frightening plan of letting loose dinosaurs all over the world and killing even more people. But the nagging sense of guilt remained. He couldn't forgive himself for the way he'd exploited Lady Jane and then callously betrayed her. He couldn't escape the fact that he had provided the spark that set off the day's conflagration.

In the late afternoon Pascal was driven out to Penward Hall in an army jeep. The authorities wanted him to see Penward's establishment again in the hope that it would jog him into remembering some vital piece of information he might have forgotten.

Pascal's feeling of gloom deepened when the jeep entered the courtyard and he saw the rows of bodies, covered in black plastic sheets, laid out on the ground. Obviously very few of Penward's staff had escaped alive, if any. He wondered if Lady Jane's corpse lay beneath one of the shrouds.

A senior army officer and a government scientist met Pascal and took him down to the underground laboratory complex. 'It's important you remember exactly how many dinosaurs Sir Penward told you he'd hatched,' said the army officer as they went downstairs.

Pascal, who'd been asked this question several times before, sighed. 'I'm pretty certain it was ten. I distinctly remember his saying they'd successfully hatched ten dinosaurs.'

'Well, if that is the case we've accounted for all of them,' said the scientist. 'The army found four here on the estate. What with the ones already killed and the baby Brachiosaurus it gives us a total of ten.'

'You killed the Deinonychus, I hope,' said Pascal anxiously. 'The one with the claws?'

'We killed all of them,' replied the officer.

'Good.' Pascal shuddered. The small, red-coloured dinosaur had scared him the most, even more than the giant Tarbosaurus. He could still see those wicked-looking scythes on its hind feet.

'The problem now is accounting for the eggs in these incubators,' said the scientist as he led the way into one of the laboratories. 'We want to make sure no one's taken any away.'

'You still haven't found Sir Penward?' asked Pascal.

'No,' said the officer. 'Nor Lady Penward. The trouble is that a lot of the bodies are very badly mutilated. In some cases all that's left is some bones or a single limb. Until we open up all the dinosaurs and examine the contents of their stomachs we won't know for certain how many people died.'

'You think there's a possibility Sir Penward escaped?'

'We do. A check on the vehicle registrations has revealed that there are two Land Rovers and a Bentley missing from the estate. It could be they were all taken by members of Penward's staff – one of the Land Rovers was found abandoned in Kettering a few hours ago – but it's also possible that Sir Penward took one. We want to know if he's got any of the eggs with him.'

Pascal peered into the glass window and saw a row of eggs inside the incubator. There were six of them and they looked smaller than the ones Pascal remembered Penward showing him. He looked helplessly round the lab and shook his head. 'I only saw inside one of the incubator rooms,' he told them. 'I don't think it was this one. I saw four eggs, that's all. Large ones. Sir Penward said they were Tyrannosaurus eggs.'

They took him into another lab. Here Pascal saw two eggs sitting in the incubator. They looked familiar. 'I think this is where he brought me. But there were four eggs there before.'

The two men exchanged a sombre glance.

'Are these eggs still alive?' Pascal asked them.

'No. The power to all the incubators was switched off when our men got here. Deliberately, we suspect,' said the scientist. 'It seems Sir Penward didn't want his creations to fall into other hands.'

'So they're all dead . . .' said Pascal quietly. 'All the dinosaurs . . .'

'Yes. With the exception of the young Brachiosaurus,' said the scientist. 'My colleagues at the Natural History Museum tell me it may weigh as much as eighty tonnes when fully grown. It's going to make quite a tourist attraction if it survives to adulthood.'

'And we've now got to face the possibility that someone may

be shortly hatching two more of the monsters,' said the army officer grimly, indicating the Tyrannosaurus eggs, 'If those missing eggs are still alive.'

Pascal was driven back into town and, after yet more questioning by some new arrivals from the Department of the Environment, he was finally told he could go; though he was to report back early the following morning. It was now 7 p.m. He first went to the newspaper office, expecting to find Jenny there. She wasn't, but he did find a message from her asking him to call her at home, and a copy of the story she'd typed out that afternoon aimed at a sale to one of the quality 'Sundays'. He called her and learned she'd been even busier. Excitedly she told him that she'd sent a copy of the story to the press agency and they'd already negotiated a deal with the *Sunday Times* for £20,000. 'I went ahead and accepted it on your behalf. Is that okay?'

'Sure,' he said wearily. 'It's fine.' He was puzzled why the knowledge he was suddenly about £10,000 the richer didn't seem to have any effect on him. He felt oddly numb.

'That's not all,' she said. 'A literary agent by the name of Lesley Farson rang me up and asked if we'd be interested in writing a 'quickie' paperback about our experiences. She said she thought she could probably push the advance up as far as £50,000. I said I'd ring her back tonight and let her know after I spoke to you. We'd have to do it pretty fast. Within a month, she said. What do you think?'

He tried to absorb this new development. He didn't fancy the idea of having to relive the events of the past forty-eight hours on paper. 'I don't know, Jen,' he said. 'I'm not sure if I'm capable of writing even half a book in less than a month.'

'Oh, I'll do most of the work,' she said breezily. 'You know how fast I am. You can just dictate your stuff to me if you like.'

'Well, in that case,' he said hesitantly, 'I suppose it's okay.'

'You don't sound very pleased. What's wrong?'

He sighed. 'I'm just very tired, that's all. And I want to *forget* all about dinosaurs for the time being. I can't take any more Jen. Do you understand?'

There was a silence on the line for a few moments then she

said, in a sympathetic voice: 'Yes, I understand. You've been through a lot more than I have . . . Look, why don't you come out to my place right now and spend the night? It'll be fine with my parents. I'll cook you a meal then you can collapse in the spare room. What do you say?'

He sighed. 'It would be heaven. I miss you desperately already. But I'd better go home and check on my mother. Besides, I don't think I'd even have the energy to drive all the way out to your place. I'm almost dead on my feet.' So they arranged to meet in the newspaper office the next morning before he resumed his interrogation ordeal at the police station, and then he hung up and headed for home.

To his annoyance he found a TV news crew and a crowd of reporters in his mother's small front garden. He had to physically force his way through them to the front door, and once inside his mother told him the phone had been ringing non-stop. All of the callers were journalists requesting interviews. Pascal immediately took the phone off the hook.

After expressing her shock at his appearance she too demanded to hear the whole story. He gave her a quick, watered-down version while he ate some of the casserole she'd prepared for him. Despite not having eaten much during the day except for a couple of sandwiches he found he wasn't hungry. And when, half an hour later, he went to bed, he couldn't get to sleep even though he felt exhausted. There were too many things going through his mind. Every time he closed his eyes some horrible image would appear – the keeper being torn to pieces by the Tarbosaurus; the butler with his arm missing; the red Deinonychus hissing and slashing at them with its clawed feet; the other dinosaur coming at them through the stained glass window . . .

He couldn't shake off the terrible sense of guilt either, and on top of that there was a worrying feeling that he'd forgotten or overlooked something very important.

Finally he decided it was no use, he was never going to get to sleep. So he got up, called Jenny and told her he'd changed his mind about coming to her place. 'I need you badly,' he told her – and meant it. It seemed that being with her was the only thing that would bring him peace of mind.

Ignoring the protests of his mother he left the house again. There were still some journalists hanging round in the front garden. He muttered 'No comment,' to them as he hurried by. *Bloody reporters!* he thought as he climbed into his car.

The Stamper residence was located in the fairly exclusive Flagon-glen district and was a handsome two-storey house built in the late 19th century. It stood in four acres of gardens – Mrs Stamper's main joy in life – and behind it sprawled the picturesque Ashton Woods.

As Pascal approached the house a police car passed him going in the opposite direction. He had encountered several police and army patrols since leaving home. According to the radio reports the danger was officially over – the last of the big cats having been killed or recaptured – but the police and army were still on alert in case they'd missed one and people were being advised to stay indoors. Pascal had been stopped by one of the army jeeps and told, very politely, that it was inadvisable to be out, but he'd flashed his press card and said he was on newspaper business.

He parked in the Stamper driveway and got out. He expected the front door to open before he reached it; the sound of a car always brought the suspicious-minded Mr Stamper out to investigate. But the door remained closed.

Pascal rang the doorbell and stood remembering the last time he'd been here months ago. It was the day he'd broken up with Jenny and the memory made him uncomfortable. Thank God he'd got her back.

Pascal rang the bell again. Nothing. No sound of voices or footsteps. Somewhere in the house he could hear a radio but that was all. Perhaps they were all out in the big, old-fashioned kitchen at the rear. But even so they should have heard the bell.

He rang it for the third time, keeping his thumb on the button for a long time. Still nothing. At this point the first tendril of fear touched him. He decided to try the back door.

He hurried round the house, praying that everything was all right, that he was just imagining things.

He almost burst into tears when he saw the kitchen door. It was nothing but splinters of wood. All pointing inwards. 'Jenny!'

he screamed as he rushed into the kitchen. She wasn't there – but her mother was. She lay on the kitchen floor in a pool of blood. Her neck, chest and stomach were sliced open.

Pascal slipped in her blood and had to grab on to the back of a chair to keep from falling. Then he picked the chair up, using it as a shield as he entered the passageway. He expected to come face to face with a lion or tiger. Somehow one of the damn animals had slipped through the net.

But no big cat appeared. Pascal continued down the central passageway, looking into rooms as he went. He yelled Jenny's name over and over but there was no response.

He found Jenny's younger sister, Janet, in the doorway of one of the bathrooms. She was naked. A blood-stained towel lay nearby. He saw the bath was full of water. She must have been having a bath when she heard . . .

Pascal picked up the towel and covered her with it.

He found Mr Stamper at the foot of the staircase, his head almost completely severed from his body.

Pascal, expecting the worst, went upstairs and checked all the rooms but there was no sign of Jenny. Or of any big cat.

As Pascal came back down the stairs, trying to avoid looking at Mr Stamper's body, he realized with a start that the house was filled with a familiar odour. A pungent, deeply unpleasant smell. The smell of dinosaur.

But how could that be? They were all dead, except for the baby one that looked like a Brontosaurus. And even if the ones from the missing eggs had hatched they wouldn't be big enough yet to cause this sort of carnage. So what was the answer . . . ?

He returned to the kitchen and stared out through the shattered door. The perfectly manicured lawn stretched off into the darkness. In the distance he could see the outline of the greenhouse but nothing else. He yelled Jenny's name again and waited, hoping she might be hiding somewhere out there. But there was no answering cry.

He debated with himself whether to go out and search for her or to first call for help. He decided it would be wise to phone first. He put down the chair and reached for the phone that hung on the kitchen wall by the refrigerator. He had just started dialling when he heard the sound of someone running across the back lawn towards the house.

Presuming it to be Jenny he dropped the phone and turned, filled with relief, to the doorway. But it wasn't Jenny who came hurtling through the doorway; it was something five feet tall with a scaly skin the colour of dried blood. And from its hind feet rose wicked-looking, scythe-like claws. *The Deinonychus!*

But *how?* The army officer said it had been killed . . .

With a shriek the thing sprang at Pascal, one of its hind claws rising up for a death blow, its forearms reaching out to hold him while the scythe gutted him . . .

But, as Pascal had done, the Deinonychus slipped in the pool of blood around Mrs Stamper and went skidding across the floor to collide with the refrigerator. Pascal ducked past it, narrowly avoiding the claws that swished through the air as the creature struggled to regain its footing, and ran for the doorway.

As he ran out into the back garden he suddenly recalled Penward's exact words: 'We have hatched ten dinosaurs to date. Eleven if you include the plesiosaur . . .'

Eleven of the monsters, not ten as he'd told the authorities. That's what had been nagging at him all this time. And that meant there must have been *two* of these scythe-clawed devils . . .

He heard the parrot-like shriek behind him. He glanced over his shoulder and saw the Deinonychus come leaping out of the kitchen doorway, its tail held rigid to give it better balance for running.

Pascal ran as fast as he could towards the greenhouse. He flung the door open and began to search frantically for a weapon. Almost immediately he saw a pitchfork leaning in a corner with other garden implements. He snatched it up and turned to confront his pursuer . . .

He was just in time. The reptile was already springing at him through the doorway.

And then several things seemed to happen at once. Pascal felt a tremendous jolt in both his arms and a strange icy sensation that ran from his neck down to the top of his stomach. Simultaneously he felt himself being flung backwards with great force. There was a sound of glass breaking, a tremendous shriek from the dinosaur and then an explosion of pain along his spine as he landed heavily on something hard.

Pascal lay stunned for several moments. When he was finally able to struggle into a sitting position he saw that the dinosaur was dying. The prongs of the pitchfork had penetrated deep into its thorax. It was lying on its side, kicking feebly and making hoarse rattling sounds.

Pascal staggered to his feet. That's when he discovered he too had been hurt. A long gash stretched down the right side of his chest. It was deep – he could see the white of his ribs in places. Blood was pouring out of it.

Making every effort not to pass out he stepped past the twitching reptile and went outside. He *had* to find Jenny . . . Ignoring the agony in his ankle which had flared up again he stumbled on . . . At the edge of the woods he glimpsed something white lying among the leaves. He climbed over the low wall, his arms wrapped around his chest as if to hold himself together, and staggered over to the object.

He screamed. It was Jenny's arm.

A few yards further on he found the rest of her – a blood-soaked bundle of clothes. He sunk to his knees beside her and started to cry. He was certain she was dead. Even in the darkness her wounds looked hideous. But then he heard her whimper.

She was still alive.

Somehow he managed to pick her up. He got her over the garden wall and half-way to the back door before he collapsed, all his strength gone. It was no good. He couldn't make it. And they would both be dead, he knew, before anyone found them.

He crouched, sobbing, over Jenny. He didn't hear the approach of someone coming over the lawn towards them. But he did hear the gasped 'Jesus!'

Pascal looked up. A frightened-looking man in his early thirties stood there. Pascal recognised him as one of the reporters he'd seen in his front garden. He guessed the man had followed him to the Stampers in the hope of still getting an interview.

Pascal smiled at him. 'Bloody reporters,' he muttered – then passed out.

25

The farmhouse lay at the end of a three-mile long lane. The lane was in a bad condition; large potholes were everywhere and the hedges on either side were so overgrown that in some places they met in the middle of the lane. A casual observer might have thought it was impossible to drive a car along it.

The Bentley was parked under some trees by the farmhouse. Penward had covered the car with branches and leaves. The farmhouse itself was derelict. No one had lived in it for years. And as far as Penward knew no one had even been on the property in years. It was perfect. He was glad he'd never got around to developing the place as he'd planned to when one of his companies bought it very cheaply back in the late '70s.

Inside the farmhouse he set things up as best he could. He felt very weak but he succeeded in building a big fire in the fireplace and soon the temperature in the small, garbage-strewn living room was very high. He was confident the eggs were still alive; he'd kept the heater in the Bentley turned right up and had wrapped the eggs in an overcoat. It wouldn't be long now, he was sure. His only fear was that he wouldn't live long enough to see it happen.

He collapsed into a dilapidated armchair and stared at the two eggs by the fireplace. But by the time the first shell started to fracture Sir Penward was dead.

Lady Jane woke up in a state of complete confusion. Her head throbbed, her throat was horribly dry, she felt sick and she couldn't move.

The reason for the latter condition, she quickly discovered, was that her hands and feet were securely tied. There was also a chain wrapped tight around her ankles and padlocked to the base of a radiator pipe against the wall. There was a rope around her neck too, tied to something behind her. She was lying on her back on the floor. There was a low ceiling overhead. The plaster was cracked and stained. Where the hell was she? she wondered as she tried to sit up.

Then she saw Penward sitting in the armchair facing the dying fire. She yelled his name but he didn't stir. Finally she realized he was dead. There was a puddle of blood on the floor near the chair. He'd bled to death.

Something rustled in a corner of the room. She wasn't alone. Some animal was in the room. A rat, probably. She grimaced and strained to look. The floor was covered with old newspapers, providing lots of hiding places for rats . . .

She tried again to sit up but couldn't. The rope around her neck prevented her.

There was another rustle of newspaper from somewhere else in the room. Somewhere behind her.

As she twisted desperately to see, she noticed, for the first time, the broken eggshells by the fireplace. They were lying on Darren's overcoat. 'Oh no . . .' she moaned.

Something pitter-patted over the newspaper towards her. She looked round and saw what it was. As she feared, it wasn't a rat – it was a baby Tyrannosaurus Rex.

It was small – it only weighed seven pounds – but already its jaws were powerful and its teeth very sharp. Nature had designed the baby Tyrannosaurus to enter the world as a fully operational killing and eating machine.

It bit Lady Jane in the calf then ran off, taking a small chunk of her leg with it. The reptile's brother, emboldened by his sister's success, followed suit . . .

Lady Jane's screams carried for a long way across the untended farmland, and continued for almost twelve hours, but no one heard them.

It was a week before they let Pascal out of hospital. They told him to spend two weeks at home resting but the following day he went to Cambridge to see Jenny. She'd been taken to a hospital there that specialised in micro-surgery.

She was still in Intensive Care, but they let him see her. He tried to mask what he felt when he entered the room and saw what she looked like. She seemed to be full of tubes; there were tubes in her arm, up her nose, there was even one plugged into her chest. Another tube ran out from under the sheet and into a large glass bottle on the floor. Even Pascal could tell that the urine in it shouldn't be that colour.

He forced a smile on his face as he approached the bed. 'Hi!' he said cheerily. 'Don't bother getting up for my sake – stay right where you are.'

A faint smile appeared on her face, which was puffy and the same colour as the pillowcase.

He leaned over her and gave her a quick kiss on the lips. Her breath smelt strange. Then he took hold of her left hand. Her right hand, and her entire right arm, was encased in a white cocoon.

Her voice was a whisper. 'You don't look well,' she told him. 'Should you be out of bed?'

'Me? I'm fine. How about you? You *look* okay. I was expecting to see a really sad case, and then instead I find a malingerer . . .'

'You can't fool me. I know what I look like.'

'You look great.'

'I'm going to be scarred.' Her eyes indicated the thick dressings that covered her chest and stomach.

'Nonsense,' he told her firmly. 'They'll fix you up as good as new.'

She shook her head. 'No. I know what I'm going to look like. And my arm . . .' Her voice faded. She squeezed her eyes shut.

'Your arm is going to be okay. You'll be playing tennis with it again in a couple of months.' The reality was different; her surgeon had told Pascal it would be another week before they could tell if the eight-hour operation to sew back her right arm had been a success. If the blood wasn't circulating properly they would have to amputate. And even if she kept the arm she'd never have full use of it again.

'I'm going to be ugly. Horrible. You'll leave me.'

'Leave you? Don't make me laugh. I'll bust my stitches. All hundred and thirteen of them.'

Tears welled up in her eyes. 'Don't leave me, David. You've all I've got now. Mummy, Daddy, Jan – they're . . .'

'I promise I won't leave you,' he told her, touching her on the cheek. 'Now stop this. You're upsetting yourself. Think of something else. Like how you'll spend your half of the royalties from our bestseller.'

'Bestseller?' she said blankly. Then, 'Oh, the book ... you're going to write it?'

'Already started. I'm not enjoying it, but I figured we should get something out of this mess. Trouble is I don't have an ending for it yet. They still haven't found Penward, or Lady Jane.'

Jenny's eyes went wide with alarm. 'David, he took those eggs with him! Do you think he's making more of those monsters? I don't think I'll be able to stand it if there's a chance that more of them will be on the loose ...'

'Easy, easy ...' he soothed, squeezing her hand. 'The police think Penward skipped the country. He's still got powerful friends apparently. He's probably hiding out in South America. Don't worry, you'll never see another dinosaur again.'

A short time later, as he left the hospital, he wished he felt as confident as he'd sounded. He had the horrible feeling that the story wasn't over; that the world would be hearing more of Penward's dinosaurs.

www.ingramcontent.com/pod-product-compliance
Lightning Source LLC
Chambersburg PA
CBHW030333030726
47499CB00003B/754